DEFECTION
GAMES

Other thrillers by Haggai Carmon in
the **Dan Gordon Intelligence Thriller**® series:

Triple Identity
The Red Syndrome
The Chameleon Conspiracy
Triangle of Deception

Visit www.sleepwithoneeyeopen.com
www.dangordonspyclub.com

DEFECTION
GAMES

A DAN GORDON INTELLIGENCE THRILLER®

HAGGAI CARMON

THOMAS & MERCER

Text copyright © 2012 Haggai Carmon

Published by Thomas & Mercer, Seattle

www.apub.com

ISBN-13: 9781477848432
ISBN-10: 1477848436
Library of Congress Control Number: 2013909774

To my family

INTRODUCTION

In 1985 I received a recommendation to hire Haggai Carmon, a well-known and skillful Israeli attorney. At the time, as the director of the Office of Foreign Litigation in the Civil Division of the Department of Justice, I was responsible for the worldwide defense of lawsuits against the United States and for finding private lawyers to protect US interests.

I had reason to be glad I picked Haggai. In our Israeli litigation he was hard to beat, winning all cases for the US government. From the beginning, Haggai and I developed a special relationship. As soon as a case was filed, he was full of ideas and ready to develop the best strategy in our defense. I quickly realized that Haggai had additional expertise in the intelligence-gathering field that would prove to be of great benefit to the US government.

The money-laundering work I asked Haggai to do was new to me and I believe for the US government as well. And the scope of the work was indeed global in nature—we had reports of stolen funds in many different countries. He was given a relatively free rein to do his work with several general restrictions: 1) Don't do anything to embarrass the US; and 2) Comply with the laws of the foreign country you are working in. I never heard complaints about Haggai's work internationally, and I never had reason to doubt that he was operating within the law of the country where he was working. He was commended for his recovery efforts by a number of federal agencies, including the Postal Inspection Service and the IRS, and from a number of US Attorney's offices throughout the country.

Somewhere along the line, I realized that his investigations were providing great material for thriller espionage novels. I looked forward with great anticipation to reading every report he submitted to the office. You can see from his four novels how successfully he accomplished his work. To me, the best feature of his books is that you are reading true-to-life accounts written by a professional who knows how to give the reader a firsthand feeling and authentic description of how undercover agents do their work—and what is really happening behind the scenes.

Haggai once told me that "white-collar criminals are different from robbers and burglars who want cash to hide their criminal behavior. White-collar criminals want their activity to look legal, so they leave a paper trail. Somewhere along that trail, they are bound to make a mistake, and I'll be waiting there to catch them." And we, the readers, are excited to learn about his latest adventures.

David Epstein
Washington, DC

I

December 2, 2006, Agarak, Armenia

A chill mist blurred my view, mist with freezing showers. They obscured the figure approaching me from a hundred yards or so down the hill. He pushed through some thorny bushes and looked around. Nervously, I glanced at my wristwatch. It was nearly sundown, not that I could tell from the thick, leaden coating of sky.

I was two miles from Agarak, a small town on the left bank of the Araks River, on the Armenian side of the border with Iran. More than misty weather blurred my vision. Blood oozed from the crease where a bullet had grazed my skull. Thick red drops mingled with the rain and dripped through my eyebrows. It burned my eyes when I wiped at it with my sleeve. Had I been a few inches taller than my six feet four inches, or had the bullet been a few inches lower, it would have gone right between my eyes.

I waved my hand at the man. I even risked calling, "I'm here," in his direction, but not too loudly—*It's an oxymoron, you moron*, said the little devil inside me. Some people hear voices. Some see invisible people. Others have no imagination whatsoever. I hear a little devil.

I'd survived the shooter's first attempt, and I might not be as lucky the second time. But if I had to go, I was going to take a few of them with me. I had the will, the anger, and enough ammunition to make it happen: I'd learned a thing or two in my three-year stint in the Israeli Mossad, and in Israel's Special Forces before that.

I wasn't too concerned that my attackers would reemerge from wherever they were holed up. I knew they were waiting for me to move, and waiting to finish the job they were probably ordered to do: kill me and the man who came to meet me, never mind who dies first, as long as we both die today. *Hey, hold your horses,* ordered my inner devil, *Who says both of you should die? Maybe the bullets were meant only for you? Consider your options.*

Maybe they would reemerge, maybe they wouldn't. Should I retreat? Run away?

Never.

Not yours truly.

As the man came closer, I could make out his thick mustache. He was limping on his left leg. I wondered if a bullet had gotten him, too. The CIA operational brief hadn't mentioned any physical disability.

He continued slowly but steadily toward me. He was in khaki military gear, black boots, and black-rimmed glasses. He looked younger than fifty-three, his listed age in the CIA fact sheet. Serving for almost twenty-five years in the Iranian Revolutionary Guard had given him a soldier's upright poise, even when he was on the run. He came closer, but so did a sudden, short barrage of bullets over my head, just when I thought that the pursuers had given up on us. I ducked, taking cover under the nearest scrubby bushes. The man couldn't be more than fifty yards away.

I gripped my Para Micro-Uzi submachine gun and looked around to identify the source of the fire. I knew I could return hellfire. This little toy, only 3.3 pounds and 19 inches long, was designed in Israel especially for counterterrorism activities. It could fire 1,250 rounds in one minute. However, the Micro-Uzi's range effectiveness was only 100 feet. That meant that your target had to be close, very close. Oh, yes, you must also be brave, because at that range you still don't know what kinds of weapons your enemy carries. While you must be less than 100 feet away to hit him, a gun with an effective range of 300 feet can hit you. You'd be dead before your bullets got a third of the way toward your enemy, wasting their short lives for nothing.

"This is Orange. I've just been under fire and took cover. I saw Tango about fifty yards away, but no contact yet," I reported to the command post. My handheld device's AES 256 key length encryption automatically scrambled all communications. NSA had approved that symmetric key cryptography for top-secret communication. Although I relied on it, as an added precaution I also used code words.

"Report location," came the response.

How the fuck should I know? I was in a remote point on Earth, 6,000 feet or more above sea level, huddled on the ground with the Uzi in my left hand and the handheld in my right, barely hidden by a pair of scrubby bushes. The land was arid; it was now night, blade-cold, and—arid land or no—it was pouring rain. My GPS navigation gear had stopped working, probably because of the massive, sharp-edged mountain slopes around me, and any minute the barrage could start again. What else could go wrong?

Sheltering my handheld GPS from the rain with my body, I tried to reactivate its personal locater beacon. The internal GPS receiver signal was, I hoped, reacquiring my position and transmitting it through the SARSAT satellites to HQ.

The GPS stayed dead. Rain mixed with blood ran into my mouth, and I yielded to the whining question that my inner little devil kept asking: *How did you get yourself into this mess?* The truth was, I *had to be there.* Sense of mission and tenacity—those I had in spades.

So, who the hell had been firing at us? The Armenians? Unlikely, because the shooting seemed to come from the Iranian side of the twisting river. If Iranian border patrol guards were shooting, there'd been a serious breach of security. However, without identifying the shooters, we wouldn't know if Iranians were pursuing the man I had come to pick up. If they were, that was bad, bad news. It was bad, bad news as well if an Armenian border patrol was in fact shooting: whenever someone tries to cross the border, they shoot first and ask questions later. From my perspective, it didn't really matter who was shooting—if they hit me, I was dead, regardless of their nationality.

A cold breeze chilled my skin, but my blood was boiling with expectation and rage. In a few days, if all went well, I'd be back in a warm room sipping a hot drink, savoring the accomplished mission. That is, unless I was zipped up in a black body bag stretched on a metal slab in a coroner's freezer. I hunched forward from underneath the bush to gain some visibility, and at least some view, in case Tango came closer.

More than ten minutes of silence, and then—nothing. Tango should have reached me by now, and I'd lost sight of him. Where did he go? He was a trained soldier, I told myself. He knew how to camouflage himself, how to hide, and how to dodge between the bushes and boulders littering the slope. It was now completely dark. I was losing patience, and my feet and hands were turning to ice. How come the command post was in a heated apartment overlooking the painfully modest village square, while I was soaked with water and blood, freezing my ass off? Next time, you shouldn't be the first to volunteer, or agree to be "volunteered," I told myself. And my inner little devil, opening just one eye, added, *Don't whine. You were ordered to be on the forefront because you didn't function well as a team member, remember?*

Of course I remembered. It had always been my problem, or maybe should I say my advantage. I can still remember Dr. Deborah Katzman, the fat Mossad psychologist, whose hairs on her upper lip made her look older than her real age of somewhere between fifty-five and sixty. She ran personality tests during my Israeli Mossad admission process. A few years later, when a careless Mossad human resources staffer left my file unattended, I'd had a chance to glance at her report. The doctor had suggested that the Mossad should give up on me.

He's too independent, tends to work alone, and challenges authority. Katzman was right, of course, but, lucky for me, the Mossad figured that those character traits would make me a better operative. Square-minded bureaucrats are a dime a dozen, but original thinkers with conniving minds and a bit of entrepreneurial flair are hard to find.

The night stayed silent. I rose partway, crouching and peering around, searching the area for any movement that could mean either the man I had come to pick up, or my backup unit, but I couldn't see any movement. He had to be near. I hoped he hadn't taken a bullet, which would mean that all our efforts, in this joint CIA/Mossad operation over three continents and months of hard work, would be doomed. Visual was the only way to communicate with him. He wasn't carrying any radio device, and unless he made it through and met us before our pursuers' bullets met him, he was history. Well, either way he'd be history. Not just the idiom, the real fact.

Historians would remember the defection of General Cyrus Madani, aka Tango, from the theocracy of Iran as the single most important event that helped derail the Iranians' nuclear arms development program. Or at least to slow its completion substantially. So much work, so much sacrifice. He had to be close. Would it now be for nothing?

"Change of plans," I heard the voice in my earpiece. "Return to point Sabra immediately." *Good God, why?* I wanted to ask, but contrary to my nature, I knew this was no time to question authority. Somebody else from my team would probably pick up General Madani if he'd made it through. We were not going to give up on him, not now.

I backed slowly around bushes and boulders, giving a final look downhill for any sign of Madani. When I didn't see him, and the gunfire didn't resume, I stood upright, turned, and continued silently at a slow pace up the hill toward the village, my Uzi at the ready. It could fold to fit into a flat box no bigger than a hardcover book. But I wasn't about to do that with the shooters perhaps still around. Whoever they were, they had tried to kill me or even Madani. That was enough to elevate them from "opposition" to "enemies," and I don't treat my enemies well. Especially when they fire first. And even when they are second to shoot.

I finally reached the unpaved road and followed it to where a rental Nissan Pathfinder, picked up earlier at Zvartnots Airport in Yerevan, Armenia's capital, awaited me. The driver was a thuggish-looking, bearded agent with bulky pockets that barely hid his own Para Micro-Uzi. I jumped into the Nissan and he sped away.

"Let me have that," said Brad, pointing at my Uzi as he drove. "We might be stopped by a police roadblock."

I folded my Uzi and handed it to him. Driving sixty miles an hour, he steered with his left hand and used his right to lock the Uzi in a compartment between our seats, together with two PC9111 Professional handguns and one Glock 23 that he pulled from his right pants pockets.

"Where is everyone?" I asked. There were seven of us in the team.

"They'll leave separately. We don't want to draw too much attention."

"Why the hell was I told to leave Tango? He was less than fifty yards away," I asked, barely masking my frustration. "Did someone else pick him up? Have you heard from him?"

Brad turned his head toward me. "You're bleeding," he grunted, as if telling me I had something stuck in my teeth.

"I know," I said. "In our profession, the target remembers but the gun forgets. The bullet grazed me. Tell me why already."

"It was a trap. That was Eric's conclusion, and he gave the order to cauterize the operation."

"A trap? You mean Tango wasn't going to defect?" The thought of all our hard work going down the drain chilled me.

"We don't know, but the fact the opposition was waiting for us—and in fact from three different directions—told us it was a trap. All we knew was the direction from which Tango was to arrive. That tells us that something got botched. So Eric gave the order to pull you out."

"Three directions? Then they were aiming from behind his back?" I thought back, trying to remember exactly where the gunfire had come from.

"Yes, but if they were in a lower altitude, and Tango was climbing toward you, they could shoot above his head and get you. It's also possible that whoever the shooters were, they didn't care if Tango was hit, too."

"Is the Agency giving up on him?" I tried to digest the news. All that time. All that work.

"We don't know," Brad said, as he searched in the dark for the main road that avoided the village. "We also had a problem with Tango's visual. The telephoto snapshot we took found some serious image discrepancies when our computer compared them to Tango's photos taken in Iran."

I wiped my wet head with a tissue pulled from my pocket. The wound still hurt. So had Tango just been dangled by Iran? Had he been lying about his desire to defect?

"Maybe there was a leak from our end, tipping off the Iranian Revolutionary Guard and that caused the case death?" I asked.

Brad gave me a strange look. "Exactly. And if that leak came from us, maybe we have a mole?"

There was something off about his tone. Did he mean me? What the hell? I leaned my head against the seat's headrest. *Keep your mouth shut*, my little inner devil suggested. *Ignore the provocation.* "Whatever the case," I said, "it's bad."

Brad just nodded. We'd arrived at the airport. The sign said Զվարթնոց Միջազգային Օդանավակայան, ZVARTNOTS INTERNATIONAL AIRPORT. We met an Agency representative at the newly built modern arrivals hall. He got quickly into the Nissan, directed us to the parking lot, and surreptitiously transferred the arsenal from our car to his car's trunk. Brad and I returned our SUV to the rental company and boarded an Armavia airline commercial flight to Moscow.

———

After a stale five-dollar tea in a café at Moscow's Sheremetyevo Airport, I boarded a Delta flight to New York. I had more questions than answers, but couldn't decide what pissed me off most—that we'd come home empty handed; that–I'd been a wet, cold, bleeding sitting duck on the Iranian-Armenian border for nothing; or my feeling that nobody was bothering to tell me what exactly was going on. Something wasn't right. To quell my mounting suspicions, I slept most of the flight.

By the time I got to my New York apartment and was welcomed by Snap, my tail-wagging golden retriever, I was just as tame. As I was playing with him, I thought about my divorce in Israel from Dahlia and made an unholy comparison of the respective relationships. Snap was always happy when I came home. In fact, the later I came, the more excited he was. Snap never complained when I left my stuff on the floor. In fact, I think he actually preferred it. And if I said to Dahlia, "OK, I'll pick it up," her response was always, "That's OK." That was one of the most dangerous warnings Dahlia could send me. *That's OK* meant she wanted to think long and hard before deciding how and when I would pay. Finally, I knew that if he ever left me, he wouldn't take most of my property.

II

December 2006, Washington, DC

After spending a few days with my children, Karen and Tom, I flew to Washington. I was determined to get some answers.

The people who could give them to me were Eric Henderson, my sleek, eel-like supervisor; Paul McGregor, a down-to-earth officer from the CIA's National Clandestine Service; and Benny Friedman, my buddy from my Mossad days and now the head of Mossad's international division.

I was ready for them, but were they ready for me? They'd seen me angry before, so maybe that explained their conciliatory tone as we exchanged the usual small talk. Eric met Paul's eyes across the table.

Then I got to the point. "Eric, what was going on in Armenia? Why was I kept in the dark, thereby making me a moving target?" I demanded. The words came out more sharply than I'd planned. In fact, I was shooting in the dark. I had no proof, just a hunch, that there were undercurrents to the events in Armenia that Eric knew about but "forgot" to tell me.

Though Eric wasn't known for his warm and fuzzy demeanor, he seemed to want to calm me. At fifty-seven, Eric headed the Special Operations Unit at the NCS, the National Clandestine Service, which centralizes the collection of human intelligence (HUMINT) services, and he had stature beyond his title. After successfully leading several CIA covert operations—most still unknown to the public—when Eric talked, his peers listened and others would cringe. It didn't help that Eric was imposingly tall and had a bulldog expression; the deep grooves in his face gave him a permanent scowl.

Eric would never win a Mr. Congeniality pageant, but he didn't seem to care, while others around him did—and they were increasing in number and hostility. In recent years, when Eric became a high-ranking NCS executive, his authority to manage overseas operations expanded, and now, his disregard for even basic niceties had become almost legendary.

Eric had moved into NCS when that organization absorbed the CIA's Directorate of Operations and, with it, Paul McGregor's Covert Action Staff or CAS subdivision. Eric reported to the assistant director of NCS, and the Director of the NCS reported to the CIA director, but Eric's unofficial authority went beyond his pay grade and the formal chain of command.

"Dan, you know as well as I, we're all pawns, every one of us," he said. "We follow instructions, sometimes without knowing what's happening in the room right next to us. I'm sorry you got screwed, but we're not running a daycare center here. In our business, unhappy customers don't file polite complaints—they shoot you. You know that."

I nodded, the graze wound on my head still hurting.

None of this was helping except for a tacit admission that he knew that something was wrong. The question remaining was, when did he know that? Before the operation? Or after it was botched?

"You haven't told me why essential intelligence about me walking into a trap was kept away from me," I said.

The intelligence jigsaw and the other hoards of crap Eric was loading on me didn't provide me with the answers I wanted and deserved.

Eric kept his mouth shut. He didn't answer my question, and I knew there was no point in pressuring him on that.

"Was there a leak or any security breach?" I asked, trying another angle, remembering the odd look Brad had given me when he picked me up in the misty mountains of Armenia.

Again, Eric didn't answer but Paul did. "We can't rule it out. The Iranians tried to engage us in a defection game." He paused and added candidly, "Frankly, between you, me, and these walls, so far, in the current game they have the upper hand."

"Let's stop being cryptic. How about you just tell me what happened," I persisted.

"The Iranians sent a decoy," said Paul. "The man you expected was a plant, a fake Tango."

"Who?" I was confused.

"A decoy, probably an Iranian agent," he repeated.

"Are you sure?"

Paul nodded grimly, drumming the table with his fingers.

"That means we've been duped," I said the obvious, realizing but not caring that I was stepping on somebody's toes.

Eric gave me a look that could instill the fear of God into anyone, but I was used to it by now.

"Actually, the problem is more serious," Eric said. "It means the Iranians knew about Tango's planned defection—genuine or staged—and ambushed us. I wouldn't be surprised if the intention was to kidnap you and any member of your backup team they could snatch, to dissuade the US from soliciting and extricating any defectors, and then trade you for major benefits."

"Ambushed *us*?" I said. What the hell was he talking about? I'd been the one under fire. I'd been the one bleeding and cold and under fire. So what was this *us* shit? Just the mere thought of being kidnapped and spending one second in an Iranian prison, with the notoriously brutal VEVAK—the Iranian secret service—chilled me to the marrow. Even being in a so-called five-star hotel in Tehran while chasing the Chameleon during a previous case was no picnic. Iran was notorious for its bad operational climate, and I had no interest in checking out the country's prisons.

Eric said nothing, avoiding direct eye contact that could result in conflict. He saw how mad I was. Benny had sat quietly throughout the exchange. Now he suddenly interjected, "Mossad's security is conducting a thorough review of all channels of communication with Tango during the past four years."

Paul added, "Separately, an independent joint team of the Agency and Mossad is trying to obtain intelligence regarding the Iranians' recent moves, whether there was a security breach, and, if so, where. They're also exploring the possibility that the shooting incident in Armenia had nothing to do with Tango."

"Meaning?"

"Theoretically it's possible that Tango couldn't make it to the border for whatever reason, or even changed his mind, and at the same time, some smuggler with or without connection to Iran's security forces tried to cross the border."

"And the gunfire?"

"Border patrol. Anyway, we can't jump to any conclusions just yet; we have to stay put until results of the investigation are in." I sensed that Paul didn't believe in what he'd just said. Neither did I. Therefore I wondered why the show was necessary. Just to appease me?

"Let me get this straight," I said in a belligerent tone. "There were communications with Tango while he was in Iran, right?"

Paul nodded.

"Then why wasn't that communication channel maintained to verify we were getting the real Tango, without an entourage of bullets seeking my person? Maybe the Iranians got him earlier, dead or alive?"

"Maybe. Dan," said Paul in a low voice, "you know the trade. The Mossad's contacts with Tango during the past years have been sporadic. He didn't have a transmitter or any direct device of communication. He met their men once every several months. He was very cautious, and rightfully so. He'd made many enemies. He knew that VEVAK was watching him."

Eric got to the point at last. His permanent scowl seemed even deeper than usual. "Before the incident in the Armenian-Iranian border," he said, "Mossad combatants finally met Tango in Tehran. Benny, care to fill us in?"

Benny leaned forward. "After months without contact, our combatants met Tango in Tehran. They had to take extraordinary measures to keep out of the prying eyes of VEVAK agents, which my men spotted in three different locations around Tango's house."

"How did they make contact if Tango was under such close surveillance?" I asked.

"We rented a house next to Tango's, but obviously I couldn't let my men just walk over to his house. We needed a plausible excuse."

Knowing Benny for so long, I patiently waited to hear his inventive trick. Benny continued—his patented sly fox smile spreading across his face—and delivered the goods.

"We clogged the main sewage line linking the houses on our side of the street, flooding the street with raw sewage. Two of my men, who were native Farsi speakers dressed in city workmen's uniforms, came with a "borrowed" city truck to pump the line. They entered three houses, including Tango's, purportedly to see where the backup came from. The VEVAK agents saw what was happening, but didn't dare leave their car and dip their feet in the filth. The stench was awful." Benny chuckled.

"Once inside his house, they gave Tango oral instructions on how to contact us. Tango had insisted earlier that he wanted ten members of his family to leave Iran first. My men gave him enough money to pay for his and his family's separate foreign trips and bribe payments en route, if that might become necessary. Under our instructions, he had earlier filed an application for a permit to exit Iran and go to Syria to visit the Shia shrine of the tomb of Sitt az Zaynab, a daughter of the Prophet Muhammad. It's located in Al Ghutah outside Damascus. The shrine's become a major pilgrimage destination for many Shiite Iranians. So the request shouldn't have raised any suspicion in Shiite Iran.

"But with Tango it was different. He was already under suspicion."

"If he was already out of the military and government service, why did he need a permit?" I asked.

"Because it hadn't been five years since he'd left his office, a must requirement under their rules. So he received a limited time and a limited destination passport, valid for thirty days' travel to Syria only. Obviously, we had no plans to extricate him through Syria. That was just a small maneuver to demonstrate to anyone watching him—VEVAK in particular—that Tango was above suspicion. He'd go to Syria, do the religious tour, and return to Iran. There were no contacts planned during his Syrian visit, as most probably VEVAK would have been tailing him. You can call the scheme 'confidence building tactics'," said Benny with his signature smile.

I knew Benny well. What he was telling me was just the tip of the iceberg, but I made no effort to press him on that. I knew that I wouldn't get anything more.

"What happened at the Armenian border?" I asked.

"We had a problem." Eric added but stopped and looked at Benny, who nodded and then said somberly, "After Tango met Benny's combatants to discuss the defection procedures, two men came over to his house in Tehran. They made believe that they were also Mossad combatants. We know now that they were not ours, but most probably Iranian VEVAK agents. They apparently knew of Tango's intended defection and spun a web to frustrate his plan, and at the same time embarrass the Mossad and the CIA by exposing their—or our—incompetence."

"And?" I asked, when he stopped all of a sudden, like a good drama director would.

"And the VEVAK agents, posing as Mossad combatants, told Tango that there'd been a change of plans and that he'd have to wait in Tehran before he could leave Iran through Iran's northern border with Armenia."

"How do you know all that?" I asked.

Benny smiled, "I had a surveillance team just behind Tango at all times. First, to make sure he wasn't double-crossing us, and also to protect him. And finally," his sly smile broadened, "the fake city employees had installed three listening devices in his house before they left."

I chuckled. "Low output devices?" I asked matter-of-factly, thinking back to our Mossad Academy training days. Benny and I used to break into apartments to install such devices. Once, we'd broken into the wrong apartment, only to surprise a couple making love. We barely escaped.

"Yeah, very low output," Benny confirmed with a smile. "We'd rented a nearby house. There we picked up the signals, and forwarded the messages home reencrypted."

"So your people were in the neighborhood the whole time."

Benny shook his head. "No, once they completed the installation in Tango's house, my men left Iran. The technical team from our Keshet unit in the next house installed a relay device that picked up the signals from Tango's home and forwarded them to Israel through a hidden Internet hookup, using Wi-Fi. The relay device used the house electricity with backup batteries recharged by a small solar panel, and could theoretically work for years. The devices were hidden in the house's outside wall. When our lease expired and an Iranian family moved in, the devices stopped transmitting. We didn't care because we had no interest in the private conversations of an uninvolved Iranian family, as Tango had left his house as well."

"Where did he go?" I asked. "I thought that VEVAK's fake Mossad combatants told him to stay put."

"They took him to a safe apartment in northern Tehran, purportedly 'to protect him from VEVAK agents,' when in fact they were VEVAK agents and Tango found himself in a golden cage. It was an apartment in a high-rise building, guarded twenty-four seven by VEVAK personnel posing as Kurds with contacts with the Mossad."

"How do you know that?" I asked wondering if these explanations were another decoy, this time to fool me.

"A new team of my men followed them to the new location, but that's where their journey had to stop. They had no access to the safe apartment."

"How did VEVAK know of Tango's defection plans?"

"We aren't sure. But if we look at the broader picture we might find a direction. Tango was bitter at the regime that ousted him from his high-ranking military position, and must have made his rage known. An angry former general with deep knowledge of a country's innermost secrets is a potential security risk. Therefore, most likely, VEVAK had also made him a person of interest who had to be supervised, and installed listening devices in his house. If true, Tango's home may have become the rival intelligence services' dream recording studio.

"Maybe Tango talked and was doubled."

"We don't know that, but sure would like to," said Benny.

"So where is Tango now?" I was about to accept these explanations. I knew Benny well, and could tell when he was lying. This time he was telling me the truth, although I suspected that I wasn't getting the whole truth. It was quintessential Benny.

Benny continued, "When he understood that he was in VEVAK's hands, he managed to escape from the safe apartment and move to another location provided by a Kurdish rebel with whom he knew we had contacts. This Kurd sheltered Madani in a secret location in a high-rise building in Tehran. That could be proof that the man you saw on the border was an imposter planted by VEVAK, but we can't be absolutely sure that we are not being maneuvered again."

"If VEVAK is actively looking for Tango, does that mean that he's lost to us for now?" I asked.

"Not so fast," said Eric, breaking his long silence. "The Mossad had a plan to extricate him, and they are going to stick to it." I sensed that Eric was laying the groundwork to accuse the Mossad for any failure, if not in Benny's face, then in Eric's reports to the front office. Eric wasn't known to concede mistakes or admit failures.

I wondered, how could we be sure that VEVAK wasn't still holding Tango—and that maybe Tango's renewed, indirect contact with Benny's men wasn't meant to lure us into the snake pit? In other words, how could we be sure that Madani's Kurdish savior was for real and not a VEVAK agent? If he wasn't for real, that could heighten the chances that the man at the Armenian border was an imposter operated by VEVAK. I could appreciate the Iranians' sophisticated cunning.

"I know what you're thinking," said Eric, surprising me. Being intuitive wasn't his strong suit. "The point, from our perspective, was that it was important to make sure that you were going to meet an imposter. From their perspective, if we sent a welcome party to Armenia, it could serve as proof that we had engaged Tango, and they would make us look like a bunch of idiots whom future potential defectors cannot trust."

Ha! Eric had just confirmed, with a straight face, that before I'd left for Armenia he'd known that I would be a sitting duck. My rage was brewing inside, but I kept quiet, for now. Future eruption expected.

In the intelligence world, "incompetent" is a dangerous label. People cooperating with you rely on your competence to keep the relationship secret and to exfiltrate an asset at a time of distress. If the Mossad or the CIA were exposed as unprofessional—as nincom-poops—it would further diminish potential assets' willingness to do business with them, in a business where the lifespan of operators isn't very long as it is.

"OK," I said, trying to digest all this and appear calm, "what do we do now, or rather what do you want me to do?"

"We want you to go to Iran, meet Tango through the Kurds who are sheltering him, and extricate him to freedom. You'll get your instructions soon."

Three minutes later the meeting ended, leaving me baffled.

———

Back in my New York office, I read the encrypted memo that Benny had just sent to me and the other team members:

The following is our report regarding the failed attempt to extri-cate Tango. As per our earlier post operation estimate, VEVAK got a double to pose as Tango and sent him through the route that Mossad/CIA designated. We now have his name: Parviz Farrokhzād, a drug smuggler with some military experience (to account for military bearing) and a physical appearance similar to Tango's. VEVAK caused his release from prison three months before his prison term was up. Parviz was released with $2 in his pocket. Outside the prison, a VEVAK agent posing as a drug dealer approached Parviz and made him an offer: to cross the border into Armenia with a smuggled 5 kg of Heroin. Payment for the job: $25,000 when he completes the mission, in addition to the $5,000 the agent gave him. Since Parviz had only $2, and these amounts are substantial in Iran, he didn't need much persuasion. He was told that cooperative border control soldiers could be shooting, not at him but into the air to justify their inability to stop him. They were paid as well. His leg was injured during the exchange of fire *and he hid in a small cave. Armenian Police were patrolling the area and found him. Parviz is now in Armenian custody. We were allowed to interrogate him.*

I called Eric on a secure phone. "How do we know that the man in the Armenian prison isn't Tango after all?"

"Our liaison on Benny's team participated in the interrogation, took his fingerprints, and sent them to the FBI's National Crime Information Center in Clarksburg, West Virginia. They ran it against their database. This includes fingerprints that Benny's 'city sewer inspectors' lifted when they met Tango in his house. The man in the Armenian prison is not Tango. Therefore, the provisional identification of Benny's men—that he is probably an Iranian drug dealer with a criminal past and a grim future—could be accurate."

"So the question remains, is the person held by the Kurds in the safe apartment Tango, or just another decoy?" I asked.

"You'll be dispatched once we have a good answer to that question," said Eric.

III

October 2006, Manhattan

The Iranian-defector whirlwind had all started when an encrypted message arrived at my office in midtown Manhattan: *Dan, read file 2004-1197 and prepare for an operational meeting later on this week. Eric.*

With the overflow of intelligence reports, sometimes it was difficult to ascertain what was important and reliable and what wasn't. So it was often difficult answering the most frustrating question: What was imminent, and what was not? I went to the heavy safe at the corner of the office, signed in, punched in the combination, stuck my index finger in the fingerprint reader, and, after the seven-second verification process, opened the thick metal door and pulled out file 2004-1197.

I sat at my desk, a rich mahogany worn smooth over the years. It always calmed me. I started reading. Although the file was not operational but informative, and a man like me definitely needs action to survive in a bureaucratic environment, I became captivated for the next two hours. So why was I captivated? Because I saw the potential, and I saw my next hair-raising operation being born.

That night, when I was sound asleep, the phone rang. It was Eric, practicing typical Eric behavior. I peeked at the clock radio on the night table. It was 2:30 a.m. I mumbled a few four-letter words, but my rage subsided when I heard his instructions.

"Unexpected change of plans. There's an eight-thirty meeting at my office with Agency operatives, Benny Friedman is also attending. Be there." He hung up. Although I was angry at Eric's total lack of consideration, manners, etiquette, or whatever—a man needs his sleep—I also knew that a meeting with Benny, my old Mossad Academy buddy, meant action. It has always been like that: official meetings with Eric and Benny meant a joint CIA/Mossad operation, of the kind that even fiction writers can't invent.

Yawning but curious, I took an early flight from New York's LaGuardia Airport to Reagan National Airport in Washington. An Agency minivan met me and drove me to Langley, Virginia, through some of the most moneyed neighborhoods in the country—lush-lawned colonials with former servants' quarters turned to stables, ornate gates, BMW after BMW. I especially liked seeing the front gardens of this area of Virginia, lush but understated, never allowed to burst out of what human hands had designed. I thought of my parents' garden in Israel, so different but beautiful as well: the some-times arid weather coaxing out date palms; and poplar trees; and the ancient desert flower, the rose of Sharon.

Upon arrival I was jolted out of my reverie. The new Agency building was a utilitarian structure of cement and smoked glass, an anonymous building in an anonymous office park. After I went through the strict security screening precautions and identification process, Eric's aide escorted me to the second floor in the new main building and into Eric's office. Benny and Eric were seated on office chairs around a small coffee table, drinking coffee from paper cups and chatting.

The third man there I didn't recognize. With no chair available, I sat on Eric's worn-out, brown leather sofa, a government seniority status symbol, and tried to engage in small talk with Benny. He was unusually reserved; I couldn't get more than two words out of him, even with a "How are you?" Soon I realized that, unlike in previous cases where the CIA and Mossad had cooperated, Benny wasn't going to give me a head start about the purpose of the meeting.

"I'm Paul McGregor," said the man sitting next to Eric, when he realized that Eric wasn't going to introduce us. McGregor was wearing a blue blazer and a yellow tie. He was in his early fifties with raven-dark hair—a full head of it—and blue eyes. He looked like an aging football player, stout, well-built, just slightly gone to seed. He gave me a firm handshake.

"Paul McGregor is with the Agency's Directorate of Operations' CAS subdivision, Covert Action Staff, handling covert actions," said Eric. "Are we all ready?"

"I am," I responded, nonchalantly leaning back on the sofa in a pathetic attempt to hide my interest, and anxious to see Benny's cat-that-ate-the-canary smile that appears when he describes a clever, conniving plan. Instead, Benny's broad face displayed nothing. With his receding gray hair, medium height, and growing belly, Benny looked like the family doctor about to tell a worried parent that his child needed to be admitted to the hospital. There were none of his usual side comments or cynical remarks that, regardless of their acidic content, always came with a friendly smile.

Benny and I had become buddies during the first operational course of the Mossad. Benny came from a Jewish Orthodox family, while I came from a non-religious Jewish background. My parents belonged to the well-established turn-of-the-twentieth-century Mayflower generation of Israel. His parents were Holocaust survivors who had immigrated to Israel from Poland after World War II with only the clothes on their backs. Yet, despite our different backgrounds, we became the best of friends.

Unlike Benny, however, I'd decided to leave the Mossad after three years when my identity was exposed during a rendezvous in Europe with an Arab informer. The informer was accompanied by an Arab whom I immediately identified as a landscaper who had worked on my parents' garden in Tel Aviv. He recognized me as well, and signaled his partner that I wasn't the European journalist I pretended to be. They turned around and left without saying a word, but their eyes said it all: *Dir Balak* (كَلَأب ريد), Arabic for a threatening *Beware!*

That botched rendezvous doomed my future at the Mossad. I could never again participate in field operations. My mere presence in the field with other Mossad combatants, regardless of the cover I assumed, would contaminate my fellow Mossad agents and could doom them. Therefore, I knew that if I stayed with the Mossad I would be forever confined to a desk. "No, thanks," I said, and left. I went to law school and, after a few years of practicing law, I divorced my wife relocated to the US, took the bar exam, and started working for the US Department of Justice, gathering foreign intelligence on white-collar US criminals who had absconded abroad with many millions. When cases I handled turned out to be espionage or terror-related, I was co-opted to the CIA. Benny, on the other hand, climbed up the ranks of the Mossad until landing in the prestigious position of Head of the International and Foreign Operations Liaison Division. That gave us the opportunity to work together again.

Eric turned to me. "We're here to discuss your role in a new joint CIA/Mossad operation. You are assigned to a location in Armenia, a former Soviet republic, to participate in the extrication of a defecting key individual from Iran. Tomorrow evening you'll travel to the US Air Force base in Ramstein, Germany, for a week of operational training with seven additional agents. Once the Ramstein training is over, you'll go to another location in Germany for additional individual briefing and training. Questions?"

Without waiting for comment from me, Eric turned to his right and said, "Benny?"

Benny leaned forward in his chair, looked me in the eye, and asked, "Are you ready for this?"

"Whatever it is," I said, "I'm ready. Even if it's another crazy plan, even if *'My bone cleaveth to my skin and to my flesh, And I am escaped with the skin of my teeth'.*" I quoted the verse in Hebrew, knowing that Benny, as an Orthodox Jew, would immediately identify its biblical source—Job 19:20.

Benny smiled. "OK, Dan, I know I don't have to tell you this, but the things I'm about to tell you are 'for your eyes' only, or rather 'for your ears only.' We can't allow any security breach. I'll use the key person's name only here between closed doors. All future references to him, use his code name, Tango. Only a few know his identity and it must stay that way. Understood?"

I nodded. I've been through this routine many times before. Who was Tango? Eric gave me a bunch of papers. "It's your Access Permit to handle top-secret documents, sign here." It was a newly worded oath of secrecy. I signed. Life in prison was deemed to be the lightest penalty in the list of hellish futures I could face if I betrayed my oath.

Benny continued in an almost ceremonious tone. "Lately, we had the opportunity we've been waiting for: recruiting a disgruntled Iranian general with a lot to tell and a rage to motivate it. He is General Cyrus Madani, a retired deputy director of the Ministry of Defense of Iran."

I let out a sigh. I knew something about Madani, enough to know he wasn't a small fish easily caught. He was a leviathan.

Benny continued, "Madani is an Iranian national, fifty-three years old. During the Islamic Revolution of 1979 he was a mid-level operative in *Sepáh e Pásdárán e Enqeláb e Eslámi.*" Benny pronounced the words in a perfect Iranian accent. My limited command of Farsi was enough to understand their literal meaning: Army of the Guardians of the Islamic Revolution, more commonly known in Iran as Sepah, a branch of the Islamic Republic of Iran's military, kept separate from the regular armed forces. According to Benny, Madani had been assigned to their intelligence branch. After successfully infiltrating his agents into the *Mujahidin-e-khalk*, the violent Muslim opposition to Khomeini's regime, he was promoted and assigned to the Al Quds Forces that were provoking the Kurdish rebels to launch attacks against Saddam Hussein's Iraq. There, Madani met for the first time a dangerous rival: a young intelligence officer, Mahmoud Ahmadinejad. In the early 1980s, Iran decided to establish a Shiite militia in Lebanon, and Madani was one of the major forces behind the Iran-Hezbollah link. He became the right hand of Major General Mohsen Rezai, commander of the Revolutionary Guard Corps, and took part in the establishment of Hezbollah. With Madani in there, Hezbollah was founded and the first step in the Iranian plan to put Lebanon under Shiite control was completed."

Benny went on. "Madani subsequently returned to Tehran, assembled teams of expert instructors in sabotage and guerilla warfare, and dispatched them to Lebanon. In coordination with Imad Fayez Mugniyah, the Hezbollah military mastermind, and his assistant, Ibrahim Akil, aka Tashin, Madani's first test for his recruits was in how effective they would be using their new 'skills.'

"On October 23, 1983, an Islamic terrorist drove a bomb-laden truck into the US military compound in Beirut, Lebanon, killing 241 US Marines. That attack coincided with an attack on French peacekeepers' barracks in Beirut. Madani's students had passed with flying colors. The attacks achieved the Iranian goal—all the soldiers of the multinational force sent to Lebanon by several countries were pulled out and returned home. Madani returned to Lebanon in 1992 as one of the commanders of an Al Quds division, a position he held through 1995. Ever ambitious, Madani then moved to the central command of the Revolutionary Guard in Tehran as a general. In that capacity, he incorporated dummy companies to disguise the Iranian destination of embargoed technology. Subsequently, Madani was transferred to the Ministry of Defense in a top position, responsible for the logistics and armaments of Iran, including overseeing the activities of a secret key company engaged in the development of Iran's nuclear bomb manufacturing capacity.

"In other words, from our perspective, Madani was, as they say, an evil man, with a lifetime's worth of dangerous information."

As Benny paused, I sensed he was about to tell us when Madani became a Mossad "subject of interest."

As if on cue, Benny said, "Lebanon is just around the corner from us, and his activities in training and arming Hezbollah were, for obvious reasons, of serious concern. We picked up on his trail when he used a false passport to travel."

I felt my stomach contract. My adrenal glands injected my veins with an extra dose of that heart-racing hormone. Benny, however, continued with his dry recounting of these otherwise very intelligence-juicy details. "Madani then became an assistant to Hojjatoleslam Ali Fallahian, head of the Ministry of Intelligence and National Security, *Vezarat-e Ettela'at va Amniat-e Keshvar.*"

There was no need to introduce that "ministry." It is the central intelligence and security agency of Iran, commonly known by its English acronym MOIS and its Farsi acronym, VEVAK. I didn't need to be reminded who Ali Fallahian was either. He was frequently mentioned in secret intelligence reports. He also starred in the published INTERPOL Red Notice list for "crimes against life and health, hooliganism, vandalism and damage." Such laundered words in fact hardly described his activities—or rather, atrocities. They put him on the short list of "people we'll be happy to meet in a dark corner" of many intelligence services around the world, with dreams of offering him instant rough justice, by bullet or bomb.

Benny continued. "In 2003, Madani uncovered several cases of embezzlement in the Republican Guard that made him unpopular, and officials involved in the thefts turned against him and forced him to resign. A year later, whatever friends he had left in the government tried unsuccessfully to win him back by offering him work as a consultant. But his enemies were still in power. Madani's chances to rekindle his government career were finally killed in 2005 when his old-time rival, Mahmoud Ahmadinejad, became Iran's president. So Madani retired."

"And he didn't take up gardening." I said.

"Right. After retiring, Madani tried to inject himself into the arms trade and weapons industry. He was trying to peddle his connections with the Iranian government to foreign companies who wanted a piece of the action."

"But let me guess," I said. "Madani was dead in the water." Retired generals, I knew, often successfully touted their government connections after retiring. But what could Madani say? *Oh, and by the way, although the president is my chief enemy, you can hire me anyway.*

"Right," Benny said. "It became pretty clear to any potential client that, as long as Ahmadinejad was president, Madani's 'connections' were worthless. Angry and bitter, he started a small business trading in textiles. However, with his credentials, Madani became ripe for recruitment by foreign intelligence services. They scout for exactly such individuals, like sharks smelling blood a thousand miles away. Before Iran learned of Madani's dissatisfaction and put him on a watch list, Madani got permission and made a trip to Italy while he was still trying to peddle his military connections.

"When he was finally realizing that he wouldn't be able to, we had our opportunity. My men made a cold approach in subterfuge, and after a long and slow recruiting process, we persuaded him to work for us. Now, obviously, my case officers couldn't risk asking him to spy for Israel."

"Right," I said. "An Iranian general spying on Israel, his country's archenemy? It's a possibility, but it could also be too big a bait to swallow."

Benny nodded. "Exactly. We decided not to take the risk, and therefore Madani was led to believe he was being offered work for NATO. No specific member country was mentioned." Finally, Benny let out, for the first time, a fleeting smile. It lasted only a second, but in that second I could sense some of Benny's pride. Madani was, after all, huge. Huge!

"General Madani is no fool," Benny continued. His tone remained serious, even a little grave. I knew that tone. Benny's work, our work, had only just begun. "I think he suspected that his recruiters worked for the US, and of course we did nothing to dissuade him from that thought. In fact it was partially true: this was our joint operation with the CIA.

"The short end of it is that Madani became a Mossad/CIA asset. However, after being cultivated for some time, he now wants to defect from Iran immediately. He refused our offer to live in any European country, and told us that we must extricate him and his family from Iran and resettle them in the US as originally promised. Eric and Paul have played major roles in the delicate dealings we've had with Madani." Giving credit to others was Benny's forte.

So, I was the odd man out here, the only one without any prior knowledge of what was going on. Maybe, I thought, that will change now. Getting the full picture was not a childish insistence, but a necessity—albeit one that could backfire. My years in undercover operations, most of the time as a lone wolf, always reminded me of a Navy SEAL operating under the ocean's surface. He has his mission, but if circumstances change he must improvise, because communication to HQ is either very limited or nonexistent.

On the other hand, limiting the information given to the operative to a "need to know basis" helps reduce a potential domino effect if he's captured and forced to talk. And everybody talks, after a few hours or a few days. Nobody can withstand violent interrogation tactics such as forcible extraction of the fingernails or toenails with pliers used by intelligence services officers who do not have an

Inspector General or Internal Affairs Office to second-guess their activities.

"Why such an urgent request for relocation? Why now?" I asked the inevitable question. An asset the caliber of Madani is almost always more valuable while on location. Once he's removed from his home turf and debriefed, and any remaining information is squeezed out of him, his intelligence value becomes zilch. His information is nothing but shopworn goods. In the Mossad, the term we used to describe thorough debriefing was *peeling him like an onion.*

Eric answered, "He's reported that he's been under heavy surveillance by VEVAK and could likely be arrested within a short time. He doesn't know whether the chatter around him relates to his contacts with us, but he's scared."

"Iran hangs spies in public," Benny said. "Sometimes they hoist them up with a crane with a noose around their neck." The room went silent for a moment.

"We think," Eric said, "that the increased security scrutiny by VEVAK most likely resulted from the sudden deaths and unexplained 'accidents' in strategic locations and against key nuclear scientists—both those that have already happened, and those that just could happen very soon. We simply can't allow him to stay in Iran any longer. If we abandon him, nobody would ever work for us. Period."

Those that could happen soon? What? I found Eric's premonition funny, but I didn't laugh. I tensed up.

"Got you," I said. "What's my role in this operation?"

"You'll run the extrication operation on location."

I felt proud. Benny noticed it. "In the Chameleon Conspiracy operation, you successfully infiltrated Iran, identified a potential defector, and managed to leave alive—all of which made Eric put you on board and at the helm on location. We supported that decision."

I nodded in thanks, remembering the chase of the evasive Chameleon and his conspiracies throughout Iran, Pakistan, and Australia.

"Where do I sign?" I asked.

"Read this." Eric gave me a thick blue folder with the CIA's golden emblem embossed on the top. I opened it. Inside were approximately one hundred pages of intelligence reports and a faded photo of a man with a thick mustache. He looked to be around fifty, with a roundish face and hard eyes—hard even through the faded photo.

"This folder doesn't leave this room," said Eric. "That put you on the bigot list, a short list of people privy to that information. You can take notes, but the notes stay here as well." Eric and Paul got up to leave. "We'll be in the adjoining office if you need us," said Paul as he stepped out, "I'll see you in the afternoon. Lunch will be brought in an hour."

Eric didn't bother to say anything. He just scowled and left.

IV

October 2006, Washington, DC

I poured myself a cup of water from the cooler and read through the folder labeled *Tango Defection*. Tango's access to real-time intelligence on Iran's progress in developing nuclear arms and sponsorship of terrorism made him invaluable. His fear of being captured created a real dilemma—pulling him out to save his life and getting our last bit of intel when he's debriefed in Langley versus leaving him there, hoping that the chatter he noticed around him was just cicadas, not VEVAK agents closing in on him.

Madani would be an incredibly valuable asset to lose. And Iranian assets were hard to come by. Very hard.

The most important part of the Tango folder was the section dealing with the strategic timetable. It gave a new meaning to the word *urgent*. According to the brief, the world would have little time to stop the Iranians before it would be too late. Your arsenal of strategies against a rogue state armed with nuclear weapons is ill-stocked if not empty. The year 2015 could mark the turning point—by then, Iran was expected to have nuclear weapons that would deter any potential attackers, as well as the means to deliver them. Iran would deploy the Russian-made air defense system S-300PMU2, serving as an advanced Ballistic Missile Defense in addition to an advanced SAM air-defense system. The Iranian Navy would be able to threaten commercial shipping and military naval forces in the Arabian Gulf, and stop oil tankers passing through the Straits of Hormuz.

By 2012 or 2013, Iran would also have accurate short, medium, and long-range ballistic missiles, which could carry nuclear warheads and reach Europe and the US Eastern Seaboard. Finally, Iran will increase its support to its proxy terrorist groups to launch attacks against American interests and allies anywhere.

Urgent? Maybe the terms *critical* and *burning* would be more appropriate.

Eric returned to the office with Benny. "Have you read it?"

I nodded. "What's my specific role?"

"You'll be the person to meet Madani face-to-face in a crossing point on the Iranian-Armenian border, identify him, and escort him to safety. A seven-man unit will be around you as backup and security. You're leaving tomorrow for a week of training in Ramstein, Germany, and then a few more days in another location in Germany where you'll also get the final operational instructions."

We spent the next seven hours reviewing the master plan.

"Any more questions?" asked Benny.

I had plenty, but I kept my big mouth shut for once. I was certain that they would be answered during the final instruction session in Germany. I've been through the process before. Almost nothing is left for self-initiative. In the Mossad operations, on the other hand, there was always room for improvisation as conditions in the field changed. It was where Israeli operatives excel—and sometimes fail.

Paul McGregor gave me a travel folder. "At Frankfurt airport, an Agency representative will give you a duffel bag with a US Army uniform and documentation. Change into the uniform and travel by train to Ramstein Air Base. There are travel vouchers in the folder."

Ramstein Air Base, in the rural district of Kaiserslautern, Germany, was the headquarters for the US Air Forces in Europe and a NATO installation.

"Bear in mind that besides Americans, the base also includes Canadian, German, British, French, Belgian, Polish, Czech, Norwegian, Danish, and Dutch personnel. Only if asked, say that you are a part of a US Army teachers' team that travels to US bases outside the United States to teach Civics. See further details in your travel folder. Use that cover story only if you can't shake the person talking to you in any other manner, polite or impolite.

"And"—he looked me in the eye—"stay out of trouble."

———

Dozing off on the plane, I was in awe at how the Mossad had been able to recruit Tango. I recalled how Alex, my Mossad Academy instructor, taught us the art of identifying and cultivating a defector. "Think of MICE," he said. "Money, Ideology, Compromise, and Ego." He looked intently at our cadet class with his watery blue eyes, and added, "Motivating an asset to defect is a huge leap forward, even when compared with turning a person into an intelligence asset. Pushing a person to defect means uprooting him from his country, language, culture, friends, and sometimes even from his family. Above all, he will have to live in fear for the rest of his life that his old compatriots would find him, and—"

He moved his hand across his throat.

This was a different case, however. There was no need to motivate Tango to defect. It was his own decision. Nonetheless, the mere fact that the Mossad, and later the CIA, were able to recruit him was a considerable achievement. I was hoping not to screw things up and compromise the very end of this case—bringing him to freedom.

I could picture Alex at his lectern, in his glasses, always rubbing the fabric of his aged tweed jacket:

Forget the stories about kidnapping the enemy's top generals. We cannot afford Soviet Cold War practices, and besides, that could backfire and force the enemy country to retaliate in kind. Very recently, we successfully completed Operation Diamond. Munir Radfa, an Iraqi pilot, defected to Israel with his MiG-21 fighter jet, the pride of the Soviet aircraft industry. Up to now, no country outside the Soviet Bloc could closely inspect a MiG-21. After the Israeli Air Force completes the review of the aircraft's capabilities and drawbacks, the MiG-21 will be sent to the US.

Indeed, shortly after Alex's presentation, that defection made the headlines. Few people outside the intelligence community know that these defections rarely end well for the defector. Their home countries don't forget, and definitely don't forgive. An Iranian pilot who defected with his missile-armed plane to Iraq during the Iran-Iraq war in the 1980s was traced by Iranian agents to Europe and was killed. Captain Mahmood Abbas Hilmi, an Egyptian pilot who defected with his plane to Israel, was located by Egyptian agents in Buenos Aires, Argentina, six months after he left Israel, and was killed.

Alex trained us in how to collect nuggets of information, or to sniff out a potential asset for recruitment. He concentrated first on the rules of recruiting, cultivating, coaching, motivating, and finally going in for the kill—motivating the asset to work for you as an informer, or to defect, or both. Decades later, true to the saying "Difficult during training, easier at combat," I remember the rules vividly. Most intelligence services maintain special sections tasked with identifying potential assets or defectors within an enemy's ranks. Spotters survey enemy ranks for a weak link—people who were passed over for a promotion, or those with personal or financial troubles. A spotter is like a vulture on a treetop waiting for a sick or weak animal to lose its ability to defend itself. Once a suitable location is identified, an approach plan is devised. This is a very complex and detail-rich scheme of deceit.

The recruiter's "legend"—his cover story that enables the contact with the target—must be carefully crafted. Obviously, the recruiter's identity can be anything but that of an intelligence operative, unless of course he has a death wish or aspires to dine on local prison food for the indefinite future.

A team of psychologists and intelligence experts analyzes the potential asset's background to create a suitable legend. Who should approach the target? A male or a female? Young or old? Where will the contact be made? Under what pretext would the recruiter initiate the first conversation? What to do if the target recoils and refuses any cold turkey contact, or luckily appears to be open to the dynamics of the contact? How would the relationship continue, and for how long? When will the target become a real asset—that is, shift from being a valuable person within an enemy's ranks, to becoming a spy or a defector?

According to Alex, motivating an asset to defect is always a serious consideration for the recruiting intelligence service. What would serve its interests best? Leaving the asset in place as a spy, or extricating him to debrief him thoroughly? But what do you do with him once the information he has is squeezed out? Maybe engage him as an instructor for intelligence combatants intending to infiltrate the asset's former country? Would he qualify? Would he risk the combatants if he returns?

Alex used to lean on his lectern, and say in his English-accented Hebrew, "*Listen to me, don't take notes; we'll rehearse all this in the field so many times that it'll be engraved in your minds.*"

And indeed it is. Alex's first rule of recruiting: "Be careful." I listened to him from the front row:

Did I already say careful? I mean extremely careful. Any potential asset who you think is ready for the move could betray you when you least expect it. It's happened before and it'll happen again. In the intelligence business in general, and in recruiting in particular, there are no morals, no ethics, no sentiments, no friendships—only interests. That means you can't trust anyone. Therefore, all recruiting attempts should be made outside the target's country. If you try recruiting a target in his home country, you never know who he'll be bringing to the next meeting—it could be half of his country's counterintelligence agents to make your life miserable for years, not to mention that they may be scoping a potential target for their own recruitment. Therefore, Rule Number Two is: 'If at all possible, approach a potential asset when he is out of his home country.'

With that wisdom in mind, it was clear to me why international conventions attended by scientists, government officials, or anyone with access to national security secrets are recruiters' favorite safaris. In these circumstances, the approach can be especially well disguised, with the spotter or the recruiter actually participating in the convention as a bona fide professional. A nuclear scientist won't be nearly as suspicious if he's approached during a convention by another scientist wearing the convention's ID tag.

"I've read your recent work, and I'm really fascinated by your findings" could be an opening line. A little brown-nosing never hurt anyone. Then comes more talk about the "findings," maybe a few drinks at the bar. You exchange business cards and depart as friends. Then you send him a short courtesy letter with a benign question: "On page one hundred twenty-three of your article you said that . . . could you elaborate a bit?" When an answer comes—and it always comes because scientists love talking about their papers—you thank him, suggesting you'd like to return the favor regarding his "articles" and asking whether he'll go to the next convention.

Once you meet again, you're already good friends. You suggest jointly authoring an article to be published in a top peer-reviewed scientific magazine. You say, "The editor was my brother's classmate.

It doesn't mean that he'll publish an article not fit for print, but with so much congestion on his desk, it might put ours on the top of the pile waiting for peer review."

And so on.

In a class of twelve cadets in the Operational Course at the Mossad, only three were sent to international conventions to try out recruiting techniques. The rest were told that budgetary constraints prevented their going. Luckily, I was chosen to go—not as a scientist, since I was too young to pass as one, but as the son of a fifty-six-year-old microbiology professor who attended a convention called "An Annual Update in Allergy and Autoimmune Diseases" in Joao, Paraiba, one of the oldest cities in Brazil. The hotel was constructed as a circle; each room had either a view of the internal gardens, or of the beach. The sand was bone-white and stretched as far as the eye could see. My window faced the beach. During my entire time there, I saw absolutely no one on it. This was a convention of serious scientists who, it seemed, preferred the semi-dark interior of the hotel's lecture halls.

My legend for this convention described me as a sociology major at UCLA, joining my Canadian mother who was attending the convention. Professor Janice Webber, my "mother," was a tall, willowy woman who kept her hair back in a bun. She could have been an aging model, but she wasn't. She was the real thing, a genuine scientist who didn't ask too many questions when her close friend, a Mossad confidant, asked her to allow me to pose as her son: "He's doing research on interactions among strangers during short-term multinational conventions, and how social barriers are removed. He couldn't ask the organizers to enroll because he doesn't qualify as a natural sciences researcher, and couldn't reveal he was doing research, fearing that any disclosure could tilt the results."

To this day, I don't know if Janice bought the story, although she had no reason to suspect any ulterior motive. Once, she looked at me with probing eyes and asked me about my research methods.

Luckily, I was fresh out of the Tel Aviv University Political Science faculty. One of the most hated classes there was Research Methods. But now it came to my aid.

Now: Whom do you recruit in a scientific convention when you are not a scientist, but a man in his late twenties posing as a student who came to meet his mother? The answer: recruit a young man or a woman in a similar situation.

During breakfast, I carefully viewed the tables to see if there were any young men or women who were too young to be university professors. There were three tables with such individuals. I passed by their tables and identified the name tag of a young woman sitting next to an elderly man. Their last names were identical. She must be his daughter, I assumed. She was rather plain, blonde with a Russian name, and stout in that way some Russian women seem to get, though the process had started early with her. She couldn't have been more than twenty-five.

I later examined the list of the convention participants and saw the man's name, Professor Igor Malshenkov from Ukraine. The woman, Anya Malshenkova, was not on the list. OK, I said to myself, Russia and Ukraine share a border, so maybe she was Russian after all, as if it mattered. During lunch, I found an excuse to approach and befriend her. She was happy to talk to me, and soon we were walking in the hotel's gardens, walking and talking. I told her what I knew about "my mother's" research and then asked her about the area of expertise of her father.

"Father?" she giggled. "Igor is my husband."

When she saw my embarrassment, she smiled and said, "Never mind, many people make that mistake. I was his student and we got married." We stopped at the pool bar; she ordered a drink I didn't catch the name of, but it was blue and came with a shish kebab of tropical fruits. I ordered soda water. I never drink alcohol while on assignment unless it is part of the role I'm playing.

It became clear why she was happy to talk to me: She was deeply bored. She made vague allusions to the "difficulties" that come with having a much older husband. She said she'd relinquished her studies to keep house, and was trying to give him a child. We ended up back in their hotel room, "to have coffee," as she suggested. When she excused herself to the bathroom, I used the opportunity to take photos of documents that were on the coffee table. This was my proof to Alex and my other instructors that I could obtain documents from a scientist. I had no idea what I was copying; the documents were handwritten in Cyrillic. Anya came out from the bathroom wrapped barely in a towel. She sat next to me and said, "To be around my own age, very nice," with that guttural Russian accent. Her voice was low, and I could smell rum.

I quickly told her I had to meet my mother for dinner, and slipped out. There was a limit to the things I was willing to do for my country during training—and having sex with an unattractive married woman wasn't one of them, particularly when I already had what I really wanted, which was copies of documents.

The sad end for me was that I actually failed in my mission. It turned out I had copied documents that were worthless from an intelligence point of view; and the truth was that I was supposed to have recruited an asset.

"Not enough time" was my excuse. Now I know that such an excuse was so bad that it wouldn't even warrant inclusion in the volume I intended to compile one day of My Kids' Excuses: why they'd skipped school, or didn't do their homework, or clean up their messes, or practice the piano.

Obviously, Alex didn't buy that excuse. "You had a mission and you didn't perform." He was so serious that I thought I was about to be expelled from the operational course. At the end, only a derogatory notation was entered in my personnel file.

"How can I redeem myself?" I asked, feeling deflated.

"I'll give you one more chance to recruit an asset and obtain valuable information," he said. "This time it will be in Israel. We can't spend more money on futile trips."

"Do I choose the target myself, or will you assign me?"

"Devise a plan and submit for my approval," he said.

That night I went out with Benny for a beer, taking the opportunity to pick his brain for suggestions. We hit our favorite bar, Puerto Rico, across from the Tel Aviv City Hall. It was small, dark, with a few couches in the back. You could order chicken schnitzel—not quite like my mom used to make, but good. The food wasn't kosher, so Benny just ordered beer.

"OK," Benny said, staring into his beer, thinking. He looked up. He had the look, that Cheshire cat smile. "What about that friend of yours whose mother is having an affair? Isn't it with an ambassador from some African country?"

"Recruit him? I could cause a diplomatic incident if I fail," I said, weighing it.

"Alex said to make a proposal. So make a proposal. He doesn't have to go with it."

Surprisingly, after consulting with his superiors, as well as with SHABAK, Israel's internal security service, Alex approved my plan.

So I rekindled my friendship with Rina. She and I had had a short romance a year or so earlier, and had remained in touch after it ended. She was earning an economics degree at Tel Aviv University, and was planning to open a chain of "hip kosher" bar/restaurants, beginning in Tel Aviv and expanding to New York. She lived with her parents in Kfar Shmaryahu, a posh neighborhood just north of Tel Aviv where diplomats and Israel's higher echelon live, five minutes from the Mediterranean shore. I once more became a welcome guest at their house, a spacious family home with a lush backyard, complete with poplar and olive trees and a sky-blue pool. It was early fall, and Rina was busy studying. I soon discovered that the African ambassador visited Rina's mother each Tuesday at noon, when her husband was at work and Rina at the university. On one Tuesday, after I spotted the ambassador's car parked in a side street a block away, I came into Rina's backyard and dived into the pool, as I had done many times before.

Wet, with my bathing suit still on, I went directly upstairs "to look for a towel," and surprised his Excellency, the very startled and embarrassed ambassador, leaving the master bedroom buck naked. I could see he recognized me from the family's parties; he looked stricken. He had a diagonal scar on his chest, and I dimly remembered reading a while ago how had been in a serious car accident in Tel Aviv; it had made all the papers. Besides the scar, though, he was, as the cliché dictates, tall, dark, and handsome, deeply brown with almond eyes, slightly Asiatic almost. They gave him an exotic look—at least that's what Rina called him, "exotic." Even *she* thought he was cute; though, no doubt her opinion would change if she knew her mother felt the same way.

I pretended to look shocked, didn't say a word, and turned to return to the pool.

He called me a day later and asked to see me.

"How did you get my phone number?" I sounded intentionally defensive.

"Rina's mom gave it to me," he answered. "We need to talk."

We met in central Tel Aviv, at a café at the top of the Shalom Tower. Back then it had been the tallest tower in the Middle East, before Dubai's massive construction boom hit. The view from the observation floor of the tower was spectacular: you could see up and down the Mediterranean coast, and as far east as the Judean Hills.

Aside from the observation floor, though, the tower was a big office building with an American-style department store, all utterly nondescript, bustling, and anonymous. Here you were swallowed by the crowd.

"I hope I can trust your discretion," the ambassador said as we sat at a corner table.

"I understand that," I said, giving him a non-answer.

He waited for my consent, guaranteeing my silence, and when it didn't come, he said, "I know it must have shocked you, but these things happen. What can I do to make things right?"

I let him simmer in silence for a minute and finally said, "I have no idea."

I had to let him sweat. "I've always really liked Rina's dad," I said. "But I mean I almost feel like I'm screwing him over by *not* telling him. Or does he know already?"

The ambassador started. "No, it's a private matter between me and Varda." He used the first name of Rina's mother.

"Don't you think he should know? I mean, isn't honesty always better?" I played at being righteous.

"That could make things worse. I'd really appreciate it if you'd be discreet and keep what you saw to yourself." He paused, and as if he was talking about a side matter, he asked, "Did you confide in Rina?"

"No, but don't you think I should?"

Now he was sweating. "No, it'd be just as bad. In my position, I could be very helpful to you. Anything I can do for you?" he asked.

I paused for a minute before answering.

"Well, I'm in a very competitive class of Developing Countries at the university. If you could help me get ahead of the other students, I could beat them in the race to enter the law-school quota."

He looked relieved that I wasn't asking for money. "Sure, I can do that."

"Fine," I said. "Let me go over my papers and see what would help me most. I'll call you later on this week.

Two days later, I called him and asked to meet again.

"Although I believe it's public record, I wasn't able to track down the minutes of the Security Committee's session during the Non-Aligned Movement convention held very recently in Lusaka, Zambia. I know that your country attended the convention."

His eyes widened, "That's a confidential document!"

"Really?" I played dumb. "So why did my professor insist I use it as an example of the dynamics involved in the emergence of a third major block of non-aligned states?"

He didn't answer.

"I'll only take a quick peek. I promise I won't tell where I saw it, and by now you know I can keep a secret."

I had already graduated and didn't need these records, but that didn't matter. I was holding the cards. If he confronted me on that, I could say I was writing a thesis proposal for a master's degree, or whatever. He didn't have to believe my story. All he wanted to do was to shut me up.

The Non-Aligned Movement of the Third World Countries, convened in September 1970, had decided to prevent the West and the Eastern Bloc countries from stationing military bases in member countries. The detailed information on the decision and the deliberations, albeit not directly important for Israel, could be traded with the US and other Western countries for information they might have on the PLO. That, Israel needed.

No further pressure was necessary. I met him again in the Shalom Tower, and he gave me a magazine. Between its pages, he had inserted eleven pages on the deliberations and decisions of the 1970 Non-Aligned Movement convention. I submitted it to Alex with my report. Alex then asked me to "introduce" Gideon, a SHABAK agent, to the ambassador. Gideon would take over the handling of the ambassador. I needed to tell the ambassador that Gideon was my academic instructor at the university who wanted to ask "a few further questions."

When I tried to contact the ambassador, I was told by his staff that he was out of the country. Three months later it was announced that the ambassador had resigned from his country's diplomatic service and moved to Europe to work for a mining company. Obviously, now he couldn't care less if we threatened him with disclosing his clandestine romantic interludes.

"Good job," were the only words I heard from Alex when that case was over.

Good job. Why the hell would I remember that now?

———

After spending a week in training and briefing in Ramstein and another week in another location in Germany, after undergoing the fiasco in Armenia, and coming out empty-handed, no way could I tell myself "good job." I had a throbbing scar from the graze wound on my head; I was pissed off and frustrated as hell.

Good job. Right.

A month later, with the Tango matter still up in the air, I headed to Dubai on my next assignment in another case.

V

On the plane to Dubai, crammed in next to the window, I finished a package of dry crackers on the tray table. Two of the great universals of flying: dry crackers and narrow seats.

My new assignment had come quickly. The Agency had received a green light to cooperate with Mossad on identifying and cultivating Iranian scientists and key military personnel to defect. It had created a special operational team, code named TEMPEST. And best of all, it even had a promising contact. The "contact" was the sender of a letter to the US Consulate in Dubai, from someone calling himself Refigh, "a friend," in Farsi. He'd offered his intermediary services in liaising with an Iranian nuclear scientist who apparently wanted to defect to the US, and he'd asked the consulate to keep a lookout for a letter that he'd mail later. My first assignment: gather pointed intelligence on this potential defector and the intermediary, of the kind that only human assets can provide.

Unfortunately, there was nothing in the fingerprints department. Forensics had found zilch on either letter. We were pretty confident of a few things, however. According to the Agency's handwriting experts, the person who wrote the letters was educated, right-handed, in his late twenties to midthirties, and frequently wrote longhand in English. They thought that he was not Anglo-Saxon, but had learned English from a British teacher. Each letter carried a Dubai stamp and postmark, and appeared to have been mailed from Dubai City. Which was exactly where I was headed.

There was also a third letter, received recently at the consulate. I looked my copy. Like the previous two, its envelope had had no return address. The third letter consisted of just one line: PO Box 7233-11 Dubai.

I was familiar with that security procedure. The first letter mentions only a general intention; the second includes the actual approach; the third letter includes just a POB address with nothing else. Only the intended recipient—or someone who hijacks all of them, a lower probability—can link the letters.

The second letter had read:

Attention CIA station manager:

Sir, I am an Iranian national scientist working in one of my country's nuclear development centers. Pardon me for not identifying myself as I have already taken significant risks just by writing this letter. I wish to leave Iran and relocate to the US. I maintain substantial nonpublic information on Iran's nuclear arms development, which I am willing to disclose in return for American citizenship and a suitable job and housing for me and my family.

Thank you.

Refigh

Anonymous letters were often pranks, or, worse, traps—and therefore dangerous. Only rarely were they the real thing. My job was to see which it was: a prank, a trap, or, hopefully, the real thing.

Reviewing the letters, I identified a discrepancy. The initial letter was purportedly from a person who claimed to know the potential defector. However, the writer of the second letter claimed that he was the potential defector. That reminded me of questions posed to a doctor on a radio talk show purportedly for "a friend," when the subject matter is too personal for the caller to admit that he's in fact "the friend."

Dubai. It would be my first time there. On the surface, it was known as a banking and respectable regional center. Beneath, however, it was known as an international hotbed of money launderers, smugglers, and arms dealers. During my briefing I was shown evidence that it was teeming with mobsters—Indian, Asian, and Russian thugs; Arab terrorists; and Iranian government agents.

Over the past few weeks, Eric, Paul, and Benny had given me even more information about Dubai: it also had, apparently, a whole lot of Iranian traders trying to broker arms deals. Dubai's underground banking channels were used to transfer money for the 9/11 terrorists. Even A. Q. Khan, the Pakistani nuclear scientist, used Dubai to distribute his nuclear technology. And, according to Eric, Dubai was such a global rat's nest that Dubai's emir, Sheik Mohammed bin Rashid al-Maktoum, had just recently vowed to honor UN sanctions against Iran. Apparently he was trying to make sure that Dubai didn't wind up facing sanctions.

"Why?" I'd asked Eric, while we were in his office. I had just received my mission.

"Dubai is just across the bay from Iran. I think he finally understood the risks his city-state was taking if it continued to allow embargoed goods to be shipped through Dubai to Iran. Most of the Dubai banks have announced that they will no longer be taking new business from Iranian banks. And worst of all, at least from the Iranian perspective, Dubai is cooperating with the United States to uncover dummy corporations used by the Iranian Revolutionary Guard and other governmental or private entities to import embargoed goods.

"It's also harder now for an Iranian citizen to get a work visa, and the Dubai government is harassing arriving Iranian travelers by subjecting them to physical searches, even eye scanning. To bypass embargo restrictions, Iran has started placing orders for some dual-purpose goods, which can be used for civilian as well as for military purposes, to be shipped through Dubai."

According to Eric, there had recently been a case in which the Iranians attempted a circular transaction, placing an order through China to a European company for dual-use vacuum pumps. These can be used in civilian industry, but they're also essential for enriching uranium via thousands of centrifuges. There was another transaction, this time by Aban, an Iranian company. From Chinese companies it bought thirty tons of tungsten, used in the aircraft industry but also used to build missiles. Aban wanted the goods shipped to Dubai and then to Iran.

"That failed, though, when Dubai recently decided to cooperate with the US in stopping these bogus 'dual-purpose' shipments. Obviously, that decision seriously pissed off the Iranians, making the situation in Dubai extremely volatile. The Iranians aren't going to give up that easily on their stronghold in Dubai. Their undercover operatives in Dubai are trying to identify American agents who are collecting evidence of embargo violations. The Iranians know that the US and its allies will use any such evidence to increase pressure on Dubai to stop these practices, or else suffer sanctions for violating UN decisions.

"So, Dan, although your assignment is completely different, you are still a US agent, therefore you should watch your back," Eric concluded.

Of course I would. *I'll be watching my back, and front*, I thought. *I can't trust you guys too much. Not because you don't care, you do, but because you're so entangled in bureaucracy, writing reports and adhering to procedure. Hell, by the time you'd answer my cry for help, I could be on my back on a slab in the freezer, toes up.*

The Iranian government had been sending its agents to Dubai to threaten, attack, and even kill anyone who might be helping the US. So running into Iranian agents in Dubai would be a very real possibility. I knew that Dubai was dangerous territory for people with missions like mine; I even expected to be dealing with some very real, very nasty covert operatives, because Dubai was a place where huge interests and money were at stake. As were lives.

"I'm careful regardless," I said nonchalantly, although I sometimes wasn't.

An elderly Agency staffer came in and gave me a travel folder. "This is your Sheep Dip."

"My what?" I was sure I'd heard "deep shit." Only later I discovered it wasn't too far from the truth.

"Sheep Dip," he repeated. "that's an old Agency term taken from farming. On farms, sheep are dipped in chemicals to kill any disease-bearing lice or to clean their fleece before shearing. In tradecraft, it means disguising your identity by placing you in a legitimate setting. We give you clean documents—your sheep dip—so you can operate without suspicion." I had to admit that I'd never heard that one before. In the Mossad, we called it *Sipoor Kisooy*, our legend, or cover story.

I knew that for my short-term assignment, there was no need to go into "backstopping" an elaborate and expensive array of bogus identification documents and background info that would hold water if thoroughly investigated by a suspicious counterintelligence service. Basically, the old Five Freedoms of Cover had to be met, Freedom of Action: what I can do; Freedom of Movement: where I can go; Freedom of Leisure: how much time I will have for my "hobby"; Social Freedom: what kinds of people I can associate with; and finally, Financial Freedom: how much money I can spend.

"Inside the folder you'll find your new European passport, credit cards, family photos, and pocket debris. You also have an electronic ticket confirmation for a United Airlines flight out of Dulles International Airport."

"Please put me on another airline," I said, "I don't fly United, and anyway, I want to fly from New York, not Dulles. I need to run some errands with my children and dog in New York."

"There's a direct flight from JFK Airport with Emirates. You'll be undercover. So federal government rules about flying a US flag carrier won't apply. Should I book you on that flight?"

"Good, please do."

All went as planned. I went home, kissed my children good-bye over dinner, made dog-sitting arrangements for Snap, and returned to the airport to catch my flight to Dubai. And so here I was, leaning back in my too-narrow plane seat, crunching dry crackers, thinking what a fitting cryptonym TEMPEST was for the operation. I expected it to start quietly and end with a bang.

My favorite Beethoven piano sonata, No. 17 in D minor, nicknamed Tempest, also alternates between peacefulness and unexpected turbulence turning into a storm.

As we approached Dubai's international airport, I could see the famous palm-tree shaped man-made island, with its glittering villas for the rich and famous on each side. They look like something you'd see in South Beach, only whiter, much taller, much grander—all against the blue sea water on one side, and an empty desert backdrop on the other, like some kind of mirage. As I exited the sleek airport terminal, a wave of hot air hit my face. It was a fifteen-minute cab ride to the Hyatt Regency Hotel on the Deira Corniche, overlooking the Arabian Gulf at the mouth of Dubai Creek.

"Welcome, Mr. Van der Hoff." A neatly and modestly dressed receptionist smiled at me. She quickly gave me my room key card. Hearing her use my new name was strange. *You'll have to get used to it, as you did many times before, to other odd names assigned to you,* declared my little inner devil as I walked to the elevator. I'm now Jaap Van der Hoff, a trader in electronic spare parts with an office in

Rotterdam, and an apartment in Paris, where I rarely stay because my business requires constant travel. I roam Europe and the Middle East looking for business opportunities. Divorced, two adult children. One lives in my Paris apartment while he attends the Sorbonne University.

I had a delicious dinner at the hotel's Al Dawaar, a twenty-fifth-floor revolving restaurant. The views of the Arabian Gulf, the Creek, and the city of Dubai were spectacular. On one side was black glassy water, with the ancient desert horizon behind it cut by sharp palms. On the other was sleek metal and glass structures, whirring and lit, like some self-generating machine.

———

On the following day, playing the part, I scheduled an appointment with the manager of United Gulf Trust, a private banking subsidiary of the Swiss Alps Bank and Trust.

"My letter of introduction," I said, handing him a sealed envelope. Hamid Al Zarwai invited me to take a seat in his palatial office. He was a trim man in his late forties, with salt-and-pepper hair and wearing a dark, superbly tailored lightweight wool suit with a vest. His small, gold-rimmed glasses gave him an almost academic air. The temperature outside was 100 degrees Fahrenheit, but the windows were tinted and his office was cool.

He quickly read the letter that Eric had arranged. It was on the letterhead of Templehof Bank, Zurich, a Swiss bank secretly controlled by the Mossad as its proprietary company, without the Swiss government's or the bank management's knowledge.

"What can I do for you?" Hamid Al Zarwai asked in a polite tone. His English was British, and he sounded like the product of a private school.

"I own a company trading in electronic components for industrial use, and I'm closely affiliated with a much bigger company," I said. "We are looking for a way to"—I paused, as if looking for the right word—"penetrate into the Iranian market, without alienating the Americans." I waited for his reaction, but he just continued to listen. The buzzwords, *alienating the Americans,* delivered the message that the type of trade I had in mind was embargoed. It could mean business that violated the laws against sponsoring terror, or those against nuclear proliferation, or even both. I was very familiar with the rules of the US Treasury's Office of Foreign Assets Control, and I had no doubt that he, too, shared that knowledge.

Al Zarwai nodded, expressionless, his eyes on me.

"I need your help to assess how to go about it. We have very strong ties with German, Belgian, and Dutch manufacturing companies. They had previously traded with Iran but had to stop under international pressure. However, they now realize that Chinese and Russian companies came in their place, and the sky didn't fall. I think these manufacturing companies would agree to resume their exports to Iran if they could be guaranteed safe passage, to keep them out of hot water with their own governments as well as the US government. They conduct substantial trade with US companies and, for obvious reasons, don't want their plans to resume trading with Iran to wind up being public knowledge.

"I myself have nothing to lose by pissing off the Americans—my company operates out of Europe and has no American interests—but unfortunately the companies we represent could lose many millions if they wind up blacklisted by the US government."

"I understand," Al Zarwai said, very calm, very cool. Still his face remained expressionless. Had I piqued his interest? His eyes betrayed nothing; he had an excellent poker face, but his body language betrayed his effort to express no emotion. He *was* interested.

I went on. "European newspapers have written quite a lot recently about how the American government is banning American banks from doing any business with Iranian banks. So when I was talking to my affiliated companies about potential business with Iran, the first question they asked me was, how do you prevent business with Iran from being identified by the US? Can we use European banks without branches or ties with the US to avoid trouble?"

I was trying to convey that I knew that the US Treasury had compiled a list of Iran's major banks, such as Saderat, Bank Melli, and Sepah, and had blacklisted them along with many other banks and individuals, so, obviously, these banks were out.

"Why?" he asked, again with placid eyes, although I was certain he knew the answer.

"Because the European companies we work with insist upon receiving letters of credit and bank wire transfers for the goods sold. They know that the US is monitoring the world's banking activities to detect illegal trade with Iran in violation of US and UN sanctions, and they don't want to get caught doing business with Iran. The US reaction is likely to be—well, painful." I paused, waiting for a comment, but Al Zarwai just sat there nodding without saying anything.

A moment later, he finally reacted. Slow gears? Or did something about me finally click? He'd sized me up and liked what he saw?

"Don't worry," he said almost casually as he took his glasses off. He began cleaning them with a lens wipe. "We use intermediary banks for these purposes. Iranian banks know how to do it."

I knew what they were doing: "stripping." Asking intermediary foreign banks to remove any markers of the transactions' ties to Iran or to Iranian banks.

"As you must know, Mr. Van der Hoff, we like to help our customers meet their legitimate goals. I think that what you are looking for is possible. However, that is not the type of business we do."

Our research had definitely shown Al Zarwai's bank as being active in financing hush exports to Iran, and now he was playing hard to get? When he saw my slightly raised eyebrows, he added, "We finance transactions, issue letters of credit and other documentary financing. Regarding all other aspects of your commercial relationship, I suggest you meet Mr. Kamiar Nemati."

That name sounded very Iranian to me. Nonetheless, his extra cautiousness was obvious and understood. He couldn't risk his bank and its Swiss parent by discussing ways and means to bypass UN sanctions with every Tom, Dick, and Harry who barged into his office, particularly when the visitor could be a US government agent, like me.

"Who is Mr. Nemati?"

"The very respectable president of Cross Gulf Trading Ltd., a Dubai company specializing in trade with Iran."

"Thank you. Please make the introduction," I requested.

"With pleasure. Please give me your business card. I'll have Mr. Nemati contact you."

I gave him my business card and wrote on its back my hotel's telephone number. "I'll be in Dubai for another week, if he could call me."

He got up. I shook his hand and left. Outside his office, I wiped my hand on a tissue. Al Zarwai's hand was clammy.

VI

January 2007, Dubai

If I was being monitored—and I was certain that I was—I was satisfied that I'd taken the first step to make my visit look legitimate, doing what a trader was expected to do. And if suspected of being a foreign agent, my conduct could not support that. It was time to move to the next step. It was part of my "trader" legend. It was also the real purpose of my trip. I went to We Forward Unlimited. According to the Dubai postal records, this company owned the postal box that the third letter to the consulate gave as a point of contact.

We Forward Unlimited occupied half of the third floor of a modern office building in a commercial area filled with similar buildings, one giant gleaming office park. More than ten people were working in an office with sleek leather couches in the waiting area. Everything here, just as in the rest of Dubai, seemed hypermodern. The air conditioning was glacial. A quick glance down a large hallway showed state-of-the-art computer equipment.

A man dressed in typical Arab garb—a tunic, in his case bright white with blue trim—but without the *kaffiyeh* headdress, welcomed me.

"Welcome, sir, how can I help you?"

"I need office services—"

"Please follow me." He brought me to a small office with glass walls.

I began: "I frequent Dubai several times a year on business and intend to increase my presence here in the future. However, I don't have a local office where I can pick up my mail. I don't really need an actual office in Dubai for the time being, but I want my Dubai address on my business cards and letterhead to look respectable."

"We are perfectly fit for your needs, sir," he answered. "You can use our street address or our post office box."

"Can you tell me a little more about how it works? Thing is I travel constantly and don't want to risk missing any business opportunities."

"No problem, sir, here's how it works. First, you pick an address."

"Well, as I said, I don't have an address here, that's the problem. I stay at a hotel each time I visit." I played the confused businessman who keeps asking questions.

He smiled patiently. "We can provide you with an address in Dubai. You may also want to consider our services in other countries as well. We can help you with the same address service in any of the Gulf States, in some European countries, and even in the US. You can give any of these addresses to your business contacts, if you need more than one address."

"I think a local post office box is better. I don't want to be embarrassed if someone actually comes to your office and realizes it isn't mine."

"Not a problem, you can use our POB address."

"Do you have only one?"

"In Dubai? Yes."

"Tell me about your mail procedures."

"When we receive your mail, sir, you decide what mail gets opened, scanned, e-mailed, and then shredded, or forwarded unopened to you by postal mail. When we receive mail addressed to you, we first scan the sealed envelope, and post the image on a website that only you will be able to access by entering a password. If you wish to delete the image, you can do that with a click of the mouse. You can also leave us a message on the website to scan the contents of the envelope and e-mail them to you. Once you read the contents, you can delete or print it anywhere.

"See, the great thing about our service is that no matter where you are in the world, you can read your mail. You don't need an e-mail address to receive important mail, you know," he said in a low, confiding tone. "E-mail boxes can be hacked and business opportunities stolen, because your business rivals will know where to look. But with our system nobody but you and us knows that you have a dedicated website where you can read, delete, or print your mail."

"What do you do with the originals after scanning?"

"We follow our clients' instructions, of course. Forward to another location, keep them in our archives until the client comes to pick them up, or shred them.

"How much is the service?"

"A one-time setup fee of one hundred fifty dollars, and twenty dollars monthly. Additionally, we charge a nominal fee for each scanned letter."

"Let's do it," I said. I had to appear legit, and my inner little devil was already making suggestions about how the service would benefit my investigation. Their prices seemed excessive compared with similar services, but I came there for the role they played, not to get a cheap deal. Besides, with the Washington bean counters' generosity, I could afford to be a little lavish, provided I didn't spend more than fifty dollars a day on "miscellaneous." Otherwise, I'd need to submit a receipt for each dollar I spent. Each dollar! Just the thought bugged the hell out of me. Auditors never participate in overseas operations. The only physical risk they take is possibly breaking a nail on a keyboard. They don't understand that by making me ask for receipts for every dime I spend, I might expose myself as a government bureaucrat. Most businesses don't treat their employees that way. Never mind I might be endangering my life, as long as an audit doesn't catch me spending an extra ten dollars! Think an IRS audit is scary? Try my bean counters' review of my monthly expense account. Sometimes I think I should use them as prisoner interrogators—they would drive even the most stubborn cons out of their minds and make them sing.

My new friend at We Forward Unlimited photocopied my European passport in the name of Jaap Van der Hoff. It was one of the "throwaway" identities that I've used when involved in deep cover clandestine operations. This showed my home address as 1359, rue Beccaria, 75012 Paris, France. In fact that was just my "clean accommodation address," a requisite for building me a new identity.

After the formalities were concluded, he gave me a copy of the service agreement and a website address. "Log into www.weforward unlimited.com/vanderhoff and create your own password. Then, whenever you log in, just enter your password and you'll see your incoming mail."

"Oh, I have one more question. I travel in Africa and sometimes I don't have access to the Internet. I'll need physically to get my mail."

"Not a problem, sir. If you can't log in, just call us to give a forwarding address."

"That's perfect, thank you."

Had I observed the Moscow Rule, *Everyone is potentially under opposition control?* I wasn't sure that I had. But I wasn't sure what to do about it if I hadn't. These rules were originally created for CIA agents operating in the Communist Soviet Union, during the Cold War. The Cold War was over. The need for the rules was not.

A day later, I met the anxious-for-business Mr. Nemati. He was in his late fifties, chubby and friendly—even jolly-seeming—with a disarming ear-to-ear grin. He seemed to smile constantly. We sat in his plush office, a block from my hotel. After I described my company's activities and "our wish to extend our trade and become intermediaries for sales of machinery, compounds, and technology to Iran," he went on to explain why I had made the right move in coming to Dubai, and, of course, in coming to see him.

"Dubai is an international marketplace," he said, standing at the window of his twenty-fourth-floor office and looking down on all of Dubai. "Since we are the only country in the region without oil, we use the advantage that Allah has seen to provide us: proximity to Iran."

Nemati didn't mention that though Dubai's citizens were mostly Sunni and Arab, the geographical proximity to Iran was so dominant that Dubai's economy was practically run by people of Iranian descent: Shiite and non-Arab.

"This is little Tehran," he said with a smile, like a proud father telling me about an exceptionally accomplished son. "You know the history of Dubai? It was once filled with Bedouins—nomads. A steady diet of camel, and more camel, and camel milk. But today! Today there are 450,000 Iranians living here who have family ties to Iran. There are also thousands of Iranian-owned businesses. We have more Iranians here than any other place outside Iran." I knew that California had more Iranian expats, but I decided not to look too knowledgeable in these matters.

"The sanctions the Americans are trying to impose on the world do not exist here. Therefore, if you can't trade with Iran directly, the next best place to do business with Iran is Dubai." He smiled in self-satisfaction, patted his belly, then suggested lunch at the Iranian Club. I expected another nice restaurant on a higher floor of a modern office building. Hence my surprise when we entered a large compound on Oud Metha Road, not far from the Indian Club.

The Iranian Club was a small city unto itself. It included an elegant hotel and theaters with intricate Moorish architecture; a large shimmering swimming pool; a restaurant; even a sports stadium. In the restaurant, pictures of Ayatollah Khomeini and Hassan Nasrallah, Hezbollah's chief, hung in the entrance. Everyone around us spoke Farsi; the menu was in Farsi. At the host station, two customers—European-looking blonde women—were putting on headscarves provided by the restaurant. Head covering was mandatory here.

After settling in, ordering soft drinks and lunch, and dancing around the issues, we got down to business.

I recited my legend and gave him copies of brochures and catalogs, finding myself once again impressed by the Agency's professionalism in creating such an extensive legend. The manufacturing company I was representing was a real and viable company. Thankfully, the owner had agreed to hire my "company" and thereby unwittingly provided a plausible cover story for my borrowed identity. The Agency had arranged the representation through a third party, supposedly acting for me and with his own legend. The terms were simple. I would act as an intermediary: I would not be able to bind his company in any agreement, and all payments for sales made would be wired directly from the buyer to the manufacturing company's bank account. When funds were cleared, the manufacturing company would pay my "company" a commission. The benefit for his company would be any business I could drum up while I conducted my real job—snooping—about which he was totally unaware. It was a win-win situation, or was it?

"How would you like to proceed?" Kamiar Nemati asked, in front of him a plate of spicy Persian rice, lavash—a thin flatbread that is the most popular type of bread in Iran—with chopped tomato and minted yogurt sauce. I had ordered a lamb stew; it came bubbling hot. "You'll have to advise me," I said, "though isn't incorporating a local company generally the way to go?"

"If you're planning to operate outside our new free-trade zone—"

As he spoke, the waiter came to refresh our water and fumbled a little, dribbling the water down the side of my glass. Nemati barked sharply at him in Farsi. His tone was so sharp, his chastisement so swift, that I was startled as well. The waiter flinched and wiped my glass down; I gathered that he was apologizing profusely.

Without missing a beat, Nemati turned to me, smiled another wide, disarming grin, and finished his sentence, "Indeed, yes, you'll need a local partner to own fifty-one percent of the company. That's the law here. I can suggest several names, if you wish."

"Please do. Whom do you have in mind?" I asked.

"Well, it could be me. I'm a Dubai citizen," he smiled again.

"What would you bring into the company?" I asked, I couldn't look too eager, although I was.

"Your ability to incorporate," Nemati said, eating a piece of lavash. He ate with surprising delicacy for a large man, almost daintily patting the corner of his mouth with his napkin. "But, obviously, I will bring business as well, certainly. I do have strong ties to Iran."

"Any connections within the Iranian government? The reason I ask is a few other companies I represent have on offer some complex technologies and equipment. Governments are their typical clients."

"Of course, I have connections in most ministries of the Iranian government. In what areas might you need them?" Nemati asked.

"Nuclear research and energy production. For peaceful purposes, of course."

He observed me for a while and carefully selected his words, without hiding his excitement. He placed his hand on his belly, lightly tapping his fingers on his vest.

"This is a matter I will need to discuss with my colleagues," he said. "I should ask, though—there are so many aspects to nuclear energy—any specific areas you have in mind?"

"From reactor cooling equipment to electric and electronic machinery, from enrichment equipment to chemical compounds used in the process."

"I see," he just said and looked at me, trying to measure me up. His broad smile had diminished but had not disappeared; it was now more of a smirk. "I'll get back to you on that. I'm sure we could do business together."

Well, at least he did not brush me off like Hamid Al Zarwai, the banker who elegantly suggested I speak to Nemati. In fact, I didn't expect Nemati to agree immediately. Once I mentioned the word *nuclear* I was going to be cross-referenced and checked a hundred times over. The Iranians in general are not a stupid people, and Nemati was no exception to the rule. There was no question in my mind that the moment I said *nuclear* I became an immediate subject of interest to several intelligence agencies, first and foremost VEVAK. That was part of the risk involved in the trade. I couldn't offer him sewing machines or fruit-juice extraction machines and get the kind of interest I wanted. I'd put my head in at the snake pit, hoping to survive the inspecting hissing.

Still, I felt that the TEMPEST seeds were planted. I had no doubt that I'd hear from him soon. I was too big a fish to throw back into the sea, whether I was the real thing or a foreign agent. Under either hat I'd be an interesting subject.

I sauntered back to my hotel. The Iranian influence was visible wherever I looked. From the Iranian mosque to the Iranian hospital, from the signs on the stores to the Iranian merchants in the Spice Market, from the Iranian restaurants to the Iranian banks. Everywhere, huge, beautifully landscaped buildings and crowds of well-dressed people. The city's economy seemed booming.

Back at the hotel, I used my laptop to e-mail Eric an encrypted report on my visit to We Forward Unlimited: *It will help if you can hack into* www.weforwardunlimited.com *and surreptitiously download its customer list. I don't know the extension of the particular client who sent the letter to the consulate, but suggest you try the extension 'Refigh.'* I hoped that Refigh had opted for the website option, rather than physically forwarding incoming mail to another location. Then

I inserted a one-liner asking about the Tango defection case. I was anxious to know when it would be resumed.

A few hours later, Eric's response arrived: *See the attached spreadsheet with the customer list. The name Refigh doesn't appear.*

I reviewed the attached list. It contained 1,609 names of customers. Hell, I thought, how do I sort it out?

I sent Eric another encrypted e-mail: *Thanks, but the list can't help much at this time. Can you match the names on the list against any existing list of Iranians associated with the nuclear program?*

I waited, ordering one, then two beers from room service. Finally, I heard the beep of an incoming message. The decrypted message read: *Dan, see the revised list, only 16 names remain, but it's possible some are aliases, and we may not have a complete updated list of all Iranians associated with their nuclear program. Eric.*

I looked at the list he had attached. It contained sixteen Iranian names, all male. Each name was followed by a short description of the man's occupation. There were six chemical engineers, two chemistry researchers, six physicists, and two mathematicians. Although the list was short, on its face it was a bridge to nowhere.

I walked out onto the small balcony off my room to do two things: look at the Gulf views, and think. What should I do next? Send a letter to the Dubai POB and ask Refigh to contact me? That would call for a carefully preplanned operation; this was also outside the defined duties of my mission. All I was instructed to do was identify the true owner of the box. I couldn't see a solution, and I was frustrated. *What's the matter,* nudged my inner little devil. *All of a sudden, you decided to follow orders to the letter? What, have you become a wimp? Where's the notorious defiance? People who behave don't make history.*

He was right, of course, but I decided to postpone any decision until after I had eaten. Never make an important decision when you are hungry, says an old Chinese proverb, I advised my little devil. *There isn't such a proverb,* he responded. Well, then I've just invented one. Frustrated, I locked my laptop's keyboard, applied the safety measures against attempted use even with an external device, locked it in my room safe, and went out.

Knowing nothing about Dubai for ordinary people, I went to the Gold Souk, a dazzling walk through all manner of gold, with vendors selling earrings, rings, necklaces, pendants. The streetlights made the gold shine in the night. Shops sold oils and perfumes, spices and fish—the same goods people might have found in a marketplace right here thousands of years ago.

And there were shawarma stands. Shawarma is lamb cooked on a rotating skewer, then cut into thin strips and placed into warm pita bread with vegetables and white Tahini dressing; the scent-rich roasting lamb was irresistible. I stopped at one stand and got an Iranian version of the dish for AED 5—approximately one dollar and thirty cents. I decided not to itemize that meal to the bean counters in Washington; they might get ideas about my ability to save on the cost of food.

I strolled through the market, enjoying my shawarma immensely. Soon, though, I realized that a man was walking just behind me, slightly off to the side. I could see him out of the corner of my eye; he was in his early thirties, and wore a black shirt and pants. As I kept him surreptitiously in sight, concentrating on my food, the man passed me, making the kind of brush-contact usually performed when two undercover agents meet in a public place, and quickly and discreetly transfer or exchange documents with no word other than "Sorry." Only a professional would notice. For any bystander, the incident would seem accidental and meaningless. He shoved a note into my pocket, and disappeared into the crowd. *Mr. Vanderhof,* read the note. *Please meet me at the parking lot behind the food stand. I have information for you.*

I kept on walking and thought about it. Usually I don't meet strange men in dark parking lots, not having a death wish or a desire to be robbed. However, under the circumstances, I decided to take a limited risk. I hailed a cab and instructed the cabbie to drive the fifty yards back to the parking lot behind the stand where I'd bought the shawarma. There, next to a late-model Japanese car, stood the man who'd stuck the note into my pocket. "Stay here," I told the cabbie when I'd made sure that the man was alone. Although I was armed, and had to be ready for any hostile encounter, I moved forward anyway.

The man lit a cigarette and I could see his face. He seemed to be a young Arab, no more than thirty years old, with a wide, furrowed brow. He took a hit off his cigarette, then nodded deferentially to me. He took a few steps toward me, in a nonthreatening manner and said, "Mr. Van der Hoff, thank you for coming."

I nodded, waiting for him to explain what he wanted, and why the aura of secrecy. I turned my hand in his general direction, and pressed on the crown of my watch. It wasn't just a simple, sporty-looking watch. Next to its numeral 3 was a video camera lens that could pick up clear images up to thirty feet away, and record any conversation within that range. The 32-gig capacity enabled me to shoot up to 120 minutes of high quality video. First, I took four still snapshots. The lighting, though, was poor. I wasn't sure that I would have a clear image of his face.

"I have information for you."

"Regarding the government's microelectronic chips tender bid?" I asked.

When he seemed baffled, I continued, "I'm interested, and would consider payment, but only if the information is solid." I stuck to my legend as an electronic components trader.

"Electronic parts? No, I have information regarding the letter."

"What letter?"

"The letter sent to the consulate."

True to my cover as a trader, I had to demonstrate complete ignorance. "What do you mean? Which consulate? I'm afraid you might be mistaken," and took a step back to the cab.

"Please, Mr. Van der Hoff." He was adamant.

I stopped, "What letter? And, just how did you know my name?" I said quickly in a mix of feigned fear and surprise.

"Mr. Van der Hoff, I'm talking about the letter to the consulate, and I understand you are in Dubai to talk about it."

That was a take it or leave it offer. If I continued to deny any knowledge, I might convince him he was mistaken—and pass on the contact opportunity. On the other hand I couldn't blow my cover just because a stranger in a dark parking lot was trying to tell me something.

"I know who you are," he said, a little grimly.

I wasn't alarmed, but I had to stay and see what he had to say. "How did you find out my name?" I put my hand into my pocket to feel the assuring metal touch of my polymer-frame high-velocity Glock 23 with its silencer.

"I have friends."

"OK, tell me about the letter you say was sent to the consulate. You mean the Dutch Consulate regarding my registration? Are my competitors trying to defame me?"

"Mr. Van der Hoff, I think we should stop playing games."

"I'm ready for that as well, so tell me what's it all about," I said, always leaving him the initiative to move forward and for me to withdraw.

"The letter talked about a scientist, and you came here to talk about it, so let's talk."

I had to keep my cover and act ignorant, as any normal uninvolved businessman would do. Although of course I wanted him to continue. "Thanks for the information, good-bye," I said and turned toward to my cab, expecting him to call me back as any bazaar store owner would do after rebuffing your final offer. But he didn't.

I got into the cab and returned to my hotel. I had to have him checked out; it could've been a trap by anyone, including the Dubai police. I had heard that the sanitary conditions in the Dubai prison system needed major improvements; I had no intention of finding out firsthand if the rumor were true.

But was it a trap? I couldn't tell. He certainly had an agenda with me. He wanted to make contact, that's for sure, but for what purpose? Did he want to surprise me and put my legend to the test? He mentioned one letter. There were three. The first two mentioned a scientist. But that might mean nothing. How did he know that I had a connection with them, or with one of them? Obviously, there had been a serious breach of security. From connecting me with any of the letters, it was only a short distance to unveiling my true identity, or at least my affiliation. That was bad news. I had to decide what to do next.

I considered my choices. Abandon ship and mission and return to the US before any damage was done, probably to my person? Or continue using my alias and let whoever was watching me monitor my actions, giving me the opportunity to turn the tables and see who they were? I know well that all reason stops at the entry points to the Middle East. But if that person was telling me the truth, his behavior was simply stupid.

Since I always hold the opposition—any opposition—in high esteem, I decided to look for another, more likely reason behind such an encounter. He never said what he wanted me to do, and didn't leave any means of future communication with him.

My inner little devil was no help. *Hey*, he said, *can't you see what he was doing? Have you lost all your senses? The man could, just could, be for real. He wanted your attention and to make you do something or go somewhere. I know, I know, how did he know to approach you? He must have had prior knowledge that you were operating under cover and might have trailed you just as he did today. That's bad news.*

No matter how many times I asked myself the question—how the hell did the man know to approach me?—neither my little devil nor I had a good answer.

In my room, I logged into www.weforwardunlimited.com/van derhoff. To my surprise, a message was blinking. Probably a routine welcome notice from the company, I thought. When I opened it, the message was unroutinely unwelcoming. *We know who you are and why you are in Dubai. You must leave immediately if you don't want to get hurt. Take this message seriously.*

The message was not signed. What the hell, I thought, I had made no progress whatsoever in discovering the identity of the person behind the Dubai PO box on the letters to the consulate. Yet whoever sent me the threat knew about my unique, password-protected web address through We Forward Unlimited. It had to be someone from within that company, or a hacker who had broken into my mailbox, or worse, into my computer. More troubling was the indication that the sender knew who I was. This meant that he didn't buy the Jaap Van der Hoff legend—or maybe he was trying to smoke me out from behind the legend, hoping that by scaring me I'd make a mistake and reveal my real identity and affiliation? That's one step before circulating to news agencies around the world the photo in which I'm blindfolded and ask the US to yield to my captors' demands or I die.

I sent Eric a message about the threat and the encounter, attaching an image file with the snapshots I'd taken in the parking lot.

What do you make of it? Eric replied.

Beats me, I responded. *There's no question that my cover was blown and that someone was able to post a message on my private box at the mail service company. The posted message isn't so earthshaking. What worries me is who knew I had that box and bothered to threaten me, and why.*

Eric messaged back: *Dan, I meant the encounter you had, not the message you received. However, since you brought it up, do you see a connection between the two incidents? As to the image file you sent, the outcome was too dark and blurred to identify the person. I'm sending it to the lab to run advanced decoding software to enhance the quality.*

I answered: *I suspect there is, but I have no basis to support the suspicion.*

Eric's next message came an hour later: *Obviously there's been a breach of security that we can't control or risk. Rent another room at your hotel for a 'business associate' who will arrive soon. Take the key, quietly move to the other room and wait for instructions. Keep both rooms. I don't want you to check out of your current hotel room and demonstrate that you have changed your behavior immediately after reading the threat. As to the Tango operation, it's still on hold.*

In fifteen minutes, I was sitting in an upgrade. When the receptionist had told me that the new room for my business associate would cost $515 a night, I immediately thought of the antacid that the bean counters in Washington would start popping when they saw the hotel bill. But I could always blame Eric. Before entering the new room, I'd made sure that no one was watching me, other than the hotel's hidden security cameras. All of a sudden, a small assignment to identify who was behind a post office box—with no apparent active opposition—had the potential to become seriously confrontational.

Other than waiting for instructions, I had nothing to do. It was late. It had been a long day. I slept.

VII

January 2007, Dubai

As I finished a late room-service brunch the next morning, an incoming message popped up on my computer monitor. *We now have a clear image but no trace on the person who approached you. Stay put for another day or two until we make further investigation.*

How could I object to spending one or two more days at the hotel's sunny pool, courtesy of Uncle Sam?

I lazed by the pool for a couple of hours, taking an occasional dip and getting sunburned in the process while I analyzed all options. That in turn called for a conversation with Eric. Exchanging e-mails was too limiting. However, the only place to make a secure telephone call would be from the US Consulate. There was still time to change my clothes and get to the consulate before it closed for the day. But even though it was in a high-rise, I didn't think it'd be wise to be seen entering it if "someone" knew who I was. The Consulate would likely be monitored by all sorts of FOE—Forces of Evil—a code I use until I identify my enemy, from Iran to al-Qaeda.

I was a European citizen visiting Dubai. What plausible business could I have at the US Consulate? Request a visa? European passport holders don't need a visa to enter the US for ninety days.

Back in my room, I got a message from Eric: *Total market change.* These were code words for *Security breached. Leave immediately. Don't use this computer until it's cleared.*

I stuffed my computer and a few essentials into my briefcase, leaving behind my small suitcase and the rest of my clothing, and walked outside. To disguise my departure, I didn't check out of the hotel. I entered an Internet café nearby and prepared a benign-looking e-mail to Eric's Gmail address, hinting about a possible source of the threat: *Maybe the trouble started with my son. I'll go and see how he is doing.*

I went to the airport, changing cabs twice. After I was fairly confident that I wasn't being shadowed, and was sure that no surveillance cameras saw me, I wiped my gun clean and dumped it in a trash can—and caught the next flight to Paris.

VIII

January 2007, Paris

I went straight to "my apartment" in the 12th arrondissement. It was occupied by André, a French student paying low rent to live there and pose as my son. The Agency subsidized the rent through an accommodating but unknowing French real-estate agent. I'd recognize André from the photos in my Sheep Dip. André was supposed to recognize me from "family" photos that the Agency gave the realtor to decorate the apartment.

Like a lot of apartments in the area, the ceilings were low, with ancient wood beams; a balcony looked out onto the standard Parisian courtyard. My framed photos—landscape shots of my "home" country, which could be anywhere in Europe—were on the wall, and my clothes and other personal belongings were in the closets. "This apartment is still under 1948 rent control laws," was the legend that the realtor had offered as to why André had to pose as my son, when all he wanted was to rent a cheap apartment advertised in the newspaper. "Monsieur needs to maintain and support the fact that he's never abandoned his residence, although he now travels constantly and is there only a few times a year, since a member of his immediate family lives in the apartment," the realtor had explained.

André hadn't seemed to care. Why should he? A furnished apartment, well below market price, with two bedrooms and an absentee landlord who visited twice or three times a year for two or three days?

"There are other conditions," the realtor had told him at the time. "When Monsieur Van der Hoff comes to Paris, he must sleep at the apartment, and you must introduce him as your father if you ever meet a third person." André had obviously agreed. For all he cared, presumably, I could be a drug dealer, although I'm sure he hoped I wasn't a serial killer.

When I used my key and entered the apartment, André wasn't in. I looked around, trying to figure out whether my security contamination had started here. I went through André's things. There was nothing suspicious. I found all the trappings you'd expect from a senior at the Sorbonne, including philosophy books, an iPod, and a small quantity of weed wrapped in a foil paper. One thing that surprised me, though, was women's clothing hung in the closet and makeup accessories in the bedroom. A woman was staying here, I realized. It was a clear violation of the agreement with André. As I sat on the living room sofa, the door opened and André walked in with a young woman. Both were dressed in black. The woman was smoking a cigarette, fouling the room with smoke. André seemed surprised to see me.

"Bonjour, André, mon petit," I said and hugged him. The woman looked at André in anticipation for an introduction.

I moved first and gave her my hand, "Hi, I'm Jaap, André's father. He wasn't expecting me," I said in French with a broad smile.

"Monica," she said and took off her dark sunglasses, revealing deep blue eyes. She had wavy, black hair, probably dyed; fair skin; a long, almost horsey face; and multiple piercings in each ear. Even so, she was attractive enough. She appeared to be twenty-six or twenty-seven years old, dressed in a tight black miniskirt and heels. So, André prefers older women, I thought; he was only twenty-two.

"Monica is my friend," said André. "She's from Germany, so let's talk in English, her French isn't that great."

I thanked André in my heart, because *my* French was also wobbly.

"Sorry I didn't call you earlier, but my plans have changed, so I decided to see how you were doing."

"I'm fine," André continued with the charade, but I sensed he had to make an effort. Realizing I had noticed that Monica was living in the apartment without my permission, he said, "Oh, Monica is staying here for a few days, I hope you don't mind."

With my earlier cursory review of the apartment, I'd already figured out that Monica had installed herself there.

"You know the rule," I said, "Even for a few days, I must report to the landlord whoever is living here, or face eviction from an apartment that your grandfather first rented decades ago."

"I'm sorry," he said, realizing that he was caught red-handed.

"I need a copy of Monica's passport, and her full home address," I said. That was bull, of course, but it created an opportunity to run a background on Monica. They didn't react.

"It's a little early, perhaps, but please let me take you both out to dinner," I suggested, "and we can find a place to photocopy her passport." Monica seemed disturbed a tad. Apparently, she wasn't aware of the reporting requirement, or maybe she felt uneasy that André had never mentioned her to me.

We dined at La Table du Marquis, a simple, excellent restaurant just a few steps down the street. The place served rustic French food, and André and Monica split a bottle of Bordeaux. After dinner we walked to a nearby all-night copy center, and I asked Monica for her passport.

She hesitated for a moment and started digging in her purse.

"I'm afraid I don't have it here," she said. I don't always know if people are telling the truth, but this one sounded like an outright lie.

"Please look again," I said. "I hate to say it, but you can't stay at the apartment unless I report you to the landlord."

She let out a sigh, "Let me see again."

I followed her hands with my eyes, and I saw the red cover of her German passport—she was clearly trying to cover it with her hands, doing a sloppy job. I said, pointing, "There it is."

Reluctantly she gave me the passport. I asked her for her home address.

"Salvador-Allende Str. 1320, 12559 Berlin, Germany," she said.

I copied her passport; Monica Mann was born in 1984, making her twenty-two years old. *She doesn't look twenty-two, no way,* said my inner little devil. He was right, I looked at Monica again. She looked much older than twenty-two.

There are exceptions of course, but in most cases, the first gut feeling is the correct feeling. That was another maxim by Alex, my Mossad Academy instructor. He must have paraphrased another Moscow Rule: *Never go against your gut; it is your operational antenna.* Here, I knew he was probably right. I scanned the copies of Monica's passport and e-mailed them to Eric from the copy center's computer via a European pass-through e-mail address: *Notification to landlord of temporary guest at 1359, rue Beccaria, 75012 Paris, France. Monica Mann, home address: Salvador-Allende Str. 1320, 12559 Berlin, Germany.*

Eric did not expect any "temporary guest" in my Paris apartment serving only as an accommodation address. He would check her out.

We returned to the apartment. I went to sleep in "my" bedroom while André and Monica slept in his. I was bothered and jet-lagged, but managed to sleep deeply sleep until garbage truck noises woke me up at an early hour. Not sure why, but being wakened by a garbage truck in Paris was preferable to being wakened by one in New York—the trucks in Paris seemed gentler, somehow. Or maybe it was the city itself. Paris was daintier than New York, trimmed with cornices. Between the two cities, I always thought of New York as the man—impressive, concrete, a solid grid—and Paris as the woman, exquisite with her narrow streets, late lunches, and pink afternoon light. I left the apartment quietly, found a patisserie with croissants au chocolat fresh out of the oven; and got a copy of *Le Monde*. When I returned to the apartment, André was sipping coffee from a mug and getting ready to go out.

"Where's Monica?" I asked. "I wanted to say good-bye, I'm leaving soon," I said nonchalantly. "Is she a student at the Sorbonne as well?"

"Oh, she just left to run some errands," he said as he went to the door. "No, she's an art student in Germany and travels in Europe taking photos of old buildings to prepare her thesis. We met when she arrived in Paris. She was looking for a place to stay, and I invited her to stay here. I'm sorry I didn't ask for your permission, I thought it was necessary only for a sublet, not for occasional guests."

"The thing is, the landlord watches me like a hawk. He's looking for any violation to evict me, so he can charge a new tenant a much higher rent."

"I'm sorry," he said again.

"At any rate, I'm leaving in a few hours."

I was bothered, but couldn't pinpoint why, exactly. As soon as André left, I bolted the door and went to André's room. It was still a complete mess, just like my own son's at that age. Sneakers strewn on the floor, a half-eaten croissant on the nightstand, fallen stacks of textbooks. I searched his closet and dresser and found nothing. Then I went through Monica's clothing. Other than some black garters and kinky underwear, all looked innocuous. I sat on the bed and looked around. I moved the prints on the wall—two Klimt reproductions— and found nothing but dust. *You're a paranoid,* said my inner little devil, *but keep on looking, even paranoids are sometimes right.* Under the bed I found a big suitcase, but it contained only shoes, some leather pumps, and high-heeled boots.

As I pushed the suitcase back under the bed, though, it was stopped by something. I turned the lights on and could see a floorboard slightly raised; its edge was stopping the suitcase. I pushed the bed aside. I found a screwdriver in the kitchen and used its edge to lift the board. *Fuck.* Was it?

Yes.

Sitting in a cavity under the floorboard was an FN Five-seveN pistol. The Five-seveN from FN Herstal is a single-action gun with a 5.7x28mm caliber, with a range of 2,100 feet, nicknamed "cop killer" because it easily penetrates body armor. I pulled the gun out using a towel, careful not to smudge or to add any prints. The Five-seveN is made of lightweight polymer, I knew that, but I was still surprised at how light it felt. In all my work with Mossad and CIA, I'd never held or even seen one up close before. So what the hell would a Sorbonne student be doing with a "cop killer"?

Or maybe the gun was Monica's? It was so light. The perfect gun for a woman, perhaps? Under the gun sat a plastic bag. Inside were two passports, seven credit cards, three driver's licenses, and a wad of euro bills, at least €10,000—approximately $12,000. There was a note attached: *Pension 1 for December.* I examined the passports: one German, one Swiss, and one Austrian. All passports and driver licenses had Monica's photo, and a DOB of June 12, 1978, in East Berlin, when it was still part of the Communist Democratic Republic of Germany. However, the names on the passports and driver's licenses were different; Gertrud Maria Schmitz, Marita Klara Haas, and Alexandra Emma Bayer.

Ha! She is *twenty-eight, not twenty-two*, I told my inner little devil. *You were right.* On the other hand, maybe these dates of birth were fake like the documents. I took snapshots with my digital camera, but had to make a quick decision: be satisfied with the snapshots or run to the copy center, risking that Monica would return to the apartment. I opted for the latter. I quickly collected the passports, the driver's licenses, and credit cards; put the floorboard back in place; and ran to the door. I stopped. *What if the gun is also Monica's?*

I returned to the bedroom, pried up the floorboard again, recovered the gun and its magazine, and put back the board. I copied the serial number of the gun and hid the gun under my coat, then went to the copy center and quickly scanned the documents and sent them to three different e-mail addresses, one for each passport. Since my notebook computer's encryption facility could have been compromised, I again used the copy center's public Internet access. For additional safety, I used the Agency's innocuous-looking e-mail boxes in Gmail, Hotmail, and Yahoo: *I attach a copy of my son's new live-in girlfriend's passport, please ask the travel agent to see if a work visa could be issued.* I sent a fourth e-mail with the gun's serial number without explanation. The fifth e-mail went to a different address. It just said, *Look what I found in my son's apartment, a serial number.*

I returned to the apartment. Thankfully, it was still empty. I returned everything back the way it was, left the apartment, and called Eric's mobile from a payphone. I hung up immediately, though, realizing that it was still night in Washington.

As I walked away, I heard the phone ring. It was Eric.

"Dan?" I heard his almost metal-sounding voice.

"Sorry I woke you up."

"You didn't. Any developments?"

I quickly reported my findings. "This is serious," I said, "The woman is either a criminal or a drunk." I used our preassigned code names for a terrorist. Under the rules, using both words meant *high probability.* "Her association with my son and my experience in the Temple," I said, using the code name for Dubai, "tend toward the latter option."

"OK," said Eric, "I'll have the office run her aliases and see if she's on our watch list." He hung up before I managed to say anything else.

Until the Agency responded with the background check, I decided to put a temporary watch on the apartment. I looked for a good observation post, preferably on the opposite side of the street. The best I could do was a café diagonally across from the apartment. Here in Paris, I told myself, that's what people with time to spend do—sit in cafés. I'd blend right in, taking my time with a very long lunch and a very large bottle of mineral water.

Watching and waiting are different in different countries. Here in France, of course, they would necessarily involve food. I had a seat and ordered. I had to decide whether to talk to Monica some more without arousing her suspicion, and considered my options as Paris bustled past. I could smell lamb sizzling from the kitchen. The waiter quickly brought out my meal: lamb merguez and fresh greens. That smell made me think of the outdoor market in Dubai, the succulent lamb shawarma. Yes, Dubai: if Monica worked for FOE and was on my tail, then she could be the one who realized I wasn't André's father or the electronics trader I pretended to be. Maybe she knew I was an undercover US government agent; that would explain how I was exposed in Dubai.

If that were the case, then who was Monica working for? My true affiliation was confidential. If discovered, it meant that "someone" had an interest in finding out, and also that "someone" gave Monica this information for a purpose. The purpose could very well mean that I had become a target.

I felt hot all of a sudden, and loosened my tie, and touched my pocket. My gun was not there. I panicked for a moment until I remembered dumping it into a trash can in the men's bathroom in Dubai airport. I never thought that I'd need a gun in Paris. As I bit into a sausage, a blue Renault stopped next to the apartment building and Monica came out. I quickly wrote down the license plate number but couldn't identify the driver. All I could see was the head of a man with black hair and dark glasses.

Time to renew an old friendship. I called Pierre Perot, an agent with *Direction Centrale des Renseignements Généraux*, the Central Directorate of General Intelligence, often called RG. Sitting in a Parisian café, how could I *not* think of Pierre? I'd worked with him on two separate cases a few years back. Pierre was easygoing in that utterly French way: he loved a good bottle of French wine (not Italian); he loved a two-hour lunch with said wine; and he loved daytime sex—not necessarily with his wife—after imbibing said wine. He also had a thing for Gauloise cigarettes. I remember him saying once that the "ladies first" courtesy was created by men to give them another opportunity to appreciate the woman's ass, then he smiled wickedly, his Gauloise smoldering off his bottom lip, his intelligent eyes slanted. There always seemed to be a Gauloise hanging off his bottom lip. Although he'd sworn to me last time I saw him that he was quitting for good.

Other than those infractions, he was a smart and efficient agent.

"Hello, Dan," he said in his strong French accent. "*Comment allez-vous?* How are you?"

After going through the niceties, I asked him to identify the owner of the blue Renault and gave him the plate number.

"Dan, are you at that age already?" he asked.

"What age?"

"They say that when men get older, they increase their interest in cars as their interest in sex declines." This was vintage Pierre—of course he would ask about sex.

"Far from it," I said, trying to figure out if he was nevertheless right. Remembering my more-frequent-than-usual activity between the covers last month, and my complete indifference to what kinds of cars I drove (as long as they were big), assured me that I was still not at "that age." Then I thought he had a point. I *had* grown older, because now I chose my cereal for the fiber, not the toy.

"I need the information for a business purpose."

He was professional enough not to ask any further questions. I was cutting corners here. I wasn't supposed to get in touch with the French government other than through "appropriate" bureaucratic channels. Which could take a week, easy. But the discovery of the gun and the multiple passports was ominous, and for me that was sufficient grounds to cut to the chase.

"We must have lunch together," Pierre said. It would be my second lunch of the day. Anything, well, almost anything, for the mission.

An hour later I met him at Café de Flore, a nineteenth-century establishment once frequented by artists and writers such as Jean-Paul Sartre.

Pierre had aged. His brush mustache had grayed, and he had gained some weight. All that wine and lunch—he had a plate of cheese and smoked sausage in front of him when I got there—had finally caught up with him. I tried not to think about my own weight. It always seemed to be moving in the upward direction, no matter what I did to contain it.

He read my mind, patting his belly.

"I know," he said, "but hey, life is short. Forget the health food. I need all the preservatives I can get."

"To life," I said, raising my water glass; he raised his wine glass in turn.

"And women."

I had to smile. It seems that as far as Pierre was concerned, growing old was mandatory, and growing up was optional.

Pierre smiled, "Why do Americans choose from just two people to run for president, and fifty for Miss America?"

I had to change the subject before Pierre got too tipsy.

"How are things at RG?" I asked.

"Fine, we're merging and our name is changing, probably next year. We'll be the *Direction Centrale du Renseignement Intérieur*, the Central Directorate of Interior Intelligence, or DCRI, tasked with counterterrorism and surveillance of targeted organizations and individuals."

A waiter came with a bowl of fish soup for me—and a bowl of mussels for Pierre, who dove right in. "Do you still eat sushi?" he asked in half contempt when I refused the mussels.

"No," I admitted. "I discovered it was a good bet to get intestinal worms, and I returned to steak and potatoes." I paused, waiting for him to finish devouring the mussels, wiping his mustache with a napkin and looking up from bowl.

"Does it mean a change in your duties?"

"No, it's just another government attempt to look efficient and cost-effective." He handed me a slim envelope, slurping at the innards of a mussel shell, although it seemed unlikely there could possibly be anything left.

"Can I open it here?" I asked, sensitive to Pierre's need to hide his informal contact with me.

"Sure," he said. "And please help yourself to anything." He motioned to his mussels, cheese, and wine.

I opened the envelope. It contained three pages of computer printouts, and one color photo with a name printed at the bottom, *Christian Chennault.*

"I think he's the one I saw in the Renault," I said after carefully examining the photo. "It could be him."

The computer printouts listed Chennault's multiple addresses and a German criminal record. A quick review showed nothing of significance. A drug charge ten years ago ended with a fine. Two convictions for disturbance of the peace, which was legalese for a bar or a street brawl, also ended with a small fine.

"He's not a criminal," said Pierre when he saw my face, "at least not in France. Here his record is completely clean."

"What is he, then?" I asked.

According to Pierre, Chennault was a man to watch. While sampling his remaining wine, salad, and cheese, Pierre informed me that the RG had information linking him to the arms trade; he was in business with a Russian man living in Germany, someone who sold embargoed technology to countries on the world's pariah list.

"Such as?"

"Dan, Dan, Dan. You know I can't tell you directly. You have to go through channels."

"OK, just tell me about the embargo lists, in general."

Pierre sighed. "Well, if you're forcing me. . . . As you know, each country has its own banned list of strategic materials exports to certain countries, but"—he added with a smile that his mustache partially covered, and in a low voice—"I can assure you that Iran appears on most of them."

That wasn't a hint. He was telling me. I knew of course that Iran is at the top of every list of rogue states sponsoring terrorism, but the way Pierre put it, there was no need to search for clues. He settled back in his chair, lit a cigarette, and when he saw my raised eyebrow he spoke.

"What?"

"I thought you quit," I said.

"Dan, if you stop smoking and start exercising, each session adds a few minutes to your life." He paused and added with a sparkle in his eyes, "So, if I follow the rule of exercising every day and make it to eighty-five like my parents did—both were smokers—I'll be able to live an additional six months in a nursing home at seventy-five hundred dollars per month. I'd rather spend that money now on good food and horny women."

I decided not to go into that territory, particularly when the exercise theory applied to me as well. "OK. But what about the quality of life that exercise can give you?"

"Dan, Dan, Dan! Life is not a ride to the grave where you must arrive in perfect shape. Me? I plan on leaving this world with one hand holding a bottle of good wine, the other the ass of a beautiful woman. I don't care if I'm in bad shape. In the afterlife, we don't have bodies at all!

"Anyway, I know I'm aging," he said with a sigh. "Inside me there's a younger person wondering, 'What the hell has happened?' Let's drink to that, shall we?"

"To old age?"

"To old age, to women, to death, to mussels, to all things that make life good, to Gauloises, to the bistro across from the park, to the girl who makes my espresso every morning, to—"

"To you telling me about Chennault, off the record."

"I've always liked you, Dan," he said with another sigh, and a sparkle in his eyes, "but if my boss catches me, trust me, the guillotine *will* be reintroduced. For my execution."

He looked at me. And then, in that very French life-is-too-short way of his, he shrugged.

"Chennault is linked to a German company that was selling nuclear technology and components to Iran, particularly for their Bushehr reactor."

"Give me the German company's name," I asked, although I suspected Pierre wasn't going to give me any *real* off-the-record information. Still, you never get what you want without asking. And I could take another rejection—I was an available man with little stability to offer women, after all. Pierre paused, and in a theatrical gesture, he pulled out from his jacket's inside pocket a single sheet of paper and handed it to me.

"Dan, Dan, Dan, what's with the third degree? What are you, my wife?" he said, tongue firmly in cheek. I gave the paper a quick look. I felt my blood pumping: the page had enough information to keep me going for the next six months. The name I was looking for was there: Leonid Shestakov, Chennault's boss and the owner of LSIT, Leonid Shestakov International Trading GmbH.

"Is Chennault a partner or an employee?" I asked before I could catch my breath.

"Leonid Shestakov doesn't have any living partners."

"Living?"

"Yes, the last one, may his soul not rest in peace, left us prematurely last year after a dispute with Shestakov over profit sharing. The partner wanted half and Shestakov offered him zero, and they settled. Shestakov took all the profits and the partner was relieved from any living expenses forever."

"Who is Chennault, then? A muscle or a higher-end operative or . . . ?"

"A jack of all trades. Chennault's father was Haitian and his mother German. He does the dirty work for Shestakov."

One thing I loved about Pierre: Beneath that devil-may-care, cheese-eating, afternoon-wine-drinking rogue exterior, he was sharp as a diamond blade. I always thought he would be great in the field; you'd never expect someone like him to have the mind he had for details. He was a walking, talking dossier.

"Anything on the operation they were running?"

As if I'd pushed a button, he gave me the full background. In 1974, according to Pierre, the Shah awarded Siemens, the German industrial giant, a contract to build two 1293 MW pressurized-water nuclear reactors. When the Shah was overthrown in 1979 and the Iraq-Iran war broke, Iraqis bombed these reactors six times. Siemens and its subsidiary company, Kraftwerk Union, ceased working on the reactors, one of which was already 60 percent complete and the other 75 percent complete.

Then, in 1990, the Soviet Union and Iran signed an $800 million protocol agreement regarding reconstruction of two VVER-440 reactors in return for three billion cubic meters of Iranian natural gas. The Soviet Union also agreed to complete the two reactors at Bushehr that the Siemens-Kraftwerk association refused to complete until the Iran-Iraq War ended. The agreement sent thousands of Russians to work in Iran to rebuild the damaged reactor in the port city of Bushehr, in southern Iran.

"But here," Pierre said, "they hit a snag: the Russians could do the concrete and steel part of the rebuild effort but couldn't re-create the nuclear technology, because German and Russian systems are technologically incompatible. The Russian components just didn't fit, so the Iranians had to continue using German technology. Either that or start from scratch with the Russians."

"Let me guess," I said. "Right about here, Leonid Shestakov shows up with an offer the Iranians can't refuse."

"Yes, exactly," Pierre said. "The marketplace was empty, or nearly empty, due to US and UN sanctions. European companies were reluctant to be seen walking hand in hand with Iran on Main Street. They needed an intermediary, and Leonid Shestakov provided a perfect solution."

"What about German laws banning exports of sensitive materials and technology? Nobody was enforcing them?" I asked.

Pierre waved his hand in the air as if shooing a fly.

"Oh, please," he said. "The German companies couldn't care less. Even if caught, and only a few of them were, they could always blame Leonid for misleading them and hiding the identity of the end user. And if that excuse happened to be rejected, the penalties were ridiculously low. Besides, the Weapons of War Control Law (KWKG) of Germany, which theoretically could stop the trade with Iran, is enforced only sparingly and sporadically."

"You have to wonder what motivates these companies," I said, thinking out loud. "I mean really, is it simply greed? Is there any other agenda?"

"Dan, you know greed isn't exactly a derogatory term in the business world. Of course they wanted to make a profit. They wanted to expand their relationships with Russian companies, and through them, with Iran. Russia is an emerging market, booming each time the price of oil goes up—everyone rushes in to take a bite of the growing pie. The German companies fear only one thing: the US government. If they are caught selling materials to Iran, they can kiss good-bye any chance of ever doing business in the US—and for the big German companies—we're not talking Adolf's Plumbing Supplies here—that is one huge deterrent. So they feel comfortable selling to Leonid Shestakov, who promises that the goods will end up in the Russian markets, knowing full well that the end user is in Iran."

"They could always say they didn't know." I said.

"Right," he said bitterly, "they didn't know? *Merde*, like hell they didn't." Pierre stopped.

"Well, go on," I urged him.

"Dan, have the Agency file a formal request. I can't say anything else."

He was right, of course, and I dedicated the rest of the time with Pierre listening to his funny stories—all crude—about the women he'd conquered and those he was about to conquer, using language that would make a Bangkok pimp blush.

"One final query," I said. "The Bushehr reactor is intended to generate electricity, not nuclear bombs, so why all the fuss?"

"Dan, that's true if the Iranians will honor their commitment to return the spent uranium rods to Russia. What if they refuse? The Russians will send their army to retrieve them? The real risk is the plants in Natanz and Arak, which are meant to facilitate the manufacture of the bomb. The Iranians are using the innocuous-looking reactor in Bushehr to obtain materials, which in fact will be used in Natanz and Arak. And of course, there's always the experience gained by Iranian scientists in operating a nuclear reactor. That experience could be used later in building a bomb."

As I left the meeting with Pierre, laughing at his jokes, I thought of my father's saying that laughing is good exercise. It's like jogging on the inside.

I went to an Internet café and logged into my private mailbox on Gmail. There was a message from Eric: *Go to the Kingdom and call me.*

I took a cab to the American Embassy on Avenue Gabriel, right next to the Place de la Concorde and a block away from the glitzy Avenue des Champs-Élysées. After a strict security check, I was led by the carbon monoxideMMO—the communication officer—to "the bubble," a windowless room, completely RF—radio frequency—proof and acoustically secure. To prevent clandestine signals from passing through the room, no wires or fiber-optic cables entered or left it. There were no loudspeakers that could mimic microphones. There were masking generators in different places, and all plenums and air vents were masked. The walls had a built-in transducer element that vibrated randomly to defeat any such clandestine distant listening devices as "laser/microwave pick-off" that detect and record audio. It also had a babbler, a device emitting gibberish in multiple foreign languages.

"Dan," Eric said, once a connection was established, "the passport that the woman you met in André's apartment gave you is fake. We identified her through her passport photo. Her name is Gerda Ehlen, DOB February 22, 1978, in Berlin. She works for Leonid Shestakov, a Russian national who runs a smuggling network of sensitive materials sold and shipped to Iran's nuclear industry."

"Ha," I said. "What the hell was she doing in my neighborhood?" I didn't tell Eric that I'd already received Shestakov's name from French intelligence. Eric was always berating me for cutting corners; I didn't want to give him yet another opportunity. Not until I could bring results, proving that my direct approach to a French government agent was justified. If I mentioned it even then.

"She could be snooping on you, and becoming friendly with André was a perfect opportunity to get into your apartment, read your mail, and maybe install a few gadgets."

"Did you make any calls from the apartment?" He sounded ominous.

"Never. I never use a landline unless secured."

"And a mobile?"

"Hell, no. Not that, either, and it was my first and only time in the apartment this year."

"It's possible there was a watch on you even before this case was assigned to you. Something to do with another case where the opposition was looking for a future opportunity to get even, and had you shadowed. If so, once you visited the Paris apartment, you unwittingly contaminated and compromised it, and it's now an arena for detecting your future assignments." Eric could be right, I thought, but said nothing.

Eric moved on. "Her home address is also fake. There's no such house number. We'll see if she got André to cooperate with her; until then, we won't shake things up there. However, in the long run, we may have to replace André with another student or abandon the apartment. I'll let you know. We want to observe her with her guard down. In the meanwhile, keep your distance from her. She's very likely armed."

That explained why she had to pose as a twenty-two-year-old, probably fearing that André, who was barely twenty-two, would be reluctant to have an affair with a twenty-eight-year-old. The person who built "Monica's" legend probably didn't remember how twenty-two-year-old men think.

"Armed, I already know. Didn't you see my report?"

"I did, but she could be carrying another gun for daily use, so to speak."

Yes, of course. That explained why she was so protective of her purse when I asked her for her passport. It wasn't the passport she was hiding. It was a gun.

"I'll send a team to cover her movements. Until they arrive, I'll ask the French to step in. I'm sending you now through the embassy's cipher room a short memo on Leonid Shestakov. Read and destroy."

Ten minutes later, a young embassy staffer walked in and handed me Eric's deciphered mail.

Leonid Shestakov, DOB May 7, 1946, in Moscow, graduated Moscow University with a degree in mechanical engineering in 1969. Served in the Red Army's Corps of Engineers and was stationed in Uzbekistan through 1989. He took a short part in the war in Afghanistan. In 1990 was discharged with the rank of lieutenant colonel and in 1991 relocated to Berlin, Germany. He currently owns several trading companies in Berlin, doing business in Russia, Libya, and Iran, which has been his major client in recent years. His companies were placing orders with German companies for sensitive nuclear materials and technology purportedly for use by Russian nuclear power plants, primarily the Kalinin nuclear power station, 120 miles northwest of Moscow.

An investigation revealed that the merchandise never got to Kalinin but was trans-shipped on the Volga River through Kazakhstan to the Caspian Sea, ending in Northern Iran, apparently without the Russian government's knowledge. This activity intensified in 2005 when Mahmoud Ahmadinejad became the Iranian president. Recently Shestakov managed to transfer fourteen satellite navigation systems to Iran. That particular type of the global positioning system is used in unmanned aerial drones for intelligence or attack purposes. Israeli Mossad reported that, during the Second Lebanon War in 2006, similar navigation systems were mounted on drones operated by Hezbollah against Israel. The Mossad reported that these systems were manufactured by a company in Baden-Wurttemberg, Germany, and could be those sold by Shestakov to Iran, which then gave them to Hezbollah. Several additional defective GPS malfunctioned and were returned.

A list of Shestakov's companies, known transactions, and key personnel was attached to Eric's cable. Eric didn't elaborate on why they'd malfunctioned, but I had my own ideas.

The memo also indicated that after the route on the Volga to Kazakhstan and northern Iran was exposed and stopped, Shestakov found a new destination in Dubai Not a surprise. The Dubai free-trade zone was declared as the end destination, while in fact it was used as a conduit to Iran, which is just across the bay.

I got back on the secure phone with Eric. "OK, got it. Does Shestakov's activity in Dubai connect to my assignment?" I asked.

Soon enough I'd have to tell Eric about my own findings regarding the unholy trinity of Monica, Chennault, and Shestakov.

"There are still a lot of missing pieces in the puzzle," said Eric, "and I don't know yet what the connection is exactly, but assume there is one."

This time, I was more cautious than Eric. I remembered another Moscow Rule, which Alex, my Mossad instructor, rehearsed with us: "*Once is an accident, twice is a coincidence, and three times is a hostile action.*" Once: Monica's presence in my Paris cover apartment. Twice: the gun and multiple passports hidden underneath the floorboard. And third: Monica's affiliation with Shestakov, "a person of interest" to many intelligence services for his trade with Iran.

I didn't need to go further, and count her fake address. I had to assume I was in active clandestine combat, and as usual in these wars, the identity and location of my enemy weren't clear. Shestakov's company? The Iranians? Some new kid on the block I hadn't met yet?

"So, now?" I asked Eric.

"Return to Dubai, stay there for a while. We need to see how the opposition got on your tail, and why. Be alert, you'll be a walking target once you return, but that's the only way to smoke them out."

Thank you very much, whined my little inner devil, *a walking target, what are you, a duck? Give Eric a piece of your mind!* I didn't listen, but soon I realized that I should have.

I did fly back to Dubai, though not until the next day. First I found a small hotel nearby and slept through the early morning hours. Then I left my luggage there and waited in the café across the street from the apartment I shared with André. At 7:45 a.m. Monica and André exited the building. Monica took a cab and André rode a bicycle. I waited for fifteen minutes, and when I thought the coast was clear I entered the apartment. It was a bit embarrassing to sneak into my own apartment, fearing detection by my "son" and his dubious guest, but I returned to their bedroom.

The arms stash underneath the bed was intact. I went through Monica's clothing again, checking all her pockets. Then I turned to the coat closet in the vestibule, and searched the coats and bags. In a small woman's bag, I found a folded piece of paper. It was a wire transfer confirmation from an account in Bank Sepah, via Barberini branch, Rome, Italy. The amount transferred was €110,000. The other details were too smudged to read.

I put the receipt in my pocket, and continued with my search. In another purse, I found three Lufthansa boarding pass stubs and a half-empty pack of cigarettes. I checked it thoroughly; it contained only cigarettes. I copied the dates and the flight numbers on the stubs. I moved to the desk and searched André's papers. Other than school materials, I found nothing of interest. I made sure I left everything intact and left the apartment.

As I walked up the street, I saw Monica coming toward me. I turned quickly and entered a store. I didn't want her to see me in the area when I'd told André that I was leaving Paris.

From an Internet café, I notified Eric about the bank withdrawal slip, using preassigned code words and making the message short.

I surfed the Internet for an hour, until Eric's ciphered response arrived, but I couldn't open it. Eric must have forgotten his order to stop using my computer until cleaned.

I sent him another e-mail: *Can't read, I'm still in Paris. I'm going to Kingdom to call you.*

When the connection in the bubble was made, Eric went straight to business. "I thought you returned to Dubai. Why the delay?"

"I decided to search the apartment again." I told him about the withdrawal slip and the boarding passes.

"What do you suggest, then?" asked Eric, catching me by surprise. Since when does Eric ask for advice? If he wants someone's opinion, he gives it.

"I think I should go back to Dubai."

"OK, go back," he said. "As long as you are in the enemy's sightline, you must exercise extra caution. Where is your laptop?"

"Here with me. I left it outside the bubble."

"Good, have my IT experts check it out to make sure it wasn't compromised. Leave it with them until you depart. Use Internet cafés to communicate using the designated code words. Report every day, or earlier as events develop. Continue using your legend as an electronics trader. Any change in your activity would signal that they were right to suspect you. Upon arrival in Dubai and before you'd pick up a tail, go to the consulate. There will be a package waiting for you with my Chief of Station."

Three hours later, I received my laptop back. *Cleaned*, said the attached note. They never said if they found anything hostile in it, and I didn't ask.

IX

January 2007, Dubai

I flew back to Dubai and returned to the Hyatt Regency. I went up to my room and opened the safe. Everything looked normal. I went downstairs, cancelled my earlier reservation for the extra room for my "business associate," and asked for a new room for myself: "Please give me a room at the end of the corridor. I'd like to have an uninterrupted view of the Gulf."

The location of the new room would give me an opportunity to see who might be coming my way, because there were at least fifty feet between my door and the door of the next room.

In my new room, I emptied my pockets. My entire legend spilled out, plus detritus from my mission. My European passport, one Visa card, one MasterCard, no American Express card—thank you very much, I've had too much hassle from them—a French driver's license, three door keys on a metal ring, two taxi receipts, airline ticket stubs, used boarding cards, a copy of the service agreement with We Forward Unlimited, and a laminated photo of my "family."

I flipped through the passport pages. There was nothing irregular there to attract attention. My driver's license had my photo and my Paris address.

Leaving the hotel, I took a cab for some blocks; switched to another; and after a tour around the city, got out a block before the Dubai World Trade Center on Sheikh Zayed Road, next to the roundabout. I walked to the original tower. After going through security, as a habit I first took an elevator to the twenty-fourth floor, and then took another down to the twenty-first and entered the US Consulate. After I'd identified myself to the Marine guard, a young man came up and said, "Please follow me."

We entered a vacant office. He gave me a bulky box. "Please sign here," he said, handing me a form and a pen. "If you intend to open the parcel here," he said, "I suggest you give me the empty box for safe disposal."

I opened the box. Inside were an M4 polymer frame handgun, the Mil Tech 12x20mm, and ammo specifically designed for the gun. The Chief of Station had also given me an unregistered mobile phone.

I returned to my hotel with the gun and the phone in my pocket.

The man who had brushed against me next to the shawarma stand a few days earlier was sitting on a couch in the lobby. How did he know I was still around? When his eyes met mine, he nodded. I approached him. The marble floors in the lobby echoed. Airy, vaulted ceilings, money secreted everywhere—you could feel it. The lobby was fairly crowded; international clientele waited at the reception desk. On my way to sit I heard at least four languages.

The man seemed to be alone, although you never know.

"Mr. Van der Hoff, please join me," he said.

I sat opposite him, saying nothing. On the coffee table between us sat a vase, with an elegant stalk of dried desert flowers.

He leaned forward across the table and spoke quietly. "I'm taking a significant risk in approaching you, but there's no other way.

The post office box mentioned in the letter was compromised by an Iranian VEVAK agent working out of Dubai."

I didn't react, putting on my best poker face. He continued. "I'm the one who sent the letter to the consulate."

I kept looking at him.

"I wrote it on behalf of my brother, a nuclear scientist. Can we talk now?"

"What is there to talk about?" I kept playing the dumb fool. It was my only available defense for a trap.

"Can you help him get political asylum in the US and a job, in return for nonpublic information about his work?"

"Sir," I said, "I don't know why you are approaching me."

He said immediately, "Because I know you work for the American government, and you came here in connection with the letter I sent. I know you opened an account with We Forward Unlimited; this is where I opened my box as well. I've just discovered that We Forward Unlimited works for VEVAK and, therefore, I wanted to stop you from responding to that box. Any incoming mail will be immediately read by VEVAK, and believe me when I say they are quite merciless."

"Well, I did open a box there for my electronic parts trading business. Is that how you found my name? Were you present at the office when I signed up?"

"No. My wife's sister's fiancé works there; he's the one who told me that the company is secretly controlled by VEVAK. He didn't know anything about my brother's plan to come to America. He told me about VEVAK over dinner, just making conversation, without realizing that the information was very relevant and important for my brother."

"How do I know you're not trying to trick me into doing something I'm not supposed to do? I'm just a merchant here trying to do business. I'm not here with any government."

"I don't know what else to tell you, I—"

He stopped here as a family paused next to us: a well-dressed man in a suit—Brooks Brothers?—and his wife, veiled from head to toe. From what I could tell, she alone was pulling the bulk of the family luggage, all of it stacked on one suitcase roller. They had two young children, one of whom was crying. The mother knelt down right next to us, soothing the young girl, gently wiping her tears with the edge of her robe. Once the child was calmed, they moved on.

"I already gave you details," the man continued, "that only the sender of the letter would know."

"How about giving me the name of your brother?" I took a huge leap forward, by revealing my interest.

He said without hesitation, "Professor Firouz Kamrani."

"Why does he want to leave Iran?" I asked.

"He has stopped working on the nuclear program originally intended to produce electricity. When Mahmoud Ahmadinejad became president in August 2005, he pushed for nuclear armament instead. The level of activities was substantially increased, abandoning necessary precautions for the sake of expediency. Mahmoud Ahmadinejad wanted to have a bomb before the world would realize what was happening and try to stop him. My brother was sending his superiors warnings about the dangers of accidents at the nuclear reactor as a result of the rushed manner of work. He was ignored.

"He also didn't like the fact that under the guise of nuclear research for peaceful purposes, Iran was planning to build a bomb. He was brushed off and warned to shut up. He is a scientist, not a soldier, and felt intimidated and afraid for his family. He told me that he was being followed, and that his mail was opened."

I had a problem with parts of his story. I knew of Kamrani. He had received military awards—and that definitely did not jibe with his portrayal as a peace-loving scientist. On second thought, maybe Kamrani was telling the truth, that his brother's troubles *had* started in 2005, when Ahmadinejad started pushing the nuclear program for military use.

I got up. "Well, I have a friend who works in the US Consulate here, I can give him that information. But I'm doing it only because I have compassion for your brother. Once I relay the information, I can no longer be involved in this."

"Sure," he said smoothly, and I could tell he thought he had me trapped.

"How can I contact you?" I asked. "Do you have a card? I may call you for business purposes."

He gave me his card. On it was the name Ali Akbar Kamrani.

"I'll meet you here tomorrow evening at six o'clock," he said and walked away. I continued sitting there, watching the exit doors, waiting to see if anyone was joining or following him—a partner or an FOE. I couldn't identify anyone fitting either category.

I returned to the Trade Center, and, after employing detection avoidance tactics, entered the consulate and wrote a detailed memo to Eric, describing my meeting and asking for a check on Professor Firouz Kamrani and Ali Akbar Kamrani. It concluded, *I can't estimate whether Ali Akbar Kamrani, the person I met, is bona fide or if he's even really a brother.*

In the morning, I had a call from the consulate to come over. "Your request for information on customs regulations in the US is incomplete," said the woman on the other end, in case we had a third person listening in. "Why don't you come over and speak with the commercial attaché?"

At the consulate, I was handed an incoming message from Eric:

Dr. Firouz Kamrani, 49, an Iranian scientist, is a professor and an authority on electromagnetism, and deeply involved in the Iranian nuclear program in Isfahan. He is a tenured professor at the University of Shiraz, holding a degree in electronic engineering, and a PhD in Physics. He has published articles in reputable peer-reviewed scientific journals and is considered to be one of Iran's top scientists. Kamrani was also a co-founder of the Iranian

Centre for Atomic Research in Tehran. We need to be sure that Ali Akbar Kamrani didn't use Firouz Kamrani's name as bait without his knowledge. We need proof that Prof. Kamrani is in the loop and is in accord with the person purporting to be his brother. We are still checking on Ali Akbar, but couldn't identify him yet. Therefore, continue contacts with him but make no promises that could expose you any further. Eric.

The following day, I bought a Nikon D80 camera with a telephoto lens and waited on my balcony. At 5:45 p.m. I saw Ali Akbar Kamrani walking from the parking lot toward the hotel's entrance. I shot twenty-four pictures in sequence and returned to my room to remove the memory card and lock the camera in my room safe. The card went into my pocket as I went downstairs to meet Ali Akbar Kamrani, who was patiently waiting.

I sat opposite him. He nodded hello.

"As I promised, I forwarded your request to a friend who works in the US Consulate. He told me to stay away. However, after I told him I was touched by your sincerity, he asked me to obtain proof that your brother agrees to what you are doing."

"How could he tell you that? I mean, my brother, he's in Iran under a constant watch of VEVAK."

"OK. My friend thought of that, and suggested that you ask your brother next time you talk to him, to suggest to his students during class to read the article of Professor Krishna Patel published in Electromagnetic Radiation magazine, Volume VII, dated November 5, 2004."

My guest had a puzzled expression on his face, but he wrote down the information. That would tell us whether there's a connection between my guest and the scientist, but obviously would not serve as exact proof that the scientist was in the loop. But, as a first step, that was enough.

He then gave me a long look. "And the Americans will know that he did that?"

"I have no idea," I said, "I'm relaying to you what my friend said. By the way, I'm Jaap Van der Hoff."

"I already know that." He smiled.

"You never told me how you know."

He hesitated. I waited patiently. "You came to We Forward Unlimited to rent a postal box."

"That still doesn't answer my question."

"Mr. Van der Hoff, please forgive me, but I will tell you only when we move forward with getting my brother out of Iran."

I decided not to pressure him, but rather to ease his tension and talk about things he'd feel more comfortable with.

"Do you live in Dubai?" I asked in a friendly tone. The business card he gave me earlier listed only his name and a telephone number.

"Yes, for a few years now."

"What do you do?"

"I work in a local representative office of a bank."

"Oh, which one?" I asked, thinking, *Maybe there's an opportunity here.*

"Sepah Bank."

"Is it a Dubai bank?" I asked, playing dumb again.

"No, Iranian."

"Are you happy there?"

"The wages are very good," he said.

"And what is your position?"

"Assistant manager in charge of export document financing."

"Interesting," I said, "I may need your services. How big is the bank?"

"It employs 18,000 people, mostly in its 1,700 branches in Iran. The rest are in branches in Frankfurt, London, Paris, and Rome."

We chatted for another ten minutes.

There was no question that he knew who I was. He called me by name; he knew I was working for the US government; he knew I came to Dubai in connection with the letters sent to the US Consulate, and I gave him answers to his questions and requested a verification to be performed by his brother in Iran. A reasonable assumption would be that the Agency would know if his brother got the message and told his students to read the particular article. Most probably the Agency had an insider at the university, perhaps even in Kamrani's class. I couldn't have been more stripped of any defenses if it turned out that the contact he made with me was a charade—a ploy by some intelligence service, most likely Iranian. And yet, I walked into it knowingly with open eyes.

Why?

Because I'm a risk taker. Not a paper pusher. Not a bean counter. Decisions had to be made; and if things turned ugly, I'd do my best to get the hell out; I've done it before, I can do it again. There's also another reason: from underneath my jacket I had a gun pointed at Ali Akbar Kamrani. If he made any threatening moves, he'd be gone so fast he wouldn't even know what hit him. I didn't think it'd happen in a hotel lobby full of people, but I was ready. I wasn't concerned with the Dubai police: I was sure that the Dutch consul could get me out of the local jail before I got used to the bad food and company.

I returned to my room and ordered room service. I decided to limit my movements until the dust settled. Before the food arrived, I went downstairs and called the US Consulate from the lobby's payphone, asking that I be met at the hotel. I couldn't risk traveling to the consulate too often and I didn't want to use the mobile phone, even though I was assured that it was unregistered, because a location could still be traced. An hour later, just as I finished my meal, a man from the consulate came over to the hotel. We met at the bar. After I identified him through an exchange of code words, we sat apart and kept to our drinks. Half an hour later, I left the bar while surreptitiously giving him my camera's memory card with an encrypted report to Eric. Several hours later, he returned and, as agreed earlier during the exchange of code words, met me in the lobby's men's room.

He handed me my camera's SD card. "Eric's response is on the card. Read it on only on your computer, it's encrypted."

I returned to my room, inserted the card into my laptop, and waited for the decryption. After fourteen seconds, Eric's message appeared on the screen:

Ali Akbar Kamrani works in an office known to be used as a front for VEVAK. That office does regular banking activities as well. Therefore, it is possible that Ali Akbar is a VEVAK agent. Regarding the withdrawal slip from Sepah Bank in Italy you found in André's apartment, we're trying to establish a connection to the bank's activities, which were a subject of the Treasury Department's attention. The bank was financing projects to develop missiles capable of carrying nuclear weapons. The bank was established with money from Iran's military pension fund. Sepah is 'military' in Farsi. The Italian branch was used for suspect transactions. It's likely that Gerda Ehlen, aka Monica, although technically employed by Shestakov, is working in cooperation with or even for VEVAK to defeat efforts to expose illegal Iranian transactions, including taking aggressive measures against those perceived as key opposition players. Wait for further instructions. Eric.

I deleted his message.

That wasn't breaking or heartbreaking news. The possibility that Ali Akbar was a VEVAK agent was real, and I took it seriously. I was still wondering about the meaning of the enigmatic note attached to the euros I'd found.

"What's Pension 1?" I asked aloud. I had no clue.

Only later did I realize that the answer was right in front of me.

I spent the whole day between the pool and my room, waiting for instructions. In the evening, I ordered room service and watched old Western movies. That's one of the many things you never see in Bond movies, or any "spy" movie or thriller for that matter—the waiting that we, the employees of a huge bureaucratic machine, have to do, the reports we have to write, the rules we must obey, and the frustration we endure when we hit a brick wall when we'd thought there was a breakthrough.

The following morning, the phone rang early. The caller spoke French, quickly using a predetermined code word to identify himself and giving me a nonsense message about a pending electronic parts delivery to Italy. He then asked about the view from my room. That was enough. I packed my bags and asked for another room.

"I want a room with a better view," I said. Although I must have been known to the hotel's staff as "the room switcher," they gave me another room. Obviously, under the new circumstances, staying in the same room for too long was dangerous. I didn't know who had visited it while I was away, or what devices might have been installed.

I left the hotel and went out for lunch at a restaurant praised by a popular website. The meal was mediocre, and I hailed a cab to return the hotel.

A few minutes later, I looked out the window and saw a sign for Mamzer Park. "Sir," I said to the cabbie, "I need to go to the Hyatt Regency Hotel. I think you just passed it."

He didn't answer and increased his speed. That was enough for me. I pulled out my gun and stuck it in his neck. "Stop or I shoot." He pulled over and stopped the car. I jumped out, continuing to point my gun at him. "Get out!" The street was flanked by glittering high-rises and the traffic was sparse.

Shaking, he came out. He was a man in his midfifties, his face deeply grooved. He wore a traditional, but very worn, tunic. Dubai had a large underclass, but the powers that be did their best to keep them hidden, on the outskirts of town—or in the drivers' seats of old cabs.

The man looked completely baffled.

"Who sent you?"

He lowered his eyes and begged, nearly crying. "Please, sir, I have a wife and six children, I don't earn much, you can take it all." He sent his hand to his pocket.

"Stop right there or I shoot," I said, "and take your hand out of your pocket slowly."

He did. I reached into his pocket; it had only a wallet. I pulled out his driver's license and put it in my pocket. I threw his wallet to the back seat. I searched his other pockets. They were empty.

"Who sent you?" I repeated, and when he didn't answer, I came closer and gestured toward his face with the gun. That made him open his mouth, "I don't know, Sahib, a man asked me to bring you to Mamzer Park, please don't hurt me."

"Who's this man?"

"I never met him before, he hired me in the street, pointed at you when he saw you leaving the restaurant, and told me to pick you up."

"Get back in the car!" I ordered him.

"Please don't kill me, I swear on Allah that I told you the truth."

"Get in!" I ordered again.

He got behind the wheel, and I got into the back seat. "How far is the park?"

"Another two kilometers, sir," he said, shaking.

"Take me there!" I ordered, "Stop one hundred meters before the main entrance."

Three minutes later I saw the park approaching. "Stop here," I said. He stopped immediately. I jumped out, and asked him, "Do you have a cell phone?" I didn't want him to report to any potential FOE what has just happened.

"No, sir." He was still shaking.

"Do you have a radio in the car?"

"Radio? You mean music, yes, yes."

"No, I mean a two-way radio, like Motorola?"

"No, sir."

I looked at the cab. It had no antenna. I gave a quick look at the front seat and couldn't see a radio or a cell phone.

"OK, make a U-turn and go back. I don't want to see you here."

"Yes, sir." He turned his cab around sharply, and sped away.

I crossed the street and walked slowly toward the park. It was at the border of Dubai and Sharjah. I was sure there would be a welcome party for me. I was ready.

The park turned out to be a beach resort with rental chalets; a swimming pool edged by a symmetrical line of tall, thin palms; and a cafeteria. I paid five dirhams to enter and walked around the fence toward the pool. The white cement of the ground shone hot in the sun. There were just a few people in the water. The welcome party I was expecting wasn't there. Did the cabbie manage to warn them I was carrying a gun?

I sat on a chair, ordered iced tea, and waited. Unlike in France, waiting in Dubai didn't involve a long lunch in a café; it involved sitting poolside in yet another sun-blasted resort area. Ten minutes later, just as the waiter brought my drink, two men approached me. They were well-built Arab men in their midtwenties. I was blinded by the sun, and put my hand above my eyes for some relief.

"Mr. Van der Hoff?"

"Who's asking?" I said with my other hand in my pocket, feeling the gun. Shooting them from this angle, with me seated, would be difficult. I stood up.

"We hear you're snooping around, and we don't like it."

I didn't answer. Thugs never understand unless I "explain" it to them with a gun. No matter which country, I run into tough guys like this. And no matter what their ethnicity, religion, country of origin—no matter what, I can count on one thing.

Thugs are dumb.

"Did you hear me?" said the taller man, trying hard to perfect an icy-threatening tone.

"I heard you," I said, and took a step back, trying to figure out which one to shoot first if things got ugly. I needed some distance to hit them both.

"People complain that American agents are looking for people doing business with Iran. What you're doing is bad for bsusiness, so get out of Dubai immediately, *wild il qahbaa.*"

That "son of a bitch" curse was said in a North African Arab accent.

"Are you representing the Dubai Chamber of Commerce?" I released the safety on my gun, still nestled in my pocket.

They looked at each other, each trying to see if the other thug understood me. One of them settled on repeating their line. "We told you to get out."

"That's why I asked if you work for the local Chamber of Commerce. You said I was interfering with business, when in fact I came to do business."

"You have one day," said the tall man. They turned around, retreating into the white-hot streets of Dubai. I continued to sip my drink. Who sent them? They could've been representatives of several hostile bodies: VEVAK, rival companies wanting to block my purported but nonexistent business efforts, or even corrupt local police paid by someone to get me out of Dubai. I returned to my hotel and e-mailed Eric about the latest developments.

An hour later his response came in: *Leave. You have no further business in Dubai that's worth the risk.*

That order flew against my best judgment, not to mention my defiant character. Funny, I always seem to become especially defiant when my life is threatened. Going home would be a bad move. Staying, I felt, I could expose who these people were, and who sent them.

As I cooled off, though, I saw the logic behind Eric's order. My job was to identify the scientist who wanted to defect. Nothing more, nothing less. And as far as the threats, they come with the territory of my real job. They had nothing to do with my legend as a trader. But that was a ploy, not the real thing, so why continue with the charade when I had no intention of playing for very long anyway?

I called my contact at the US Consulate for a representative to meet me at my hotel. In the lobby of the men's room, I gave him my gun. I returned to my room, packed my bag, checked out of the hotel, and dropped in a mailbox the cabbie's driver's license. I let two cabs pass and took the third cab that stopped. I went to the airport, and, two hours later, I was airborne. Destination: New York.

X

January 2007, Manhattan

Was my mission a success? I'd identified the sender of the letter and the scientist who purportedly wanted to defect, but failed to verify either the sender's bona fides or that of his alleged scientist brother. I was also exposed to FOE. That could hardly be called a success. Nonetheless, the results so far were worth the risk. I was curious to see how Eric would manage the answers I brought, and if he'd even bother to share his conclusions with me. I taxied home from the airport and was asleep before my head hit the pillow.

I woke up to the annoying ringing telephone. I heard Eric's voice. "Read my message." His voice was stern and I was half asleep. I wiped my eyes and looked at the clock on the night table. It was 3:45 a.m. I turned my computer on and read Eric's message:

Firouz Kamrani, an Iranian scientist, died last night of unnatural causes. Iranian media reported the cause of his death as 'gas suffocation in his sleep caused by fumes from a faulty gas fire.' Leaked information suggested that the actual cause of his death was radioactive poisoning. We are still collecting intelligence. Anything we need to know that was not included in your reports? Eric.

What the hell? How did VEVAK get Firouz Kamrani so fast, or did they? I turned off the light and returned to bed, lying on my back. It was a cold winter in Iran now, therefore the use of gas heating was expected. However, if he died at home, then did he really have radioactive material at home? Unlikely. You don't keep this in your refrigerator and mistake it for a beer.

Hey, my inner little devil broke in, as if he hadn't been dormant for some time, *what if he died from radioactive poisoning elsewhere and was then brought home, or it is also possible that for once in a millennium the Iranians are telling the truth and he died at home of accidental carbon monoxide poisoning?*

I lay in bed, piecing it together.

"No," I told my little devil, "I need more information, but, as a hunch, I tend to think that the Iranian security services killed Kamrani. Maybe they suspected him of trying to defect to escape the role he was playing for them. His purported brother was their agent; I had no doubt of that. But if VEVAK killed Kamrani, why didn't they use the opportunity to blame the CIA, Mossad, or both for the killing, particularly after my meeting with Ali Akbar, the 'brother'? Maybe fearing that if they accused any foreign intelligence service, it'd send a message that the CIA and Mossad could operate within Iran with impunity: an unthinkable move in a country where pride and honor are more important than life."

I went back to sleep.

Another phone call woke me up again. "Get ready," said Eric, "I'm sending a car pick you up in thirty minutes."

"Where am I going?"

"A meeting in Georgetown."

A car-service limo with tinted windows veered over to the curb. The uniformed driver got out, approached me, and said "Oasis," the code word identifying him as an Agency operative. I answered, "River." The driver opened the door for me and I got in. I slept most of way.

In Washington, DC, he pulled up at a brick town house on Olive and 29th Streets in Georgetown, Washington's oldest neighborhood at 250 years and counting—which, compared to where I was from, and where I had been, to me seemed like the blink of an eye. Inside the townhouse were Eric, Paul, and Benny. Benny's presence was a pleasant surprise.

After reviewing the details of my encounters in Dubai, it was time to hear whether there were any developments.

"We're still gathering intelligence," said Eric, "but word gets around quickly. Kamrani's death was announced by Iranian television days after the fact. They described the cause of death as 'gas poisoning.'"

"Did they discover his defection plans, if there were any?" I asked.

"Highly likely," said Paul, "We are sure now, based on intelligence from other sources, that he wanted to defect. We are also sure now that Ali Akbar wasn't his brother. VEVAK had concocted a plan to kill Kamrani and blame it on us, saying we killed him after he refused to spy for us. They killed him, but the blaming part was discarded, they had second thoughts about that."

"Wasn't he very important to the Iranians? Why kill him?" I asked.

"He was previously the brain behind the Isfahan plant that produces uranium-hexafluoride gas, an ingredient in the enrichment of uranium at the Natanz facility, and they realized he in fact wanted to leave. The Iranians just couldn't let him get out of Iran alive. However, we can't rule out assassination by other foreign intelligence services, or even an accident."

But if it wasn't the Iranians or an accident, that means the Iranians would be shitting in their pants because someone flattened their key nuclear scientist. The others are probably writing their wills, my little inner devil suggested. *If the Agency was involved, but neither Paul nor Eric shared that information with you, then somebody was doing overtime.*

Kamrani was a worthy target. The fact that the Iranians announced his death only a few days afterward must have been for a good reason. I wish I knew what it was. It certainly wasn't because the Iranians found him dead several days after he'd supposedly died at home. A nuclear scientist in Iran cannot just disappear without half the Iranian security force looking for him, likely even within an hour after his failing to show up for work. My inquisitive mind went further: did the delayed announcement mean that the Iranians were not involved, and in fact were waiting to see who left Iran in a hurry? Did they discount the possibility that local assassins retained by a foreign intelligence agency did the job, and that they need not leave Iran?

On the other hand, I thought back to when I practiced law, was there proof that the cause of death was in fact assassination? Maybe it was an accident? Even people whom the world wants dead might fall victim to real, not staged, accidents. I had to stop speculating. It was taking me nowhere.

Eric turned to Paul. "By the way, I read your status memo. You know you left out an important detail." His tone was gruff.

Paul looked surprised. "What?"

"Kamrani was recently employed by Isfahan's Malik Ashtar University of Technology. Several departments of that institution have been quietly involved in Iran's secret nuclear program. His boss was University Rector Mahdi Najad Nuri, also a general in the Revolutionary Guard," said Eric abruptly.

"And what's so wrong with a general getting an education?" asked Paul.

Eric, ever humorless, didn't get it. "What's so wrong is that Mahdi Najad Nuri is on a UN Security Council list of people and institutions whose activity is being monitored for alleged contact with Tehran's nuclear program. The Nuclear Technology Center of Isfahan is a nuclear research facility that currently operates four small nuclear research reactors, all supplied by China. The uranium conversion facility at Isfahan converts yellowcake into uranium hexafluoride gas, which is then enriched by thousands of centrifuges.

"As of late October 2006, the site was almost fully operational, with twenty-one or even all of twenty-four workshops completed. There is also a zirconium production plant located nearby that produces the necessary ingredients and alloys for nuclear reactors."

"So do you think the death of one scientist, as senior as one could be, would put off Iran from developing nuclear weapons?" I asked, sounding doubtful, because I was.

"It sends a message, although not by us," said Eric. "Let the ground shake under their scientists' feet. Let them fear the unknown. These deaths increase the 'white desertion' of scientists. They either continue working but their minds are elsewhere, or they resign and move to less dangerous jobs. But the Iranian regime doesn't let them off the hook that easily. In fact, some of these scientists find themselves between a rock and a hard place.

"We know that VEVAK is behind all that. When their agent, whom they named Ali Akbar Kamrani, sent us the letters for his purported scientist 'brother,' they were not shooting in the dark. We think that the entire ploy was to send a message to their scientists who cultivate thoughts of defecting: 'Watch out! Big Brother knows everything.' This time, Big Brother is Iranian. Benny?"

Benny waited a moment, and then confirmed my earlier suspicion.

"My men in Tehran tell me that they suspect Firouz Kamrani was chosen by VEVAK to fake defection intentions to the US, and when his defection 'offer' was accepted, expose the clumsy attempt of the US. This would allow VEVAK to retaliate by smearing the CIA and the Mossad.

"So, the Iranians hoped to achieve two goals from this: destroying our credibility, so that no potential asset would work with either of us, and deterring other scientists who might think of defecting, because they could never know if the offer made to them was a genuine CIA or Mossad offer, or was actually made by VEVAK to entrap them.

"When Kamrani was selected to participate in the ploy, VEVAK didn't take into account one small detail."

"Kamrani wasn't faking," I said, although I wasn't quite sure.

"Right. He *wanted* to live outside Iran, and the offer made by VEVAK to fake defection was his chance to become 'defector-in-place.'"

"Meaning?"

"He was theoretically renouncing his Iranian citizenship and allegiance, but remained in Iran as an informer until extricated. Unfortunately, things went south. Either there was a security leak and Firouz Kamrani's real intentions were revealed to VEVAK or. . . ."

Benny didn't finish the sentence. Was he hinting that there was a security breach, or worse, a mole among us? I didn't ask, and he continued. "Anyway, we tend to believe that VEVAK discovered Kamrani's defection plans and probably rigged his gas heater to emit carbon monoxide that killed him in his sleep. So here we are, having lost a potentially invaluable asset, someone who could have provided us with the intel the United States and Israel need. We were so close."

For once in my life, I disagreed with Benny. "The Mossad and the CIA were never close to getting Kamrani as an asset. This was a ploy to begin with. Even if Kamrani wanted to defect, then what? He of all people couldn't go to the bathroom without being monitored by VEVAK. He was a lost cause to begin with."

Benny paused and looked out the window, his brow furrowed. I knew he was turning over the what-ifs in his mind.

"Whatever happened," he continued, "we need to cover all bases, and therefore, our security department is investigating whether there was any security breach on our end that exposed Dan, or brought about Kamrani's early demise."

Silence fell over the room. "What's next?" I asked.

Benny, still with that stern expression, turned to me and said, "With Kamrani dead, we are dropping his purported defection case."

I was certain that it wasn't the purpose of this meeting, just to announce a closing of a case. There had to be another, forward-looking plan. I waited patiently.

"For a while now, we've been quietly spreading the message that defectors will be welcome," said Benny. "We have several combatants operating in the area, harassing nuclear scientists. And the harassment was working. When my combatants tried to intimidate a particular Iranian nuclear scientist from continuing with his research, they were more successful than they anticipated. The scientist quite plainly let our combatants know that he'd be willing to stop his research if we helped him defect from Iran and get a university research position in the US. We told the CIA, and there the idea of forming a joint agency team gained speed."

"So did you help this scientist get the job?" I asked.

Eric nodded. "His defection was scheduled to take place last week. Once in our safe house in Virginia, after his thorough interrogation, we would've announced it publicly, to make other Iranian scientists aware it would be worth their while to stop working on the Iranian nuke and defect to the US, or Europe. The plan is on hold. Now that Kamrani's died, potential Iranian defectors are, for obvious reasons, getting cold feet."

"But," continued Benny, with his sly smile, "we are revisiting old plans on talents ready to defect. It's time to Tango again."

Benny, Paul, and Eric then detailed their plan. It left me breathless.

XI

May 2007, Damascus, Syria

It was time to Tango again. An Agency car took me from CIA HQ in Langley to Reagan Airport, just across the Potomac from Washington, DC. The two weeks of training I had just had at The Farm were intriguing and extensive. Although the signs at the entry say DEPARTMENT OF DEFENSE ARMED FORCES EXPERIMENTAL TRAINING ACTIVITY, it's in fact a 10,000-acre site where CIA trainees, also called Career Trainees, take an eighteen-week course in what's called "operational intelligence." The camp was similar to many other military camps I'd seen, except that uniforms were few. Those who graduate the course begin working as intelligence and case officers for the CIA's National Clandestine Service.

After a brief stopover in New York to see my children, I flew to Frankfurt International Airport using my blue US tourist and business passport. I proceeded to the arrival hall, claimed my luggage, and met an Agency representative, a young man in his early thirties who identified with the right code word. He signaled me to follow him to the parking lot. I entered his Volkswagen van.

Inside he gave me everything I needed to assume my new identity. A European passport with my photo and biometrics, describing me as Alexander Yager, born in Riga, Latvia, in 1950. Three credit cards—Visa, Eurocard issued by MasterCard, and Diners Club. And again, no American Express, thank you very much. There was €9,000 in Visa traveler's checks and €1,000 in cash. Family photos of my late wife Anna, may she rest in peace, and of Snap, my real-life golden retriever. I also had business stationery and business cards for Yager Export and Import Consultants, GmbH. It was set up as a German firm that helps European textile goods companies penetrate new and emerging markets, and to avoid bureaucratic pitfalls whether they are buying or selling.

I gave the Agency representative my US passport. That was the only item that connected me with the US. My clothes were made in Europe, mostly in Germany, including my underwear, socks, and shoes. My watch was Swiss; my eyeglasses were made in France. My luggage was made in China and sold in Swiss department stores. Even my ballpoint pens carried European marks. I was glad to find a baggage cart next to a parked car, and used it to get my suitcase back to the terminal.

I checked into a Syrianair flight to Damascus International Airport. As we approached Damascus, I couldn't avoid thinking of my friend, an Israeli Air Force pilot, who had been captured by the Syrians during the Six-Day War and had undergone inhumane and brutal torture. He returned missing one blue eye, with a scarred face, but with a strong determination to put it behind him. The Syrians are not known for merciful treatment of their enemies. Another Israeli, Eli Cohen, a Mossad spy, was caught and hanged in Damascus in public. I shivered at the thought of what would happen to me if I were captured.

The Damascus airport was mostly empty when I arrived. The passport control officer asked me only about the purpose of my visit and the expected duration of my stay. He saw that I had a ticket for a Syrianair flight to Tehran in ten days and asked me to prove I had enough money to pay for my stay. Five minutes later, I was out in the street, practically swarmed by dozens of taxi drivers and hustlers. It was an unavoidable scene in most third world countries.

I took a cab for the short ride to the Four Seasons Hotel at Shukri Al Quatli Street and paid 1,500 Syrian pounds for the ride. I settled in my room and then took a walk to the old city, surrounded by a Roman-era wall with large oblong stones. Like a typical tourist, I looked at the tour guidebook; the old city has seven gates: Bab Sharqi, Bab al-Jabieh, Bab Keissan, Bab al-Saghir, Bab Tuma, Bab al-Jeniq, and Bab al-Faradiss. The main road crossed the city from Bab al-Jabieh to Bab Sharqi. Occasionally, I used Mossad tactics to identify whether I was drawing any particular attention. But it seemed that the coast was clear. I didn't identify any sign that I was the subject of particular interest to anyone. This was odd and unusual. Under normal circumstances, in the Middle East, people looking like tourists are usually approached by all sorts of locals, either seeking to offer services or just to be courteous.

But, here and now, nada.

When everything seems to be right, then you must be wrong, were the warning words of Alex, my Mossad instructor. I thought of the thorough briefing I had received at The Farm before leaving. Although Syria is about 55 percent Sunni Muslim, for nearly 40 years it has been governed by the Assad family, who are Alawites, a Shia sect. Although Syria has a population of nearly 22 million, the Alawites, who number only 1.4 million, have managed to keep their grip on the country—first by Hafez al-Assad and then, after his death, by his son, Bashir al-Assad.

Syria is a typical Middle Eastern police state, where the rulers are "elected" by a 99 percent majority and stay in power by playing various groups off one another and brutally suppressing opposition groups. For the past twenty years, Syria has allied itself with Shiite Iran. The pariah status of Iran in the eyes of the world was shared by some Arab states and it affected their attitude toward Syria, which became unpopular with most other Sunni Arab states.

Syria openly supports Hezbollah but also provides sanctuary for Sunni Muslim terrorists on their way to Iraq. But even this was done at the request of Iran, which was supporting al-Qaeda and its ilk, only because this was a way to kill Americans. Normally, al-Qaeda prefers to kill Shia Muslims (whom they consider heretics). Syrian Sunnis and Kurds in the north have commenced terrorist attacks against Syrian Alawite targets. The Alawites have responded, as they always have, with efficiency and savage reprisals. Bloodshed is routine in these areas.

I went looking for Hammed's lingerie store. I wasn't going to buy sexy underwear for a girlfriend. I was going to get something much hotter: information and assistance.

Syrian lingerie is famous among distributors in the US, but the consumers know nothing of it. The MADE IN SYRIA labels are cut out and replaced with labels showing another country of origin. When I first heard that during my training in The Farm, I was surprised and amused. Syrians are conservative, but they manufacture sexy underwear that would put porn magazines to shame.

I walked to Souk Hamadiya. Its labyrinthine market streets and alleys were packed with people. Many of the small stores lining the souk were cluttered with underwear sets displaying more traditional wear, such as sequined belly-dance costumes. I found Hammed's store, a shop selling outsized lingerie and other women's clothing. A middle-aged man with dark eyes and a scarred face looked at me suspiciously. I asked to speak to Hammed.

"Who are you, sir?" he responded in English.

"I'm Alexander Yager. My office received an inquiry regarding exports to Germany. Are you Mr. Hammed?"

"Please follow me," he said and took me to the back of the store. He opened a wooden door and entered an office. He emerged within seconds, leaving the door open and inviting me to enter.

"This is Mr. Hammed," he said pointing at a heavyset one-armed man with gray hair and a mustache. The man got up.

"Mr. Hammed?" I asked.

He nodded. The door was still open and the scarred-face man was standing nearby. I recited my role.

"My company in Germany received your inquiry. They said you wanted to sell women's lingerie and needed their help to penetrate the German market."

"That was a long time ago," Hammed said wearily and for a moment, I suspected that someone at the Agency had failed to do his homework.

"Are you still interested?" I asked.

"Only if you could get my merchandise into the German markets." His English was good, but with a heavy Arab accent. He didn't look local; his skin was darker. "Please sit down." He left the door open.

"We have strong ties with major department stores in Germany and in other locations in Europe," I took from my briefcase colorful brochures of German department stores. He looked at them with interest. I couldn't tell whether it was professional interest in the goods, or a personal fancy for the voluptuous blonde models.

"Nice merchandise," he said. "I can manufacture to your standards." The door was still open.

"Good," I said, "for example, how many bras can you deliver in a month. Can you ship five thousand?" I asked. "They usually prefer to work with bigger quantities."

"I can, sizes 34 to 44 with cups A to D."

"German women like pinkish colors," I said. These were the buzzwords that would confirm that he was the real thing.

"We have got that and purple as well," came the right answer. Hammed was my man.

Hammed was a Kurd, the son of a tribal leader who'd been fighting all his life for Kurdish statehood in the northern parts of Iraq,

Iran, Turkey, and Syria. Hammed was my local anchor, a Mossad contribution to the case.

"Can we talk here?" I asked in a barely audible voice.

"No," he said, "too many ears, too many eyes, and they are all bad. Come to my home tonight for dinner." He gave me his address. I sat in his office for an additional twenty minutes going over brochures and then returned to my hotel, carrying a plastic bag full of sample women's underwear.

"It's better if people see you leave my store with merchandise," he said. I didn't know if he meant it was good for his business or for mine.

———

I returned to the Four Seasons Hotel. I couldn't tell whether I had followers, but as usual and under the rules, I had to assume there were. At six-thirty I took a cab to Hammed's home. It was located less than 150 feet from the center of the old city. I rang the bell. An iron gate opened, and I found myself in a small courtyard paved with blue and white ceramic tiles. Against the wall were flowerpots, and through the big oblong windows I could see the living room. Hammed met me at the entrance.

"Welcome, my friend," he said, "*Marhaba.*" I followed him into the house. The walls were thick, and the elevated and extended window seats were used as sofas, covered with colorful Arab bedspreads. There were just the two of us. A small table was laden with pistachio nuts, sweet rolled-up baklava cakes, and small mugs with thick coffee.

I looked around. There was no sign of a dinner table, and I was hungry, expecting a Middle Eastern dinner. The street's shouts and clatters came through the windows and masked his voice. I had to move closer to hear him.

"Have you been followed coming here?" he asked.

"I don't think so, but one can never tell. Anyway, I'm a businessman and I came to do business. There's nothing wrong or suspicious about it."

"*Tayeb*—good," he said, although I was certain he wasn't satisfied with my answer. I discovered why, but not before he drained my patience. He then moved to discuss the weather, ask questions about Germany, talk about his friends that emigrated to Europe, and lament the limited number of tourists coming to Damascus. I was waiting for him to make the move: start talking business. My business. I said nothing, of course. I was very familiar with the Middle Eastern custom of engaging in small talk for a long time until you get to the point. There was a lot of wisdom in that custom: you have ample opportunities to study your guest and find his soft points.

After about an hour, he finally turned to business.

"When you land in Tehran you will be met by Khader and his men. He's my cousin and you can trust him. He is also in the women's clothing business and, therefore, your contacts will look OK."

He paused, waiting for my response, and looking at the small table between us. I took the hint. As customary in the Middle East, he would not touch the food until I helped myself. I took a few pistachios in my hand, and asked, "Will he recognize me?"

"Yes," he assured me. "He'll meet you for dinner on the day of your arrival at your hotel." He gave me additional technical details, addresses and phone numbers and emergency escape routes. The information Hammed gave me generally matched my instructions. I knew that neither Hammed nor Khader could risk any electronic communications with the Agency or the Mossad and, therefore, the specific information had to be given to me in person. If their messages were intercepted by the Syrian or Iranian security services, we wouldn't know it until it was too late.

"Any questions?"

"What about the exit?"

Hopefully, I would return within a week accompanied by Tango. I wasn't sure whether Hammed knew of Tango's identity, and I had to assume that he did not.

"It's all in here." He handed me a single sheet of paper, printed with a travel agency's stationery.

"Do I keep a copy?" I was a bit surprised at the lack of security.

"No, just memorize it. Khader has a copy as well. He will make sure you depart safely. When you arrive with your friend in Damascus, you will be staying in a vacation apartment we rented for you. My men will meet you in Damascus Airport and will take both of you to the apartment. If all goes well, both of you will leave Damascus the next day. There's no point in keeping you here and attracting the attention of the Mukhabarat, the Syrian secret police. They are everywhere, believe me, I know."

Hammed went to the next room, holding the document. I heard the toilet flush. He returned to the room without it.

"Have you had any run-ins with them?"

"Yes," he said with a sigh. He then said that he had been arrested by the Mukhabarat.

"Why?"

"They came to my store one day and went through my files, without asking permission or a court order. I'm a Kurd; we are a minority here. I had to keep my mouth shut or get on their bad side. They looked in my address book and asked why there were so many foreign addresses. I told them they were names and addresses of my clients. They didn't like my responses. They said my address book was proof I worked for the CIA and the Mossad."

That was bad news, because it could mean that Hammed was still on their radar.

"Why aren't you drinking your coffee?" he asked suddenly.

"Sorry, coffee doesn't agree with me, and the aftermath would be regrettable," I replied, hoping that I wasn't insulting him.

"Is tea all right?"

"Sure," I said.

He snapped his fingers. A young boy came in, looking humble. Hammed said "*jib chai*"—bring tea—and moments later, the boy returned carrying a polished steel tray with a pot of sweet tea and an hourglass-shaped glass with a gold rim.

Hammed continued, "The Mukhabarat questioned me as to whether I was a member in KDP, the Kurdistan Democracy Party. I denied it. They took me away and detained me with common criminals at Adra Prison, near Damascus, where I was beaten and degraded. I was not allowed to meet privately with my lawyer. I was prevented from leaving my cell, watching TV, or listening to the radio. One day I was assaulted by a criminal detainee who stabbed me with a sharpened spoon. I nearly died of bleeding until the prison guards pulled me out. This is how I lost my arm. On another occasion I was severely beaten by prison guards who shaved my head and made me crawl on all fours.

"All that happened before I was brought before a judge for crimes I never committed. I didn't even know what the charges against me were. I was sentenced by the Damascus Criminal Court to five years' imprisonment on the charge of spreading false information harmful to the state under Article 286 of the Syrian Criminal Code."

"Why? What had you done?"

"They brought a witness who said he'd heard me say that 'Soon the Kurds will have a state of their own.'"

I knew that such political trials were heard by Syria's Criminal, Military, and State Security Courts as part of their effort to suppress any hope of the Kurds for autonomy or independence.

"How long were you imprisoned?"

"Five years. The Mukhabarat promised me that I could be released sooner if I agreed to spy on my own people. I refused. They moved me to a prison cell in the basement floor, with no running water, no daylight. I was in solitary confinement. The Mukhabarat interrogators used electrical shocks on my genitals," he said, gesturing at his crotch and then his feet. "They beat me on my back and legs and I still feel pain although it's been seven years since my release."

I saw the pain in his bloodshot, yellowish eyes. They reflected his intense anger. I got the messages he sent me, direct and subtle, and I was sure that our meeting had ended. As I was planning to leave and rush to the nearest restaurant to satisfy my hunger, Hammed snapped his fingers. His servant opened the door, and Hammed directed me to a dining room.

A long oblong table was laden with many small plates with various salads and dips. "Please, please," he said, directing me to a chair opposite him. He broke pita bread and wiped it into a small plate with hummus. I followed suit, attempting to look ignorant of the custom of eating with your hands. This was strictly a case of need to know, and he didn't need to know about my Israeli background and my lifelong lust for hummus.

It was close to 10:30 p.m. when I left Hammed's home. The streets were empty. It was a cool night with a half moon. A sudden breeze chilled, or was it the steps I heard behind me? A professional would not look back. But, I was playing tourist, and I looked back. That was, of course, contrary to Rule Number Four of the Moscow Rules: *Don't look back; you are never completely alone.* But, hey, I wasn't supposed to be familiar with the Moscow Rules. I was just a businessman from Germany. Two men were behind staring at me. They didn't even make an effort to hide or "shake off the dogs," in old CIA lingo. I continued walking, hoping to catch a cab. Were they thugs looking for easy prey? Cops? I had no time or will to find out. Alas, there were no cabs.

I walked a bit faster, and they were still behind me. I passed by stores with their iron curtains down. The streetlights were sporadic and the cold wind was still blowing. We were still alone in the street. I finally made it to the main road. If they were to continue following me, it'd mean they were cops, not robbers who'd prefer a darker street. A cab cruised up, and I hailed it.

Before entering I looked back, the two men just stood there. Cops, no question. Why? Because I saw one of them holding a two-way radio and talking. That was alarming news. I couldn't have been exposed from my end for any suspicious activity. Maybe Hammed's past brought on my present situation? Was there a leak in the Mossad or the Agency? Besides, if there were, a reasonable response by any secret service would be to let me roam freely throughout the country, see what I was up to, whom I met, what photographs I took, and then apprehend me red-handed.

Other than meeting Hammed, I had done nothing since arriving in Damascus. I was also seen walking through the market with a bag full of sexy women's lingerie. Was that a heinous crime here requiring surveillance? The only plausible conclusion was that I had grown a tail because I had made contact with Hammed, who was already contaminated, and the Mukhabarat was watching his home. The only plausible explanation was that they were a deterrent tail, letting me know they were following me to scare me off from achieving my purpose.

I was upset and concerned. Why did the Mossad connect me with a "dirty" contact in Damascus? It just didn't make sense. I knew the way the Mossad operated, and security and caution were top priority. I was too tired to think about all the other options, so I just put it off for the time being.

As I inserted the key card into the slot on the door, I smelled cigarette odor combined with sour sweat. Not just cigarette smoke, but the stench locked into smokers' clothes that leave traces wherever they go, combined with the body odor of someone who hadn't bathed for a decade. I gingerly approached the door and heard noises. Someone was in my room. It wasn't a chambermaid because they leave the room door open while they work, and it was too late for that. I knocked lightly on the door of the neighboring room, hoping that someone would be up. A man dressed in European clothes opened the door, holding a nightcap in his hand.

"Excuse me," I said in an apologetic tone, "I was locked out of my room." I pointed at my door. "I think but am not sure that my wife is there sleeping, therefore I don't want to knock. I heard noise coming from your room, so I assumed you were awake . . . . Can I please go to your balcony and look over to my room to see if my wife is there?"

It took him only two seconds to open the door wide and say in an Italian accent, "Please."

I walked to his balcony and bent over the divider. An intruder was inside my room, bending over my still-unpacked suitcase. It was zipped, and a small lock linked the two zipper ends. The man used a sharp object, perhaps a ballpoint pen, and stuck it between the tiny teeth of the zipper. An old Mossad trick, now practiced also by others. The top part of the suitcase easily separated from the bottom part. My host came behind me. "Is everything all right?"

"Yes, thank you very much, I guess my wife is not in yet or maybe she's in the shower, so I'll go to the reception and get another key." I left his room and went to the lobby. I wasn't concerned with the search, because there was nothing in my room to cast any doubt on my identity. I was still Alexander Yager, a sales representative for a German export-import company. I was concerned by the mere intention to search my room, a treatment most tourists in Syria are probably spared. Although my legend was waterproof, there was no doubt that I'd attracted attention. But then, even a deep cover was no defense if I was caught doing something unconventional that an innocent businessman wouldn't do, such as meeting with political rivals of the regime.

Something was very wrong here. I thought of Rule Number Three of the Moscow Rules: *Assume that there is always hostile physical surveillance unless countersurveillance proves otherwise.* Why would the Mukhabarat risk breaking into my room when they knew I was about to return? They probably didn't mind. Where was the sentinel who was expected to be in the hallway to warn the intruders if I was returning to the room? Why did the CIA or the Mossad hook me up with a contaminated person who now tainted me as well? It just didn't make any sense to me.

But I had no time for soul-searching. I had a mission to complete and I needed to get my ass out of Syria as soon as I completed my mission, unless I faced imminent danger. Consequently, I also had to make an immediate decision about what to do next. Wait for the man, or maybe men, to leave my room and behave as if nothing had happened? What if they were planting an explosive device or some incriminating stuff like drugs or secret documents to frame me as a spy? Would that qualify as "nothing happened" as well?

On the other hand, if I abandoned my room and went to another hotel, that would be a strong signal to the Mukhabarat that I was not the innocent Alexander Yager, but someone with intelligence training. There was no point in fumigating the room for electronic surveillance devices. I couldn't care less. I was just a businessman.

As always, I confront challenges. I went to the lobby, sat on the soft couch, and waited. I rested my hand on the armchair pointed toward the elevator door. Why? Because I had to direct my wrist-watch toward the door. The elevator door opened and two men exited. Although I never saw my intruder's face while he was in my room, I recognized him by his jacket. I pressed the watch's crown three times, and put a bland expression on my face. The man exiting the elevator nodded to a third person who stood on guard next to the elevator door in the lobby, and the three of them left. I went to the door and saw them enter a dark sedan driven by a fourth person. Syrian secret service?

I returned to my room, opened the door, but left it open. If someone was still in my room, I'd better leave an escape route for him, and maybe for me if he was armed.

On first sight, the room was empty. I looked in the bathroom, the closets, and under the bed. Nothing. I closed the door. Under the circumstances, with the shadow escort I just had getting back to the hotel and the uninvited guests in my room, I had to assume a crisis was looming. I bent next to my suitcase. It was zipped up. I used the small key to unlock it and slowly lifted the back cover. All my stuff was there. But I couldn't tell whether something, such as a homing or listening device, had been added. I had no laptop computer or cell phone, and of course, no electronic surveillance detection devices.

But, hey, I wasn't going to talk on the phone with anyone, nor was I going to entertain anyone in my room. Therefore, I couldn't care less if a listening device was installed. Usually, I try to mask my plans. Now, I wanted them to be known, because why would a European businessman behave as if he's hiding anything?

———

The following morning, I checked out and took a cab to the airport. I expected that my departure could be a problem. I stood before the booth of the immigration officer as he flipped through the pages of my passport.

"How long was your visit?" he asked.

"Just two days," I answered, "I had a single business meeting and I'm done."

He slowly entered the information into his computer, and I waited for him to stamp my passport. The door behind him opened and another officer entered the small booth. *I'm in trouble*, was my first thought. They exchanged a few sentences in Arabic. Although I understood Arabic, it was too fast for me to catch. The officer who first took my passport left the booth. I was concerned as to whether he'd take my passport with him, but he didn't. The officer who replaced him just stamped my passport and handed it back to me.

"Have a safe flight," he said with a smile.

I smiled back, with deep inner relief, grateful that I'd be allowed to board the Syrianair flight to Tehran.

As I walked slowly through the airport, I wondered what it was all about. I had been followed, rather clumsily, by two men who made no secret of their interest in me. Two men had broken into my room and searched my suitcase, and yet nobody tried to stop my departure or even talk to me? Strange. Too strange to just be inefficiency. There was something else. I had to find out, but had no idea how, or when.

I glanced at my watch. With all my wonderings, I had to run to the gate. I made it, but there was a short delay. A man sitting next to me signaled me to follow him. In the men's room, after we exchanged code words, he rapidly took my Alexander Yager passport and gave me another, in the name of Hans Dieter Kraus, plus an envelope of documents backing up my new identity.

I boarded the plane, which was half-empty. I tightened my seatbelt and let out a smile when I remembered the joke about the German flight attendant who announces on the PA: "Please fasten your seatbelts, and I vont to hear van click!" In fact, here there was no such instructional language, and the business cabin crew was exceptionally courteous and friendly, which helped to slow my accelerated heartbeat. Being brave means that you are the only one who knows you are scared. And frankly, I was worried. *Who are you kidding?* asked my little inner devil. *You are terrified, I know, I'm inside you. All of your organs are contracting.*

XII

May 2007, Tehran

I looked out the window and saw Damascus disappear beneath the clouds, and then looked around me in the cabin. All passengers in business class were men in suits, although a few wore them without a tie. Most were bearded. Before landing, as my heart palpitations increased, a smell of toothpaste and clogged bathrooms filled the cabin.

This was my first arrival into Imam Khomeini International Airport near Tehran. During my previous visit to Tehran, posing as a Canadian author, I had landed in the older and poorly maintained Mehrabad Airport. As we approached the airport, I saw the surrounding Alborz range and in the center, sunk in clouds of smog, was the metropolis of Tehran with its fourteen million residents.

It was a bumpy landing. Much to my surprise, instead of going through a walkway to enter the terminal, a bus was waiting. With accelerated heartbeat and a nervous stomach, I entered the arrival hall of Khomeini International Airport. Upon entering the terminal, I was surprised to see its poor maintenance. Though this airport was new, the floor was stained and damaged, and the aluminum-framed windows were dirty. The English and Farsi signage, yellow on blue, was legible, but at least twice the English was unclear. The red illuminated letters on the black sign at passport control were only in Farsi. The men's bathroom was disgustingly dirty. There were several white flowerpots in the hallway, but the plants were nearly dead for lack of water.

I was nervous and for a good reason. I was high on the Iranian secret police "wanted" list.

A few years ago, while chasing the elusive Chameleon, I had penetrated Iran undercover, and barely escaped. To this day, I didn't know if the Iranians knew my real identity or my real professional affiliation. I wasn't using my real name now, and I didn't use it then. Even the aliases were different, as well as the legends. I carried a European passport with my photo and biometrics describing me as Hans Dieter Kraus, born in Minsk, Belarus, in 1951. Two credit cards—Visa, Eurocard issued by MasterCard (no American Express, thank you very much). Also, €8,000 in Visa travelers' checks and €2,000 in cash. Family photos, again, of Matilda and Snap. From the envelope of documents I also had business cards of *God's Faithful Followers Magazine*, a European magazine catering for the faithful of all religions believing in God.

The Iranian security services had my photo, first from when I'd applied for a visa, and then from when I was under surveillance in Tehran during my chase after the Chameleon. However, my appearance had changed: no beard, thirty pounds heavier, ten years older. I was hoping, just hoping, that the change would smooth my entry. Adding to my sense of trepidation was the risk that if I had in fact been contaminated in Damascus, then VEVAK would know almost immediately. That would earn me a swift arrest, and a slow and painful interrogation and incarceration. The fact that in Damascus I was Alexander Yager and in Tehran I became Hans Dieter Kraus would only help to tighten the rope around my neck.

I was full of dread, but determined. My sense of mission was stronger than the butterflies in my stomach. I took a deep breath and walked toward the passport control booth. Standing before the police immigration officer, who was dressed in a light green shirt with his rank embroidered on his collar, I showed him my passport. He gave me a tired look. He was unshaven and reeked of cigarettes. He flipped through the pages of my passport, and, without a word, stamped it. That was it. *Dan, you're a paranoid*, said my inner little devil. I agreed, though not forgetting that even paranoids may have real enemies.

Relieved once again, I went to the lower level to collect my luggage. An hour later, when everyone else had already collected their bags, I realized that mine wasn't coming any time soon. The carousel stopped. The area emptied of people. I went to the lost luggage counter.

"Wait for a few more minutes," the man behind the counter suggested, "and if your luggage is still unrecovered, call this number tomorrow." He handed me a printed page in three languages. Frustrated, as I was preparing to exit the terminal without my bag, thinking who might be interested in keeping it—and I had one obvious guess—a man came running, holding my bag. "I found it!" he exclaimed. Grateful, I tipped him nicely.

I went back to the lost and found office to cancel my complaint, and the attendant giggled. He then told me that this is a regular trick of the baggage handlers to increase their poor wages. In each flight, they hold on to a bag or two and when the frustrated passenger seems helpless, they bring it to him as a newly found bag, and win a generous tip. I left the terminal into a bustling crowd of taxi drivers, moneychangers, and self-certified tour guides. I knew there was no metro or train to Tehran and had expected an hour and a half of travel by taxi to the city. The air was humid and the back of my shirt was wet, not only because of the humidity.

A talkative cabbie drove me to the Laleh Hotel in Laleh Park, close to the business district. Before the Islamic Revolution it was named the InterContinental, the best hotel in Tehran. Settled in my room, I opened the curtains and saw spectacular mountain views of Damavand and Alborz. I went downstairs to have a meal. With a choice of rotisserie, Polynesian, and Iranian restaurants, I chose the hotel's Namakdoon restaurant that serves traditional Persian cuisine. Hell, I didn't come to Tehran to eat Polynesian dishes! There were many diners in the elegant restaurant, and I was busy reading the menu, when a man dressed in Persian attire came to my table. "Mr. Hans?"

I ignored the fact that he was addressing me by my first name.

I looked up over the menu. He was heavyset, in his midfifties, with a dark mustache and sun-parched face. I nodded. When he didn't respond, I said, "Yes, I'm Hans Dieter Kraus, and you are?"

"Mr. Khader's chauffer." His accent was heavy. I looked at him attentively. He continued, "Once you finish your dinner, please go outside. I'll be waiting in a white Mercedes limo." He half bowed and walked away.

The food was delicious, but I was too preoccupied with planning my next moves to enjoy it. Although I've been through these operations many times before, each time I was excited anew. I finished my meal and went outside. The man was waiting in his car, and I sat in the back seat.

He started the engine.

"Where are going?" I asked.

"To your apartment."

"What apartment?" I asked. I knew I wasn't supposed to check out of my hotel room.

"Change of plans," he said, "Mr. Khader told me to bring you over."

"I need stuff from my luggage," I said. I was concerned. Although the chauffer gave me the correct code word, identifying him as my contact, the sudden unannounced change of plan was unusual. I decided not to argue and to wait for developments. I'd just violated a Mossad Rule: *A sudden change of plans is always suspicious. Therefore, you must make sure you verify the authenticity of the instruction and abort in case of the slightest uncertainty. It could be hostile.* I thought of Rule Number Two of the Moscow Rules: *Never go against your gut.* I had just violated that rule, too. Why? Because I'm a risk taker. If I fail, then my decisions would be defined as callous and stupid.

"Mr. Khader said that you will not be returning to this hotel, and that your luggage must stay there. I have another suitcase for you here."

I said nothing, leaned back, and watched the passing streets of bustling Iran.

We arrived at a six-story building in northern Tehran. The chauffer quickly exited and opened my door. He gave me a set of keys. "One key will open the main entrance door and the other key will open your apartment door. It's on the sixth floor, apartment 6F." He opened the trunk and pulled out a suitcase, which he carried to the door.

I took the new suitcase, entered the building, and took the elevator to the sixth floor. As I entered the apartment I saw a man sitting on a sofa. The hair on my back rose. *A trap, after all,* I said to myself, quickly wondering how I'd let myself fall for it. I looked back to see if I could escape. It was too late. Behind the door was another man who closed the door, keeping me inside with no place to go.

The man on the sofa got up, "Mr. Kraus?

"Yes," I answered trying to figure out what had gone wrong, and how long would it be before they'd peel me and get my identity, mission, and maybe even details about my previous Iranian penetration. I shouldn't have ignored another Moscow Rule: *Assume that all local nationals are hostile.*

He smiled, "I'm Khader, Hammed's cousin, I'm glad to meet you." He shook my hand firmly. Was a sigh of relief appropriate here?

I wasn't sure yet. I sat next to him. The man standing next to the door remained there. After the inevitable small talk, although no coffee was served—it was *my* apartment—I asked him: "Why did I need to leave my hotel room?"

"For security reasons. You'll keep your hotel room. My men will enter it to mess up the bed and make it look like you slept there."

"I need my toiletries and clothes."

"If you have medication or anything personal you need, my men will bring it over tomorrow. Otherwise, that suitcase"—he pointed at the suitcase I brought up—"contains a complete change of clothes for you."

I didn't answer. The arrangement still seemed odd, but I decided to see how things developed. Besides, that sudden change must have been coordinated with the Agency, if they had my clothing sizes. "What about Tango?" I asked. After all, he was the focus of my mission.

"Tango has left his apartment," Khader answered.

"To where?"

"To another location. The VEVAK was getting closer to him."

I realized I wasn't getting straight answers. "What's the arrangement, then?" I asked, a bit surprised at the evasiveness.

"We will bring him over to a safe house in southern Tehran, where he can blend, and once he's there we'll get you to him."

"When will that happen?"

"Within a few days," he said. "In the meanwhile, feel free to tour Tehran, but stay out of trouble," he smiled. "Have you ever been here before?"

My inner little devil had been semi-dormant the whole time. Now, he opened one eye. *Don't answer that! But be polite.* Volunteering information, when asked a simple question that calls for a short answer, is always a bad policy. Doing that with strangers while on assignment is simply irresponsible. Why is he asking?

"I'll do some sightseeing of museums, there's no trouble there," I smiled back.

"Tayeb," he concluded. "There's food in the refrigerator and a cleaning woman will come every day." He handed me a piece of paper.

"Here is my number. Memorize and destroy." He shook my hand firmly with both his hands and left with the man at the door.

I stretched out on the sofa, trying to digest the events. An hour later, I went out to the street and took a cab to Park Saie. I crossed the street and entered a store at the Sadaf building. I paid twenty-five thousand rials—about three dollars—for one hour's use of their computer. I logged into my Yahoo account and mailed a message to Allgemeine Textile Fabriquant GmbH:

I have arrived safely in Tehran. My hosts suggested I stay at an apartment rather than at the hotel to allow them to bring models to try on our merchandise. I was told that the shipment of our sample merchandise has not arrived yet, but hope to clear it through customs shortly. Hans Dieter Kraus.

The memory of the great Iranian shawarma I had in Dubai was too strong to ignore. Despite my dinner at the Laleh Hotel, I stopped at one of the shawarma stands and helped myself to a hearty serving. Even though the white tahini sauce oozed through my fingers onto my pants, I didn't stop eating. I looked around me. Young couples were pushing baby strollers, students were carrying backpacks, bicycle riders were maneuvering through the hectic traffic amid the noise of honking cars and eye-burning smog. This was the same Tehran I had left in a hurry ten years ago. It had only gotten bigger, dirtier in some areas, and more congested. During rush hour—and it's rush hour during most of the day—walking is sometimes faster than taking a car. Crossing a highway is like swimming across an alligator-infested pool fast, hoping to make it in one piece.

I went to a nearby ATM machine and sent a two-digit code to my bank in Germany. The bank's computers were programmed to automatically and invisibly forward these messages to the CIA's call center somewhere in the US Midwest. Code 76 meant *I'm OK, but sudden changes raise concern.* This was a midlevel alert. The instructions I was given during my training at The Farm were clear: *Use it when there's no imminent danger, but increased alertness is applied. If no communication is received from you that includes a #, or number sign, within twenty-four hours, that would mean you're in distress and may have been apprehended and that communication was coerced.*

I behaved as a businessman with a few hours to kill would behave. My day tour the next day started with a visit to the Carpet Museum. Next, I went to the Museum of Reza Abbasi, named after the miniaturist in the Safavid era. It exhibits calligraphy and artifacts dating back to ancient Islamic periods and even before. Next, I visited the Crown Jewels Museum and the Archaeological Museum. There I saw a stone capital statue of a winged lion from Susa, and a sixth-century BC hall relief of Darius the Great from the Treasury at Persepolis. Nowhere did I identify anyone taking a special interest in me.

After quick tours of the museums, I walked slowly through the bazaar, buying two souvenirs—bargaining the price down a bit—and then took a cab to my hotel. My hotel? Yes, I wasn't comfortable with my instructions to avoid the hotel. Something in me said it wasn't right. Good to my notorious character of questioning authority when instructions do not make sense to me, I went up to my room, collected a few items from my baggage, messed up the room a bit, used the bathroom and left. I took a cab back to the bazaar, made sure through a few maneuvers that I wasn't followed, and took a cab to my apartment.

An hour later, Khader arrived. He opened my door with a key. That surprised me, but in fact, I should have been pleased that he had immediate access. I needed no privacy, I wasn't entertaining women there, and in case of emergency, he could enter. I was troubled though that he didn't bother telling me he had a key.

"Mr. Kraus," he said and I immediately sensed his anger.

I looked at him.

"I thought we asked you to stay away from your hotel."

"No, you did not. You said I would move here, but said nothing about not returning." Was I under his watch all the time? I decided not to ask or comment any further. He knew, and wanted me to realize it. That was probably his purpose in chiding me.

"What's up with Tango?"

"We hope to move him to a safe house in southern Tehran tomorrow."

"Just hope?" I asked. I didn't like the uncertainty.

"We'll see in the morning," he said cryptically. I didn't respond; there was no way I would challenge him. Not then, not there. Maybe later. Maybe? Err, for sure.

"If you need anything, call me," Khader said, and when I said I was OK, he left, but not before asking me not to return to my hotel.

I was anxious but not in a hurry to move the operation forward. However, the way things were progressing here made me uncomfortable. I recognized the feeling. A cloud of uncertainty was invisibly hovering in the room, telling me that something wasn't right, but I had no clue what it was. This was my second undercover tour in Iran in which I had significant help from the Kurds. I'd also had several other contacts with the Kurds. The ones I had met were fearless fighters, honest and loyal.

However, my little inner devil was restlessly moving inside me, telling me he too was uncomfortable.

I decided to play it safe. Believe all men, but cut the cards. I thought of reporting to Eric, but if Khader and his men were sour, then my communication with Eric could be captured, especially if I used the tiny communication device that Khader had given me earlier. There was no way of knowing whether he had added himself as an additional subscriber. I wasn't going to use the device other than for communicating with Khader. My other means of contact with Eric and Paul were through the Internet, using pre-agreed messages, or in case of emergency, via short messages through any ATM machine. These would end up, through my bank, on Eric's desk. At this time there was no emergency, so I decided to wait.

After watching Iranian television for an hour, I went to the kitchen, took a jar of sugar, and spilled it on the floor in the vestibule, covering it with a newspaper. Anyone entering the apartment during the night would step on the newspaper and make a grinding noise. That would be enough to wake me up.

I went to sleep in the other vacant room in the apartment. Somehow I wasn't comfortable sleeping in the master bedroom of an apartment to which other people I'd just met held keys.

I woke up to the chant of *muezzins* calling devout Muslims to wake up for the morning prayer. It was still dark outside, but the sounds, broadcast from at least three minarets and coming from three directions, reminded me that I was in a Muslim country, where believers were expected to pray five times a day. As I planned to roll over and continue sleeping, there was a knock on the front door. I froze and listened to the sounds. Khader didn't need to knock. Who else might it be?

I went to the door and peeped through the viewer. A mustached man was standing there.

"Who are you?" I asked while taking cover behind the door.

"Khader sent me," he said quietly, and gave me the password that identified him as a friend.

I opened the door. "Please be ready. We are going to see Tango."

I returned to the bedroom, quickly changed, and joined the man. We went out to the street and entered his beat-up Toyota. I looked at the streets of northern Tehran as they filled up with traffic, mostly trucks, packed buses, and taxis. We entered Sadr Highway, got off next to Qeytariyeh, and entered a beautiful residential area.

"Where are we?" I asked.

"We're in Farmaniyeh, this is where rich people live," he said in an appreciative tone.

He stopped the car next to a high-rise and used his cell phone to make a call. After exchanging a few words in Kurdish—a language I didn't speak—he asked me to leave the car.

"Go to the eighteenth floor," he said, "Khader and Tango will be there."

"Aren't you coming as well?"

"No, I need to stay here."

"Is there a doorman in the building?"

"Yes, just wave at him; he was told that a guest was coming."

"To what apartment should I go on the eighteenth floor?"

"Khader will wait for you as you exit the elevator."

I walked to the entrance. The lobby was palatial, with a twenty-foot archway at the main entrance, marble floors, stone walls, arched mosaic ceilings, and decorative chandeliers. The walls on the walkway to the elevators had brick and terracotta façades. I waved at the half-asleep doorman and went to the eighteenth floor. Khader was indeed waiting for me. Without saying a word, he turned and I followed down a long, carpeted corridor hung with oil paintings. At the end of the hallway, he opened an apartment door.

A man in his midfifties stood there.

"This is General Cyrus Madani," said Khader, as I approached. The general said nothing and shook my hand. His handshake was firm, and I could feel his farmer's rough skin. He was dressed in starched and ironed khaki pants and shirt. I looked at his face. He had dark eyes and a well-groomed mustache.

"I'm pleased to meet you," I said in Arabic.

"We can talk in English," he responded, realizing from my accent that Arabic was not my native language.

"Marhaba," he nonetheless said in Arabic. "Welcome. Please, let's go inside." I followed him to the end of the room, near tall windows. The curtains were open and I could see the nearby park. Madani sat on one end of a black leather sectional sofa. I sat on the other. Khader remained standing.

"What's the plan?" Madani asked. He had the confident tone of a person accustomed to giving orders. I was surprised at the direct approach, very much unlike the local custom.

"We are going to cross the border to Syria."

As if on a cue, Madani asked, "And who would you be?"

"I'm journalist writing an article on religious pilgrimages of various religions."

"For whom are you writing?"

"*God's Faithful Followers Magazine*," I said.

"Is that a joke?" he asked, in half contempt.

"No, not at all, that's a real magazine, and I'm listed in the masthead as a staff reporter. I fact, my previous article described the faithful Catholics' pilgrimage to the Vatican. Here, I have a copy for you," I handed him the magazine I kept in my briefcase.

He flipped through the pages, his face motionless. He handed the magazine back to me.

"No," I insisted, "keep it. You may have to show it if questions are asked."

For the next three hours, I went with Madani through a series of instructions, telling him what to say if questioned about how our contact was made, and explaining why there were no previous telephone conversations, letters, or e-mails between us. I rehearsed the legend the CIA had designed for us.

"Please memorize it," I said, "remember even the minute technical details, such as the time of day I first approached you."

"Remember," I concluded at the end, "it was your travel agent who specializes in pilgrimage tours who made the connection. My editor called him, asking for a good example of a Shia pilgrim, and he suggested you."

"You mean that my travel agent is in the loop?" He sounded surprised.

"No, he is not," I said emphatically. "He in fact was approached by my editor, but your travel agent thinks it's a real request from a genuine magazine, and in fact it is. The article about your pilgrimage will appear in print."

He gave me a long look, without saying anything. Moments later he said, "Tayeb."

"There's a train going from Tehran north and west to Istanbul, avoiding Iraq, then south to Damascus. We will take it," I said.

His face showed no expression. "And then?" he asked.

"From Damascus, we'll take the return train to Turkey and you'll be met by American agents who'll take care of you."

He slanted his eyes. "What do you mean, take care of me? I thought we had an agreement. I'm going to America."

There was more than a tad of anger in his voice.

"Of course, General," I said quickly. "What I mean is that my instructions are to bring you safely to Turkey. From there another unit is taking over. As a general with so many years in the military you know the importance of field security. I am not supposed to know about all the details of the operation, just those that concern my role. If I'm caught and made to talk, I could be forced to reveal only what I know—my limited duties, not the entire operation. That is meant to protect you."

His black eyes were still on fire, but I moved on.

"If we need to be in Turkey, why travel through Damascus?"

I was uneasy. It was Madani who had told the CIA that his Iranian exit visa was limited to a Syrian visit only. The little devil inside me moved nervously.

"Because I've been told that your Iranian exit visa allows you to visit only Damascus on a pilgrimage, right?"

He nodded.

"How are we going to Syria?" He sounded surprised. "Iran doesn't border with Syria, Iraq is in between."

"As I mentioned earlier, by train. We have reservations for a four-berth cabin on a train traveling between Tehran and Damascus through Turkey, which requires a five-hour ferry ride to get across."

"Who's traveling?" he asked.

"Just you and me."

"Then why the four berths?"

"They have no two-berth cabins. We paid for the four couchettes to avoid company." I wasn't going to tell him that we'd be guarded from a short distance by six men in the next cabin.

"It's a long ride," Madani said in a weary tone. "I thought we were flying."

"No, my instructions are to travel by train. There are fewer security checks."

"It's more than three thousand miles away," he insisted.

"I know," I said, not mentioning that the actual distance was not even half that: less than 2,400 kilometers, and so less than 1,500 miles. There was no point in contradicting him.

"It doesn't make sense."

I decided not to challenge him. "Is there a better plan?" I asked, although I knew that Madani couldn't make changes to a plan that had been worked out by dozens of CIA and Mossad researchers and analysts. Nonetheless, I had to give him the impression that his opinion was important.

I waited for a response or the next argument to come immediately. It didn't.

I continued, "We'll be traveling on an Iranian train where VEVAK has eyes and ears in every corner, showing we have nothing to hide."

"Why aren't we going from Tehran to Damascus through Iraq? It's much shorter?"

"There's no train service from Tehran through Iraqi territory. Hostility is still strong."

"Why can't we get off in Turkey en route to Damascus? What's the idea of passing Turkey, staying on the train and then when in Damascus returning to Turkey?"

There was a lot of sense in his question, but the planners thought differently.

"We'll get to Damascus, and go on a pilgrimage which will most probably be shadowed by VEVAK agents. Since we know you are under their prying eyes, they are most likely going to expect defection in Turkey and if that happened, they would shoot you then and there. No. We will travel to Damascus from Turkey and then you lose them."

"How?"

"I don't know," I admitted. "It's part of the next step."

His dark face became red all of a sudden. "What do you mean, you don't know? What kind of an operation you are running here? Are you an amateur? I'm risking my life and 'you don't know'?"

The last sentence was undoubtedly genuine-sounding, but not the rest of what he said. My stomach moved nervously again.

"When?" He asked curtly, moving on all of a sudden as if nothing had happened.

I looked at Khader, who said, "Tomorrow morning."

"Is that all?" he asked, rising from the sofa.

"I guess so," I said, "Khader will fill you in on the technical details. But generally speaking, you should pack and conduct yourself as if you are going on a pilgrimage."

"I am," he said, reassuring himself.

"Of course you are, but at the conclusion of your pilgrimage to the Holy Shia sites in Syria, you'll continue on a different pilgrimage to the US."

He seemed satisfied to hear my answer.

"I'll meet you tomorrow, Monday evening, at the Tehran Central Railway Station, in Shoosh," I said, shaking his hand, and left. Khader accompanied me down to the waiting car.

"He seemed nervous," I said.

"You can understand that," said Khader. "It's a huge step to take for a man in his position."

I didn't share with Khader my gut feeling and the messages the little devil in me was sending. The driver took me back to the apartment building and, as the car sped away, I entered a small newspaper and magazine store and bought a Farsi language daily. I could read the script, since the letters are Arabic and its grammar is similar to that of many contemporary European languages. But I could barely understand the general meaning due to my limited command of the Farsi language. Nonetheless, a man holding a Farsi newspaper is somewhat less likely to be regarded as a stranger.

I walked to the nearest bank and used the ATM machine to withdraw rials. Then I punched a sequence of keys for innocuous-looking transactions. They would immediately appear on my bank statements being monitored hourly in the operations center in the US. The sequence of keystrokes sent the message: *All well. Leaving with Tango as planned.*

I returned to the apartment and prepared for the next move. I had no idea where my backup team was located. I knew they were close, but I hadn't identified them yet. With security cameras located in most public areas and buildings, I couldn't risk being seen with any one of my team. One of us could already be contaminated, and, by meeting, would automatically contaminate the other.

———

On Monday afternoon, Khader's driver picked me up and took me to the central railway station, a palatial building with Acropolis-like heavy columns and a building façade reminiscent of the Pentagon. Holding my ticket and travel documents, I passed the gate and saw Madani standing on the platform next to a woman dressed in a black chador.

I nodded and said, "Good afternoon, General."

"This is my wife, Fatima," he said.

I smiled at her. "Good afternoon, Mrs. Madani."

Her eyes smiled. Because of the chador she was wearing, I could barely see her face.

"She doesn't speak English," said Madani.

I carefully scoured the area. I was certain that there were at least two groups of watchers, my backup team and VEVAK agents. However, I was unable to identify any of them. The sleek modern electric train was already in the station, and passengers were boarding. Madani hugged his wife and watched her walk toward the exit. Then we boarded the train and entered our cabin.

XIII

May 2007, Tehran to Istanbul

Soon the train left the station and Tehran. As we sat in the cabin, Madani seemed tense, nervous, and uncomfortable. I eventually decided not to engage in conversation that could irritate him further.

"I'm tired," I said. "I'm getting some sleep."

Madani just nodded.

I woke up several hours later.

Madani wasn't there.

I jumped to my feet and checked the bathroom. Nothing. I left the cabin with my heart pounding, searching the corridor. I couldn't see him. Many passengers stood in the aisle, smoking cigarettes that burned my eyes and charred my throat.

I was alarmed. How could Madani leave the cabin? Wasn't he aware of the risks? And where the hell was my backup team, who were supposed to monitor him and me at all times? I had a weapon of last resort, a small communication device disguised as a pen. I could transmit brief coded messages a short distance by pressing the top. That would bring the team out to help me in any distress. But that could also blow their cover and, most likely, doom the operation if we were observed. I asked the conductor which station came next.

"Zanjan," he said.

I'd fallen asleep after we'd left the only stop before Zanjan. That meant that Madani must still be on the train. I walked to the front of the train, trying to look disinterested, and peeked into each cabin. No trace of Madani. I was distressed. How could he vanish, and how could I face Eric and explain? I could almost hear Eric mutter, "An intelligence golden nugget that has been worked on for a year with considerable effort and expense slips through the hands of that nincompoop Dan Gordon."

I felt cold drops of sweat roll down my spine. That could be my CEI—career-ending incident. I took a deep breath and was more determined than ever to find Madani. I completed two rounds of search throughout the train, and even waited outside each of the occupied lavatories to see who exited, but to no avail. I pulled out the pen, getting ready to press its head and alarm my backup team.

Think outside the box were the words of my Mossad Academy instructors. Nice suggestion, I thought, but where is the box, and what's beyond it? At a time of distress, these suggestions only contributed to my confusion.

As I was about to turn around, return to my cabin, and operate the pen, I saw Madani in the corridor approaching me. I didn't know which emotion took precedence—my sense of rage or relief. I was about to yell "*Where the fuck were you?*" but composed myself.

"Where were you?" I asked in a calm tone, although I was on fire inside.

"Oh, I sat at the front engine talking to the engineers. I've always been fascinated by trains," he said matter-of-factly.

I needed to take a deep breath or else I'd scream at him with the full throttle of my lungs. "General Madani, please let me know next time you are leaving the cabin. There are serious risks involved if you leave without telling me."

He didn't respond, or even look at me. He entered the cabin and sat looking outside, clearly sending me a message to get off his back. But I wasn't going to. I also didn't like the story about the engineers, but as long as Madani was back in one piece and the train was moving, I could live with some wrinkles in the plan.

Hours later we arrived at Tabriz and customs officers boarded the train. I had just one bag with clothes, a laptop computer with articles I purportedly had written, a camera, and toiletries. They didn't bother with my luggage. Their only concern was whether I was carrying large amounts of money or drugs. When I said that I wasn't, they moved on to Madani. He was pale and I sensed a light tremor of his right hand. After reviewing his papers, they moved to the next cabin.

The train continued to Urmia, the capital of Salmas township, the last stop in Iran. I looked in my guidebook. It described Salmas township as being located 854 kilometers northwest of Tehran, and as a beautiful city with attractive bazaars and stone mosques.

I used that opportunity to start a conversation: "My guidebook says that we are already in the Iranian province of West Azerbaijan and that it has a Kurdish origin."

Madani nodded. "And there are good mineral water springs here that have therapeutic qualities."

From the train, I could see Lake Urmia. I opened the window. We were at 4,000 feet and a cold breeze went through the cabin. The train stopped. Through the window I could see a small blue sign hanging from the outside wall of a dilapidated but clean building, saying SALMAS STATION in English and Farsi. Lamp poles were painted blue and white, and the platform was paved with uneven wood logs. The cabin door opened and two Iranian Police and Immigration Control officers, dressed in green uniforms, boarded for final passport control. We gave them our passports. Although I was carrying a foreign passport, the officer holding it just flipped through the pages and returned it to me without saying a word.

The officer holding Madani's reddish-brown Iranian passport opened it, gave Madani a glance, and said something to the other officer. Madani's face went frozen, getting a grayish tint. He was visibly nervous. He should be. If this were more than a routine passport review, he could be taken off the train without much ado. I was just as nervous, stomach turning, but put on an indifferent face. There was a fast exchange of questions and answers between Madani and the officers. Although I could barely understand a full sentence, my limited command of Farsi was sufficient to understand that their questions concerned Madani's route. As expected, they asked him why he was on board a train to Turkey when his exit visa allowed him to go to Syria only.

"I'm not going to Turkey," I understood Madani to say. "The train is going to Syria through Turkey because Iran doesn't border with Syria."

I couldn't understand the officer's next question, but I gathered from Madani's answer that a train ticket was cheaper than flying.

One officer left the cabin, taking Madani's passport with him. The other officer remained standing in the cabin. Tension was in the air. If for any reason—whether related to Madani's planned defection, or any bureaucratic problem—Madani was not allowed to continue on the train, then the operation was doomed and I was toast.

I exchanged looks with Madani, hoping that he would not tie me to him. I wasn't sure what to do next. Remain an anonymous passenger who just happened to be in the same cabin with Madani, or come forward and identify myself as a journalist accompanying Madani? I decided to keep quiet and see what developed. If Madani's problems were preplanned by the Iranian secret police, then he must have been under photographed surveillance that undoubtedly captured me in Madani's company prior to our joint train trip. Therefore, trying to distance myself from Madani by pretending to be a complete stranger could potentially dig me into a hole and make me also a suspect.

After ten or fifteen long minutes, the officer returned to the cabin holding Madani's passport. He snapped something in Farsi and Madani got up, gave me a helpless look, took his suitcase, and followed the two officers as they exited the cabin. That was a time to decide: to follow him and the officers even if they got off the train, or continue the ride until the next stop in Turkey, twenty miles away, to report to Eric what had happened.

I heard doors slamming. It was the moment to act. Duty first, I concluded. I grabbed my bag and ran to the door, jumping to the platform just as the train started moving. I looked around, but I didn't see Madani. The platform was vacant. I searched around the terminal building, but there was no Madani or his police escorts. I went outside and entered a beat-up cab, signaling the driver to take me on a tour of this city of 75,000, hoping I'd see Madani in a police car.

Just as he started the engine, I changed my mind. Madani could still be in the terminal building or in its vicinity. The border control police must maintain a local facility to process and question all suspects they remove from the train in this last Iranian stop before the Turkish border.

"Stop!" I said. The baffled cabbie looked at me. I gave him a few rials, exited the cab, and reentered the terminal building. Except for a cleaning woman wiping the floor, it now was empty. I asked her where the police station was.

After a second she said, "Polise?" I nodded. She pointed her finger outside and said, "Salmas." I ran outside again and reentered the cab. The cabbie didn't seem to have too much business.

"Polise," I said. A few minutes later, he dropped me off near a small building. "Polise!" he announced.

I entered the small building. There was just one officer there behind a desk. I introduced myself, hoping in vain that he spoke English.

I heard voices of people arguing in Farsi coming from the back.

"Madani," I said, "I'm looking for General Madani."

The officer went to the back and left me standing. The door opened. One of the officers who had taken Madani emerged.

"I'm looking for General Madani," I said, without asking if he understood English. "I'm writing an article about his pilgrimage. Is there a problem I could help you with?"

"Madani is a PJAK terrorist," he replied.

I knew that PJAK was an outlawed organization with ties to the Kurdistan Workers' Party (PKK), trying to establish an independent Kurdish state. PJAK had been staging cross-border attacks in Iran since 2004. However, I didn't want to appear too politically savvy, and pretended not to understand what PJAK was or why Madani was detained.

"Terrorist," the officer said, "PJAK terrorist."

That couldn't be true, I thought. Madani was ethnic Iranian with a rich military past that had no connection, to my knowledge, to the Kurds, unless he was double-dipping. I couldn't challenge the officer without alienating him.

"Can you release him on bail?" I asked, "I could sign for him."

"Sign?" he said in contempt. "Bail money," he said, rubbing his thumb and index finger together in the too-well-known sign for demanding payment.

"How much is the bail?" I asked. To me it was clear that we were talking about a bribe.

"One million rials."

I quickly calculated the amount. It was just over one hundred US dollars.

I handed him the cash.

"No," he said, and took out a form from the desk drawer. He filled in the details in longhand, and handed me the form—all in Farsi—to sign. I signed and handed him the cash. He put it in the drawer, went to the back, and returned with Madani.

That was the first time Madani smiled at me.

The cabbie was still waiting outside. We had him drive us to the terminal. "There's another train in a couple of hours," said Madani. "Let's wait in a café nearby." He seemed cool.

The whole incident was peculiar, bordering on the bizarre. First, they tell me that Madani is a terrorist and then, within ten minutes, they release him on a hundred dollars' "bail"?

Furthermore, I was an English-speaking Westerner, in this remote area that had recently been in the news following deadly attacks attributed to PJAK—attacks rumored to be supported by the CIA and the Mossad—and yet nobody bothered to ask me anything or at least to copy my passport? The little devil in me moved nervously.

I smelled a rat. There was an abnormality here, in an intelligence lingo. First releasing "a terrorist," then not even getting the details of the person travelling with him? Unless they already had my details, which made the stench even stronger.

The train arrived and we continued our journey. I looked out the window at snow-covered mountains in the distance as the train crossed a bare plateau. Poplar and pine trees covered with snow were glistening, and herds of sheep looked for food in the few green spots between the clay and gravel roads.

After passing the border station of Razi on the Iranian side, the train stopped in the Turkish border station of Kapikoy. Time to get out again. A customs official behind a glass window pointed to a picture of Ataturk, the founder of the state, and asked a young Scottish woman tourist cheekily, "Do you know who that is? Welcome to Turkey." The Scottish woman took off her headscarf with a sigh of relief.

I remembered from my briefing that the railway linking Turkey to Iran, Iraq, Central Asia, and Pakistan goes through Kapikoy, so that Turkish officers could check passengers' visas. The next stations going west were Van, the ancient cradle of Armenian civilization, and Van jetty. In Van jetty, passengers get on a ferry for the five-hour voyage across Lake Van to Tatvan jetty. Then passengers traveling to Damascus continued with a Syrian train. I looked up the schedule: The next stopovers in Turkey were the cities of Malatya, Sivas, Kayseria, and Ankara, before arriving at Istanbul's Haidar Pasha Railway Station.

My notes said that then, after passing Fevzipasa Station, the train stops at the border station of Islahiye, which controls the exit from Turkey. Then Syrian officials check passports and conduct customs inspections at the Syrian border station of Meydan Ikbis, and the train departs for Damascus. I closed my notebook.

We arrived in Istanbul without incident, making our way through the station's bustling crowds. In the corner of the high-ceilinged station, a group of whirling dervishes were spinning in ceremony, surrounded by onlookers. For a minute, I was reminded of the street performers in the Times Square train station, back in New York. This station, however, was more storied than any subway; this station was the final stop on the famed Orient Express. As Madani and I exited the station, I recalled how that simple phrase, "The Orient Express," seemed at one time to be synonymous with all kinds of intrigue, with impeccably dressed spies in suits.

And right as I was thinking about this—in fact, right as I was specifically trying to recall the last time I was able to fit into an extra-large suit—a slob of a man swerved into me, dripping coffee all over my shirt, then mumbled an apology. As I tried wiping the dark stain off, I was almost run over by an angry old lady shouting in Turkish.

No, I thought. *My life is nothing like the Orient Express.*

Through the haze of afternoon smog, I spotted two distinguished-looking men, tall, and just this side of nondescript, walking towards us. One carried a small backpack. Madani spotted me spotting the men; he and I exchanged eye contact: *Is that them? Yes.* The men got closer, and closer—and passed us. As I turned to watch, the coffee man came up to me again, so uncomfortably close I could smell the drink on his breath.

He said, "Didn't we meet in Vienna last year?"

So this was *him*. Our contact. Could I trust him? Hot coffee or no, I was hoping so—the little devil in me was somewhat uncomfortable. Did the agency really send that slob? I looked at the coffee man and said, "No. I think we met in Paris."

The man held his hand out to me.

"I'm Scott," he said. And then he motioned to a squat, balding man in a suit, who, I guessed, had merely been pretending to look for a cab. He too held out his hand to me.

"This is Thomas," Scott said. "and, oh, sorry about the—" He pointed to my shirt. I waved it off.

So, Scott and Thomas it was. They looked at Tango, then at me, and asked, "And this is?"

"Tango," I said.

They shook his hand. Madani looked confused, trying to grasp was going on. He didn't ask and I didn't offer an explanation. I also decided not to share my doubts regarding Tango with these guys. Because if my nervous little devil's suspicions regarding Tango were proven, then perhaps there were other contaminated individuals out there, detrimental to my mission. True, we'd all exchanged identification smoothly (or, looking down at my shirt, smoothly enough). But you never know. I still had the bullet scar from the first time I thought I was bringing in Tango, back at from the Iranian-Armenian border. *That* Tango turned out to be some fake, good-for-nothing drug dealer just out of prison. I decided to keep quiet and my eyes wide open.

"Where are we going?" I asked.

"Let's talk outside," suggested Scott. They had a car waiting for us, a black Suburban with Turkish plates. Even as I got in the car, I was doing a double take. A Suburban? No one drives Suburbans in Istanbul except US Embassy personnel, and maybe a few others. Can anyone possibly be more conspicuous? There was something wrong here. At the very best, Scott and Thomas were amateurs. And at worst?

As they drove up to the Conrad Hotel, Scott turned around and said, "Here you are. This is your last stop."

When I saw that Tango remained sitting, I asked, "What about him?"

"We're taking Tango with us; those are my orders."

"Whose orders?"

"The head honcho," Scott said. He wasn't going to give me a real name in front of Tango. So why did I ask? He caught me off guard, really; I found myself dismayed and surprised that my mission was going to end so soon and that the plan to continue our travel to Syria was scrapped. Frankly, that had never made sense to me in the first place. But I was also feeling something else, something I can only describe as relief.

I exited and met Scott at the back of the car, out of Tango's sight. He took my travel wallet containing my Kraus passport and credit cards, and gave me another leather travel wallet with a new set of identity documents and a new legend in a brown envelope. The little devil inside me finally exhaled a little as I checked into the hotel with my new Irish passport.

My name today was Daniel Patrick Leahy. I settled in to my room and began to memorize yet another new identity. How many had I had by now? I began counting my past identities like sheep.

I flopped down on the bed without bothering to lift the bedspread. The second my head hit the bed, I fell asleep.

An hour later I woke with a bad taste, not only in my mouth, but also my mind. I needed to talk to Eric and Benny. I knew that I would have to wait until contact was made; I couldn't initiate. Or so they told me. Since when did I meticulously obey orders? If my suspicions had any basis in reality, I needed to know.

I went to the minibar and pulled out a can of local beer, which tasted like it had first gone through a horse, and right as I was contemplating the minibar yet again, the phone rang. I picked it up and heard Benny's voice. Although we were both raised Israeli, we always spoke English while outside Israel. We never knew who might be listening. Although with Benny's accent, he'd never be mistaken for anything other than Israeli.

"Come down now and hail a silver Mercedes taxi. The driver has a black cap on; he'll take you to meet me."

I followed his instructions, and after half an hour, we were in a quiet, residential area, a nearly deserted street lined with date palms and apartment buildings. There was no traffic. The cabbie told me to go the ninth floor. As I came out of the elevator, I turned to see my old friend and Paul.

"Hi, Dan," Benny said, smiling that broad smile of his. "You're two days late."

We began walking down the hall.

"What do you mean?"

"You're two days late."

"Let me remind you, Benny, that we were traveling through locations that haven't made it even close to the twenty-first century, some with crippling bureaucracy. And I'll tell you, along the way, I began wondering whether some of the delays weren't intentional."

We turned into an apartment at the end of the corridor. Benny sat on its white leather sofa; I sat on its white leather chair. Next to Benny on another chair sat Paul. Below us ran a wall-to-wall pink-patterned carpet. The décor was tacky in the extreme. But I wasn't here for the interior decorating.

"What do you mean, intentional?" Benny asked.

"I mean, intentional. At this point I have too many questions. First off, there was a major change of plans which I wasn't aware of."

"Meaning?" asked Paul.

"Instead of staying at the hotel in Tehran as originally planned, I was taken to an apartment. Khader said it was for security reasons. Were you aware of that sudden change?"

Paul and Benny exchanged looks. "No," said Paul. "Tell us more."

I gave them the information. "At the time I thought it was strange, but I decided to go along with it, as long as the plan to get Madani out of Iran was progressing. Then there was another major change of route, which I didn't know about."

"You mean ending the voyage in Turkey rather than in Damascus?" asked Paul.

"Yeah," I said angrily.

"This change was authorized for security reasons. If you were apprehended there, you couldn't tell about the Turkish ending of the trip, and give VEVAK enough time to give us a hard time here." I already knew about the planned, post-Damascus ending of the trip in Turkey, but said nothing.

"Next, I had suspicions concerning Tango but couldn't ask him. And there was no way I could discuss it with you. So I continued with my mission, but I still have doubts. Are you sure we're not being duped again?"

"What do you mean?

"In Armenia," I reminded him, "the Iranians had sent a phony defector; attempting to extricate him nearly cost me my life. For this mission, I was dispatched to Damascus, and Tehran, not exactly vacation spots, to deliver this man, this bona fide defector. And none of it seems right."

Benny gave me his wise, heavy-lidded, brown-eyed look, one I know all too well after decades of friendship.

"Dan," he said, "things are not always as they appear."

At this, my blood pressure began to rise.

"What do you mean?" I asked. "I risked my life again—for nothing?"

There was a knock on the door. I gave Benny a look, to which he responded, "Eric is here."

Eric wore a black polo shirt and khaki trousers. I hadn't seen him in a few months. He'd lost weight. I was jealous.

"What's up, Dan? I hear you brought in Tango safe and sound," said Eric, as if continuing a conversation we'd had yesterday. That was quintessential Eric in Technicolor, two-dimensional, with no emotions.

"Yes," I said, and brought him up to speed, repeating what I'd just told Benny and Paul.

"Good," he said. "I want you to stick around in Istanbul for a few days until we ship Tango to the US. Have some fun. Eat." He knew that eating was my favorite pastime. I couldn't believe my ears. I had just told him about serious gaps in the structure that the Mossad and CIA had toiled so hard to build, and Eric suggests food?

"Thanks, Eric. I do like Turkish food. But I'm here for the action, not the calories. And you know, when you tell me to 'take it easy,' it sounds a lot like I'm being kept out of the loop." My words were loaded with temper.

Eric shrugged. "If that's what you want to call it. You've completed your assignment. I heard your reservations, and I'll take a look at them once I see your written report. Until then I thought you might want some time to relax."

"Shouldn't I be present during the debriefing of Tango?"

"Yes, there will be a debriefing."

"Do I participate?" I asked.

"No. Two Agency interrogators will do the job."

"Don't you think I should sit in as well?" I asked. "I know this guy." Was it a good time to add that I have suspicions regarding Tango? My inner devil said, *Go for it.*

"Of course you do, but my interrogators should grill him first, and then we'll see."

"Eric, you just heard my reservations regarding this guy. I'm not sure he's for real. I raised them earlier. Then there were additional events you don't know about, which increased my level of suspicion."

"You've always been suspicious," said Eric in a surprise showing of some humor, albeit acerbic.

"I'm serious, Eric."

"We'll read your report and then decide." This was too evasive for me to accept.

I gave him a nasty look.

Eric looked quizzically at Benny and Paul.

Benny said, "Let me think about it," and before the period hit the end of that sentence, I knew he meant "Never."

"Don't give me that bull. I've earned the right. So what—I was simply a chaperone? That's what I do now? I'm some glorified slab of muscle?"

Benny shook his head. "That's not true. We needed a smart guy like you, who knows how to avoid trouble."

"What, you're kissing up now?" I knew how bitter this sounded. And I meant it. And I said again, "I think I've earned to right to participate." That was not a case of etiquette or honor that made me insist. During the few days I spent with Tango, I had noticed a few minute details that made me uncomfortable. I needed to sit in his debriefing to see how he reacted to direct questions. Tango was our prisoner now, albeit in a golden cage. If he changed his mind all of a sudden and demanded to be let go in Turkey or returned to Iran, I didn't think Eric would allow that. Not after all the effort and expense that was invested in the operation. Eric would first squeeze all the lemonade he could from lemon Tango before letting him out on the street. And that wasn't going to happen any time soon, and definitely not in Turkey, where Tango could walk to the nearest police station and complain that he had been kidnapped by American agents. The level of the political scandal that would follow can only be imagined.

Therefore, Tango would sit while a few seasoned CIA interrogators tried to get his life story out of him. Until travel arrangements to the US were completed, he would have to spill the beans, knowing he had no alternative. That's exactly why I wanted to be present.

"Why is that?" said Eric. "This isn't a competition."

"I agree, Eric, this isn't a competition."

I walked over to the window, looking down at the deserted street below. Everything I'd done for the Agency, I thought. All my work. My sweat. The bullet scar above my temple. And for what? To wind up here, a glorified bodyguard? With a pat on the shoulder, a "Good job, Dan?"

I turned to Eric.

"You're right," I said, "This isn't a competition. This is bullshit. And I want to know why, Eric. Why I'm being treated like someone utterly expendable. And worse, an idiot."

Eric looked at Benny, at Paul, then at me. Benny's eyes seemed to question Eric's; somewhere, deep down, maybe, Benny wanted to tell me something. But Eric's eyes, as usual, were steely: a quality, I knew, that made him very good at his job, a quality that alienated many and typically impressed me. Well, most of the time.

But not today.

No. Today, standing in our safe house in Istanbul, Eric's poker stare felt like some kind of heat ray, because I could feel my temperature rise. My temples began to throb. My scar began to throb. For a split second I even wanted to punch him. Isn't that what a "body-guard" might have done? Wouldn't a slab of muscle simply hit the guy? I played it out in my head: me smashing Eric's jaw with my fist, watching him topple through the glass coffee table, watching his blood stain the tacky Turkish rug below.

The image did nothing to quell my anger. Of course, I knew why; only thugs resorted to violence. And I wasn't a thug. Besides, would a punch by me knock Eric over? No. The Mossad has a saying, "Your best weapon is the mind," and of course, my mind is the reason I'm alive today. My mind, not my fists. My rage was no longer addressed to their refusal to let me participate in Tango's interrogation. I was beyond that already. I was angry because I'd just realized that they might have known that Tango was also a fake that the Iranian planted, but nonetheless they let me continue with the charade, risking my life for nothing.

"Eric. I already told you that there is something wrong here. I can smell it. Everywhere I've been, everywhere you've sent me the past few months, my cover has been blown. Dubai. The German 'girlfriend' in Paris."

"You do covert operations, Dan. That's par for the course," Eric said dismissively.

"To a certain extent, yes. But there have been so many security breaches, it can only mean one of two things: either the Agency has become completely, shockingly inept, in which case you should recommend to the Agency to do some housecleaning—you too, Benny. Or, you've duped me into a babysitting a fake Tango. And I want to know why I was risking my life—twice—when you knew it was just a game."

"You weren't babysitting him," Eric said, calm, cool, artfully dodging the most loaded part of my accusation: that I was right in my suspicion that Tango was probably fake.

"Tango needed a savvy escort. And for obvious reasons, Dan, that was you." He kept up the stare, but was now he scratching the back of his hand; it looked like a nervous tic. But no, couldn't be. I'd never seen Eric do anything I would call "nervous tic."

"Did you hear what I called him?"

"Fake? Is this is a gut feeling, Dan? I mean, he could be a fake planted by Iran, of course. If you had hard proof, if you'd intercepted any kind of communication, for example. . . ."

Proof. He wanted proof. *The best weapon is the mind.*

"OK," I said, although I was certain he had proof, but wanted to see my cards as well. "Let's apply Occam's razor. According to the fourteenth-century English logician and Franciscan friar William of Ockham, the simplest theory that accounts for all the facts will be correct. Now, I know it may seem like intelligence work is an exception to that rule; very often, the 'truth' seems tremendously complex. I go to Dubai, to Istanbul, to France, to Damascus. I have different names in different countries. But in the end, it's really not so complex. In the end, it's all about groups of people who want to do harm to other people, and I work to prevent that. Simple. I've been doing that for *you* for years—"

"And you know we appreciate the work you do Dan. You know—"

"Spare me the platitudes. Back to Occam's razor. Let's take the problem, and see what the simplest answer is. Problem: Madani had no idea why we were going through Syria, even though it was supposedly *his* idea. Problem: he disappeared on the train on our way here, claiming he 'likes trains.' My suspicion? He met someone for whatever reason, and it was not romantic purposes, and I don't think he spent some time chatting with the engineer."

My God, I wondered, *did Madani really say that to me?* That he was "chatting with the engineer"? I should've broken protocol right then and there. I should have made contact. I went on.

"Problem: Madani and I were questioned by the Iranian border police, after which they spoke to Madani privately, after which I was told Madani was a wanted terrorist, after which I was told to post a hundred-dollar bail. A hundred dollars? For a terrorist?

"Problem: these very same police didn't look twice at me, an English-speaking foreigner in an area where you seldom see tourists, traveling with an alleged terrorist? Not even look at my passport? The director who staged this folly should be sent back to school."

The sun was setting now, and blue shadows began pooling around the room. I heard a vacuum cleaner going down the hall. I felt like a prosecutor, wrapping up his case.

"The simplest. Most obvious. Is the most reasonable explanation, returning to Occam's razor: 'The simplest explanation will be the most plausible until evidence is presented to prove it false.' Therefore, Tango is fake. Need more? Problem: Madani—"

Eric interrupted. "Look, Dan, we already know, OK? We began to suspect along the way, just like you. That something wasn't adding up."

"You knew," I said, scar throbbing again. I grew quiet, my voice lower. "And you kept me in the dark?"

Eric sighed heavily.

"First off, Dan, we didn't 'know' until a few days ago. At the beginning we only suspected, and telling you was impossible because you were already traveling with him on the train. Anyway, telling you that would have placed you in much greater danger. If Tango is a fake, and he at all suspected—"

"And as I'm the only one here who knows Madani, the only one here who spent past two weeks with him, breaking bread with him, drinking tea with him—no one is better to extract that information than I am, particularly now, when we both know he's bad. There are so many details we could extract from him, that I can't even start to count."

"Wait," Benny interrupted. "Let me ask you something, Dan. Say Tango is a fake, what do you care?" The question seemed rhetorical to me. "So, we got the wrong guy. Then what? No damage was done. He gave us nothing, we gave him nothing. End of story."

"Propaganda," I retorted, again realizing they just wanted to hear my reasons, which might be different from theirs. "You should care, because if he's fake, you can't hold him, you won't give him all the goodies Madani would get. Therefore, once he walks, in Istanbul, Tehran, or Washington, DC, it will soon hit the media that the Iranians toyed with us again, and we'll be getting yet another black eye from public opinion. And if it comes out he's a fake that the Iranians sent, the bloggers and armchair counterspies will be all over it. Then the House and Senate Committees. You know that."

"Not so fast, my friend," said Benny in a measured tone. "Even if Madani is fake and what you're saying is true regarding the propaganda war, it's still not the end of the story, for one because we'll be credited for exposing his lies. And besides, fake or not, we'll take the opportunity to milk what he knows."

"Knows?" I said in half contempt. "If he's fake as I suspect, then he knows nothing, zilch. The Iranians are smart. Do you think they would risk sending someone with any information whatsoever, other than the price of a loaf of bread and the bus fare? Nonetheless we need his confession that he's fake on video in case he goes public and Iran tries to mock us."

"Dan," said Eric, "don't be so sure that he couldn't tell us anything of value. Even if he was recruited off the street, he knows who they are, and what they told him to say. He was trained some place, he could tell us that. He could tell us who his instructors were, and whether others were trained with him. There's always something."

The only problem with that reasoning: No one learns the names of their recruiters, instructors, or other trainees. They all use false names. Eric knew that. I knew that. So when Eric saw my astonished face, he added, "I know, I know, they all use fake names, but in a closed society like Iran, when many people know many others, although fake names are used, there are after-hours gatherings, a coffee and a cigarette together. People lose their defenses after a while."

Eric was right, of course, so I didn't respond. There was no point in developing the argument.

"Listen," Paul said. "Imagine an Iranian general—any Iranian general—glued to TV broadcasts of a Madani, telling the Iranian public how the CIA had offered him a cool three million to defect— but since the CIA caught him as a fake, they'd expelled him, so he has no money, but there he is telling the world about that offer. The Iranian security apparatus would not be happy to hear that on television. To say the least. It would be like a commercial to all Iranian military commanders, 'Come to us and we'll give you three million dollars tax-free, and asylum, if you are for real.'"

"Do you still think, even if Madani is a fake, that Iran would be able to maintain any kind of upper hand in the propaganda war?"

"A general?" Benny weighed in. "You wouldn't even have to be a general. Say you're a major, hardly making it in Iran. Maybe you're sick of everything, the Ayatollahs, the moral police, the oppression. All of it. And there you are, in front of the TV. And you hear of an opportunity to give yourself and your family a better, freer life. You have a wife and children, wouldn't you consider defecting, seriously?

"So I say, let the fake Madani say whatever he wants. It'll still be our best recruitment tool, enticing others with possible intel to consider defection to the US. Three million dollars turns defection into real possibility. Not just asylum—money. That's a considerable carrot."

"The world's most expensive carrot," I said. "Why tax-free?"

"Because under an Internal Revenue ruling, any bonus paid to a defector is not taxable since it's for 'work' performed before the defector came to the United States," said Paul.

It was now evening, almost dark. I could see the three of us—Eric, Benny, and me—reflected in the window, in yet another safe house, another city, another country, trapped yet again in the twisting maze of intelligence work. Once again, both sides were playing the counterintelligence game, and neither party was able to reveal its tricks. In this case, because it might tip the other side as to how the enemy might be using a defector—as if the Iranians or the US and Israel needed instruction on deception. In the Mossad, especially, deception meant survival. My Mossad days taught me that if one wants to come out ahead, he must persuade the opposition that its ranks are riddled with spies and moles. In this way, you turn the enemy on itself.

I excused myself for minute to the bathroom, to splash water on my face. I needed to clear my head. The cold water shocked me into clarity. Yes, I thought: we must persuade the opposition that its ranks are riddled with spies and moles. I knew such an approach could work. In the 1960s, the CIA's head of counterintelligence, James J. Angleton, was sure that the Soviets had infiltrated the CIA. He took measures that effectively paralyzed the CIA's operations in Moscow. A quintessential counterintelligence overreach—too much information of no use disseminated by a counterintelligence officer.

I came back to the room with Benny, Eric, and Paul and sat down, the four of us, quietly, as if digesting a full meal. All four of us were thinking, thinking; you could almost hear gears whirring.

Hopefully, I thought, the same paralyzing fear will take effect in Iran. With any luck, the CIA has Iranian counterspies turning Tehran's labs upside down. Of course, years ago it was remarkably easy to sow seeds of doubt in just about any foreign government, including Iran's. US counterintelligence agents could very simply contact a member of a terrorist organization and hint, insinuate, or just say, "Hey, Nawaf, or Abdul, or what have you, is working with us, why don't you?"

And it would work. Even if the target turned away, the "Hey, Nawaf" approach would inevitably work its magic. When the target reported the encounter, rounds of internal accusations and investigations to find our supposed "spies" would ensue.

Likewise, it was in the CIA's interest to paint the re-defector, or the fake defector, as just one of many long-term American moles—or, at the very least, as someone who gave up the names of others in the nuclear program who might be vulnerable to CIA recruitment after he fled to the West. Almost certainly, Iranian security would wring any defector dry on that score—or worse—and redouble its efforts to root out the CIA's supposed spies.

The challenge for both sides, of course, is, was, and always will be knowing for sure who is on whose side. And in the spy versus spy world's so-called wilderness of mirrors, you can never be sure.

I was still sure about one thing, though: the man calling himself Madani, whom I escorted from Iran to Turkey, was not our intended Tango, General Cyrus Madani.

"OK," I said, "OK. Fake or not fake, maybe it can work in our favor. You make good points. And, as you say, he'll have useful information for us, whatever his motives."

XIV

June 2007, Germany

Twenty-four hours later, I was in Germany, debriefing Madani, genuine or fake. Persistence wins. Well, at least with me versus Eric.

Interrogation rooms always look alike, no matter the country. Drab. Nondescript. One large one-way mirror and no window, so if your charge wants to look outside—if he finds himself looking around the room, if he needs a distraction—there isn't any, only his own reflection. Sophisticated audio and video recording equipment was buried in the ceiling, covering the room from both sides.

This room was different, however. It was the notorious grinder. A safe house used only for Madani's debriefing. Only those on the need-to-know short list were given the location. The defector, genuine or fake, had to be protected from outside attempts to kill him. Why a grinder? Because the subject is required to repeat his story again and again. His recorded accounts are then analyzed for consistency, and voice tremors to identify the subject's lies or half truths.

Sometimes, the process can take months to complete and determine whether the defector is bona fide or a plant.

I sat across from Madani today—the fake Madani, I was sure of it. He wasn't yet searching the room; he was still placid, still calm.

"And you were born . . . ?" asked one of the agents, a large, imposing man named Hank, although his demeanor belied his frame. His tone was soft, unthreatening. Next to him sat Doyle, wiry, with a mustache. He reminded me a little of a weasel. Hank, in mock disinterest—as if this were just another mundane routine he had to get through, like filing paperwork—read from the open file in front of him, and looked at Madani. I sat behind the agents, watching quietly.

"I was born in Yazd, Iran," Madani said. "But isn't that in the file in front of you?"

Hank shrugged in a kind of mock apology. "Yes, but you know how it is. We have to follow the routine."

"Oh, yes, yes, of course," said Madani, nodding and waving his hand in a conciliatory way, as if to say, *Oh, of course, I've done this myself.* Although he sounded relaxed, I knew he was not.

Behind him, just visible through the corner of his eye, sat a man in sunglasses and a raincoat, a man here without explanation. Madani could also see the man in the mirror in front of him. The man was not here to ask questions; he was not taking notes. He was simply sitting. He was there for one reason: to unsettle the person interviewed. Physical violence could often lead a suspect to man up, to steel himself against his interrogators, and therefore it was not dependably effective. To unsettle the person interviewed, though— to make him unsure of what was happening and why he was here, to make him question his own perception of what was happening right in front of him—this relatively subtle technique, unlike violence, was often tremendously effective. And the "quiet man in sunglasses" was a tried and true way of making the person interviewed very, very ill at ease, and a suspect who is ill at ease is, in the hand of a skilled interrogator, easy to trip up, to trap in his own lies. I'd seen and practiced it time and time again.

"And the street you grew up on?" Hank asked. Again, apparently reading from the open file in front of him.

"Besat Street."

"The elementary school you went to?"

"Seyyed Al Shohada Elementary School."

At this, Madani moved his head around, just slightly, for just a split second, as though stretching his neck. I'd seen this "neck stretch" move before. Because even though a suspect will always be positioned in such a way that he can see the man with the sunglasses in the mirror, for whatever reason, the suspect always seems to develop an urge to turn and look at the man in the flesh. But he has to fight that urge, he knows he has to fight that urge, because to turn at look would be to show your cards. To turn and look would be admitting there was something remiss here, that you're wondering who the hell is behind you, that you're nervous, that something isn't right.

And so instead, suspects do what Madani just did. They stretch their necks. And still, the urge, the wondering, grows.

"So, you were recruited into Iran's Revolutionary Guard, when...." Doyle asked, trailing off. As he trailed off, he shuffled through the file as if trying to find something, as though looking for something lost. Two tried and effective techniques were going here at once. One, by "trailing off," the interrogator is still, by design, giving off a disinterested air designed to lull the suspect. And two, the shuffling of papers, again by design, seems disheveled and disorganized, so the interrogator seems absentminded, a nonthreat. Until the suspect realizes yet again a man is just behind him, sitting, staring.

"I was twenty," Madani said, voice perfectly modulated to neutral. He watched intently as Doyle continued rifling through his file. "My cousin had been recruited the year earlier and put in a good word." That neutral voice: I had to hand it to him. Madani seemed, still, remarkably at ease. Even I might have mistaken his composure as true if it hadn't been for that split-second neck stretch. Madani was Iranian after all. Iranians, I knew through experience, were notoriously difficult to read.

I could feel the mood in the room shift. Hank sat up straight. Doyle stopped shuffling papers.

I wrote on my pad: *Madani is wrong here. He said he was born in 1952 and recruited to the Revolutionary Guard when he was 20—that's in 1972. However, the Islamic Revolution was in 1979 and the Guard was first established in May 1979.*

So he was off by seven years, a too substantial discrepancy. Was it a slip of the tongue or a crack in the wall that the Iranian VEVAK must have built around him to create the fake Madani? I didn't want to interrupt the flow of questions, and therefore saved it for a later opportunity. If he was indeed fake as I suspected, then VEVAK did a sloppy job here.

"How about marriage? You were how old?"

"Twenty-four."

"And where did you get married?" Hank closed the file in front of him, and slipped it into his briefcase.

"Aref, Yazd," Madani answered.

"Hmmmm," Hank said. "In fact, weren't you married in Tehran?" Hank didn't look at the file now; he looked Madani in the eye. In fact, Hank already knew everything in the file. He had never had a need to open it in the first place. It was a prop, merely another thing used to distract Madani, another thing in the room Madani could focus on. When interrogators looked at a file while they asked questions, so would the suspect. Suspects liked distraction. But now the file was closed, and Hank was looking Madani squarely in the eye, and the only way Madani could maintain the composure of someone telling the truth would be to look back.

"Oh," he said. "Tehran was the place of my second marriage." Madani's eyes met Hank's. Then he looked at Doyle. And then at me.

"Your second marriage," said Doyle. A simple technique, repeating back to the suspect what he just said. Putting the suspect even more ill at ease.

"Yes. My second wife is much younger, so of course when I think marriage, I think of her. Surely you understand." Madani half-smiled here, looking from man to man; he was making an unconvincing play at male "bonding."

"What about Yazd? You said you went to school there? But you didn't. Didn't you tell us during our initial contacts that you went to Imam Muhammad School, which was right next to your home? Now you are telling me you went to a different school that is more than three kilometers away. How did you get to school? As a young boy, you didn't drive, did you?"

Madani again stretched his neck, then squeezed it as if he had a crick in it.

"That was a long time ago. How am I supposed to remember the road to my elementary school? I've lived a lifetime since then. Please. We are all reasonable men here."

"That road didn't just lead to your elementary school. You grew up on that road."

"You don't know what you are talking about. You didn't ask me what road I grew up on!" His tone of voice was angry, even impatient. *How dare you.*

The man in the sunglasses stood up, and walked behind Madani. Madani turned to watch, and as he did, as fast as lightning, Doyle reached across the table, grabbed Madani's head and slammed it on the table, twice. With his massive hand, he held it there. Madani's nose started bleeding, dripping thick blood on the table.

"I've got a lot of other things to do today," Doyle said. "So let me make this brief. You are on a military base, which means you have no access to a lawyer. No one knows you're here. To us, unless you tell us what we need to know, you are nothing. *Nothing,*" he said in a raised voice. "I'm telling you all this because I want to make you feel

179

right at home. We've created little slice of Iran for you, right here in this room. Here you have no rights.

"You're a ghost. Anything can happen to you here. Anything at all. I think the Iranians who sent you want you dead, and we could just make that happen if you continue bullshitting us. Hey, I never thought we'd have a joinder of interests with Iran," he chortled.

At that, Hank pulled out from under the table what looked like an old-fashioned doctor's bag, a kind of leather satchel. He put it on the table, and said nothing.

Doyle slammed Madani's head down again, in his huge palm.

And again.

"Wait!" yelled the man calling himself Madani.

Doyle stopped.

"Please. Let me talk to Mr. Kraus—please."

And that is how I made my "good cop" entrance. The agents exchanged looks, nodded and left; I sat down with Madani; I looked at him gently. I told him to tell me the truth, that he had a choice here. A choice between misery and freedom. To me, it seemed an easy one. I told him so.

"I am *Cyrus Madani*," he said. "*I am.*" His eyes beseeched me. Doyle's finger had made long bruises on his cheek but his nose had stopped bleeding. Madani, I knew, had to be smarting with shame.

"Let me ask you, as a member of the Revolutionary Guard, what kind of work did you do?"

The man listed fairly accurately the various positions that Madani had held.

"And your house, surely you had servants?"

"Of course."

And we went back and forth for two hours. I needed to know if he did any kind of manual labor. Any at all. Of course a member of the Guard wouldn't, but perhaps he had a hobby. Perhaps he liked building things. Perhaps he liked gardening. Unlikely, I knew. And his answers were all no, no, no.

I looked at him. I reached over, grabbed one of his hands, turned it over. They were rough. A farmer's hands. Not the hand of a general of the Guard.

"We know, Madani. Or whatever your real name is. We already know."

He looked at me, then looked away.

"Do you know Abdul Karim Zarqawi?"

"Who?"

I repeated the name.

"I don't recall, I met so many people in my lifetime. Maybe."

"Try to think again, Abdul Karim Zarqawi?"

"Maybe."

"What's maybe? Yes, or no?"

"I don't recall."

"Abdul Karim Zarqawi was your neighbor for ten years, living one floor below your apartment. The families used to go out together, and you don't remember him?"

"Aha, that Abdul Karim Zarqawi, I now remember him, of course. I don't know how I could forget. Yes, yes, I remember him."

"What was his wife's name?"

"Help me here," he said. "I'm embarrassed for forgetting."

"Fatma," I said.

"Of course, Fatma, I remember now. Thanks for reminding me."

I got up. "There's no point in continuing. There's no such person named Abdul Karim Zarqawi. Madani never had neighbors living below his apartment because he always lived in single-family homes, detached or semidetached. You are a liar. I'll have to send in the two other interrogators," I said in faked despair. "You've given me nothing. You and I know it's bullshit. You are not General Cyrus Madani. Who are you?"

"OK," he said. "OK."

But I immediately discovered it was not "OK" because he repeated his mantra, "I'm General Cyrus Madani."

"Look here," I said, "have you heard of the CIA enhanced interrogation techniques?"

There was a frightened look on his face. But he didn't answer. Fear of the unknown is the strongest fear you can instill in an interrogated person.

"Let me tell you what they are, and you can choose in which order they will be applied to you. First, there's the Attention Grab: I'll shake you like a salt dish over a salad. If that doesn't help I'll inflict pain on your belly. That will cause you a lot of pain. I know that doctors advised against doing it because it could cause lasting internal damage. But hey, there are no doctors here to tell me that.

"And then I could waterboard you."

He raised his eyes in fear.

"You are giving me no choice," I said. "You are not a prisoner of war, or a refugee. You came here voluntarily. You have no rights, nothing. You're a spy, you came to spy on us. Therefore, we have every reason to treat you as such. You know what they do to spies in Iran? Why should you be treated any differently by us?"

I noticed that his lower jaw had a sudden tremor.

"Let me tell you what waterboarding is," I said, "You'll be bound to an inclined board, feet raised and head slightly below the feet. Cellophane will be wrapped over your face and water will be poured over you. You'll feel that you are drowning. And you might. I'm told that on the average, most people beg to confess in fourteen seconds. Al-Qaeda's toughest detainee won the championship—he was able to last two and a half minutes before begging to confess. Do you want to challenge his record?"

Madani shook his head.

"I'll give you thirty seconds to decide or I'm calling the guys to do you over. They are not as nice as I am."

"OK," he said faintly. "I'm not General Cyrus Madani. My name is Siavash Dowlatabadi."

"Go ahead," I said. "Who sent you?"

"Quds Forces."

"Who in Quds Forces?"

He hesitated.

"Tell me!"

"Khalil Mohagheghi."

"Continue," I ordered. There was no going back. I was about to peel him like an onion and nobody could stop me.

"To which unit does he belong?" I'd never heard his name before.

"To *Niru-ye Qods,* the Quds Force," he repeated faintly. "The Jerusalem Force."

I knew it was the elite unit of the Revolutionary Guard, tasked with "exporting Iran's Islamic revolution," and responsible for "extra-territorial operations of the Revolutionary Guard." The Quds Force reports directly to the Supreme Leader of Iran, Ayatollah Khamenei.

"And Khalil Mohagheghi? What's his position?"

"I don't know, but he gave me the orders."

If true, then the information this fake Madani gave me was crucially important. Usually, VEVAK, a government ministry, is entrusted with internal security. Quds Forces, on the other hand, is deeply involved with radical Islamic activities worldwide, plays a role in military operations of these groups, and provides pre-attack planning and tactical direction. That could mean that my fake Madani's role was more than just to fool the US and Israel. He may have been assigned to do a much bigger job, perhaps after establishing himself in our eyes as a "hero," a defecting Iranian general.

"Did you serve in Quds Forces?"

"Yes."

"What was your rank?"

"Captain."

"In which unit?"

"I was stationed in Baalbek in Lebanon, training Hezbollah forces."

"Is that where you met the real Cyrus Madani?"

"Yes."

My interrogation lasted three more hours, and at the end I had all what I wanted. Proof that this guy was a fake. Let the others here extract the rest of the juice out of him. I was done.

I felt a wave of relief pass over me. I'd known it all along, in spite of Eric's, Paul's, and Benny's denials. All those creeping doubts I'd had from the beginning were correct. At the end of that day, my gut was still a finely tuned instrument. I'd complied with another Moscow Rule: *Never go against your gut; it is your operational antenna.* I could still trust my gut, aka my little inner devil.

I had many open questions, but I decided to let the professionals pose them. Where is the real Madani? Is he still alive? Was the whole Kurdish connection in Syria and Tehran also a ploy? With whom he was talking when he disappeared on the train? I took a breath. I felt good.

There was a knock on the door. A woman gave me a note: Eric was calling from Istanbul. I went outside, and let two guards enter the room to watch Siavash Dowlatabadi, who had almost fooled us into believing that he was General Cyrus Madani. I was still smiling when I took the phone, feeling triumphant.

"Eric," I said by way of hello. I was thinking my sense of triumph might be infectious, even over the phone.

"Dan." His voice was low, almost monotone.

"You need to come back to Istanbul," he said. "And you need to do it today."

"Eric," I said, "I've just peeled off Tango. He's fake."

There was a moment of silence.

"Fake?"

"Yes. It's all on video. Do you want it encrypted and sent to you now?"

"No. Come here first."

XV

June 2007, Istanbul

I took the first flight out to Istanbul. As I set foot back in Istanbul, the heat, the smog and the chaos felt like an affront. Because the second you set foot in Istanbul, you sense chaos. I was waiting in front of the airport for a car; Eric said he'd brief me on the way back to the safe house. I'd begun sweating the second I stepped out onto the curb. Seems that even a mere twenty-four hours in Germany had me acclimated to a different, milder environment: mellow sun; clean, smooth streets; orderly pedestrians; orderly traffic; and fresh air.

A dark-blue car drove up, medium-sized, totally nondescript: a far cry from the Suburban that had chauffeured me before. Eric opened the door to the back seat. The AC was a tremendous relief. When I got in, he handed me a file to read, his way of updating me silently. Until we were safely ensconced back in the safe house—until we could speak in private—we'd both remain silent.

The file contained two classified memos. In these days of increasingly omnipresent electronic surveillance, a return to paper—utterly unhackable—was becoming more and more popular in my line of work. The first memo concerned a man whom both the Agency and the Mossad regarded as the "real" Madani. A third one on my count. I turned to look at Eric, incredulous. That explained why Eric wasn't alarmed when I told him I'd unveiled the second fake Madani.

I took the file but found it hard to swallow. Another "real" Madani? No way. According to the memo, before he could leave the country, authorities in Iran had discovered General Madani's plans to defect. The General Madani currently considered to be "real" had been apprehended in Tehran by the authorities and placed under house arrest. In a fairly rushed manner, they had prepared a decoy—presumably, the phony Madani I'd been with only hours ago. The Iranian authorities had to act quickly in creating their reverse-defector mole. He had to keep up the defection schedule that the "real" Madani had already worked out with the US and the Mossad, so as not to create suspicion.

Eric watched me read the first document. I looked up. We made eye contact. I could read in his eyes, *Make sense?* I nodded, *Yes.* This definitely made sense to me. I recalled my trip with Madani: he'd made a lot of mistakes along the way that the "real" Madani would not have made, though not in huge ways. I could see now they were the mistakes of a poorly trained novice.

The second memo, though, told a different story. The current "real" Madani had escaped house arrest in Tehran, then made it to Damascus with the assistance of the Kurds and the Mossad, and now he was being flown to the US. This, I found unbelievable. The "real" Madani had actually escaped house arrest? So we actually have a third Madani in our midst? And this time, he's supposed to be "real"?

I looked over again at Eric. This time in disbelief. Eric nodded. *It's true.* I shook my head. *I don't believe it.* "Third time's the charm," he said. "Be patient. There's more to the story," he said. I sat back in my seat, watching the streets of Istanbul pass by.

Back at the safe house, we could talk.

"Let me get it: we've had three Madanis? The first one on the Iran-Armenian border, a fake. The second, the guy I escorted from Tehran—a fake. And now you're telling me there's a third one, this time for real?" Eric nodded.

If there was a hesitation, I didn't notice it. *More like three strikes*, I thought. *Three strikes and you're out.*

As I turned into the living room, I said to Benny, "OK, look. I hope you realize this 'real' one has to be another joke, on us. The fact Iran would send us a novice tells me I—"

I was distracted for a moment. Benny was there sitting on the tacky white sofa. He said hello, but he was not the distraction. Rather, what sat in front of him was. In front of him, a plate of hummus, olives, and pita had been laid out on the coffee table. A bowl of cut oranges and dates sat next to it; next to that was lamb kebab. Benny wouldn't touch the meat. It was not kosher for the observant Benny.

I began shoveling triangles of pita into my mouth, having realized that I was starving. Then I had some dates, then some kebob. Oh, I knew what Eric and Benny were doing: this was a classic interrogation technique. Feeding an interviewee food he loves, especially after denying him any substantial food long enough to make him uncomfortable, puts him at ease. Psychologically, he'll begin to associate you as a "caregiver." He'll begin to trust.

"Feel better?" Benny said after I'd finished, a bit of a grin on his face.

"Grudgingly, Benny, I have to say 'yes, but not a full unequivocal yes.'"

Damn Benny. I had to admit that I did feel better, more at ease. And maybe, possibly, I felt just a little more willing to listen to whatever Eric and Benny had to say about the "real" Madani Number Three.

"So," Eric said dryly, "Madani made it to a Turkish Airways flight from Damascus to Istanbul, then to Germany, and from there to the US."

"Wait," I said. I was willing to listen, but not before I'd had my say. "Just hear me out," I went on, now matching Eric's calm. "How can you know this one, the third one, is the real Madani? Think about it. This would make a perfect setup for Iran. They send us a novice posing as Madani, someone they know full well we'll discover is a fake. Then, they fabricate a story about having the 'real' Madani under house arrest. *This* is the story we're supposed to believe? And what, are we actually supposed to believe he escaped *house arrest*? A suspected traitor just slipped out the window?"

"He didn't slip out the window," Eric said. "It was an elaborate operation set up by two of the Kurds guarding him—Kurds who have a connection to the Mossad."

Kurds were considered "brutes," far below Persians in social status, in class, in anything. They were an oppressed people. Along those lines, Kurds typically did physical work. That there were a few low-ranking Kurdish guards in this mix sounded just this side of plausible. The Mossad had been developing Kurdish contacts with amazing success since the '60s. The Kurds would usually close ranks, and were generally insular and suspicious—and who could blame them?

However, given the long-term relationship with Israel developed by the Mossad, they treat Israel as their ally. Israel and the Kurds shared common enemies, after all; and they both lived in incredibly close quarters with said enemies.

OK, I thought. A Kurdish guard or two. A plan. It was possible.

"So," Benny said. "Is the food working? Do you believe it now?" They apparently thought that food was my tranquilizer when in fact it was my energizer.

"Yes," I said, "OK. I do. I mean, it could be."

"You wanted to be in the loop, so you're in the loop. And there's one other thing—" He trailed off here, peering out the window now. Looking down at the street. Something was wrong. I couldn't say what or why. But the little devil in me was moving. I thought of a saying I heard once, *Good instincts usually tell you what to do long before your head has figured it out.*

Why on earth did Eric and Benny try so hard to persuade me that the third Madani was for real? After all, I worked for them, not the other way around. Why should they care what I think? Courtesy? Yes, but not beyond that. However, what they were doing was over-kill, and that bothered me.

I did the only thing I could do: went to my hotel to have a good night's sleep. I needed to sort out my thoughts about the third Madani and settle my baffled mind. Instincts are great, but after-thought makes them ripe for action.

In the morning I knew why I couldn't sleep well, although I was very tired. I was thinking of Ali Akbar Kamrani. I resurrected in my mind how we met in Dubai, how he approached me in a dark alley with a story about his scientist brother wanting to defect from Iran. At the time, he never really answered my question about how he knew I was an American agent. I'd let it go, because my mission was to identify who sent the anonymous letters to the US Consulate in Dubai, and I did. It was Ali Akbar Kamrani. And when his purported brother was found dead as a result of alleged carbon monoxide poi-soning, from my perspective the case was closed.

But during the long night in my very quiet hotel room, I still needed that answer. There was no question I was in the Iranian gov-ernment's sights, and even Eric warned me of that just before I went to Dubai. But I'd never cracked the code: How did they know I'd be traveling to Dubai, or at least, when I came to Dubai, how did they identify me immediately as a US agent? I reconstructed in my mind my contacts with André, my "son" in Paris, and my meeting with his suddenly appearing girlfriend with the multiple passports and hidden cop-killer gun.

Excluding a mole amongst us, the solution could be there, in the Paris arena.

At 8:00 a.m. Istanbul time, I called Pierre Perot. I expected him to yell at me for waking him up, but when he answered his mobile phone I heard traffic noises. He was already on the street.

After a brief exchange of pleasantries, I went to the heart of the business.

"Pierre, I need a quick yes or no to this question: Did Shestakov have a Dubai contact in Sepah Bank's branch in Dubai?"

I expected a formal answer; for instance, "Dan, you are my friend, but a formal request must be made through channels." Instead he said, "Yes, Ali Akbar Kamrani."

I wanted to kiss and hug him, but with my preference for kissing women and the distance to Paris, instead I promised him a hearty meal next time we met. I hung up.

Ha! My friend Ali Akbar Kamrani, you are becoming a person of interest for me. Next, I also needed to close the circle: Did Madani also work for Shestakov, directly or through Ali Akbar Kamrani?

I called Benny. He was away, but his ever efficient chief of staff located him and conferenced us. I knew she did that each time Benny didn't want to reveal where he was. The relay of the call through Tel Aviv made it possible to mask his location.

"Benny, can you check if Tango had a connection with Mr. X? I'll send you his name through channels." Obviously I couldn't do it over open phone lines.

"I'll let you know when I get it. Although the question seems redundant in light of the recent news regarding Tango."

"It's very current and relevant," I said and hung up.

I sent Langley an encrypted message asking them to relay to Benny the name Leonid Shestakov. Was he connected to Madani, through Ali Akbar Kamrani or directly?

A day later I received Benny's response through Langley:

Leonid Shestakov retained Tango to inform him on purchasing plans of nuclear components. We don't know how Tango was paid;

it was definitely not in Iran because the Iranian government was unaware that Tango was in fact spying for Shestakov. Since he hadn't left Iran, there must be a hefty bank account somewhere waiting for him. However, we have no information regarding Ali Akbar Kamrani's involvement, or even if Tango and Kamrani knew about each other.

There was no time to waste. I sent Eric a short message: I had to leave Istanbul immediately, and would return in a few days. I knew he'd go ballistic, but I didn't care. It was burning in me. I'd smelled a rat when Eric and Benny had told me about the third Madani. I just had to get to the bottom of it. The lone wolf in me, the character trait that the Mossad psychologist warned my recruiters of at the time, put the gears in a forward shift. I was on a mission. And this time without Eric's, Paul's, or Benny's blessings.

XVI

June 2007, Rome

I flew to Germany, and took a connection to Rome. First things first, I had a thick pizza Napolitano with lots of mozzarella cheese and two glasses of Chianti. That calmed one urge I had, but not my curiosity. Rome was the location of a bank that interested me: Sepah Bank. I had to find a connection, or a reason for the withdrawal receipt for ten thousand euros that I'd found in my apartment in Paris.

I called Aldo Giovanni, a senior investigator at the Financial Crimes Unit at the Italian Finance Ministry. We'd worked together when he was attached to a joint US-Italian financial task force assembled to fight Italian Mafia tentacles sent to the US.

Aldo was happy to hear my voice and agreed to meet me immediately. However, in his book, "immediately" meant next week. When I insisted politely that we should meet sooner, he relented and came to my hotel the next morning. I told him only that I was investigating a potential connection between Shestakov and Sepah Bank in Dubai.

As a seasoned investigator, he didn't ask too many questions about why I needed to know that.

I did some quick research. On March 30, 2007, financial regulators in Italy and the UK froze assets of Iran's Bank Sepah, following a March 24 resolution by the UN Security Council in response to Iran's nuclear program. Therefore, Italy's central bank effectively took control of the Rome branch of Sepah. Now the bank had an Italian overseer.

Aldo came to my hotel. We sat in a quiet corner of the lobby.

"Do you have access to the bank's records?"

"Generally yes, but normally we intervene only if we establish that there's a suspicion of criminal or other activity in violation of the UN Security Council decisions. Are you telling me that there's such a violation?"

That was way more than I'd asked for, and continuing on that path could in fact damage my case and put me in hot water with the State Department. I had to slow him down. "Thanks, but at this time all I need is records showing a connection between Shestakov and Bank Sepah Dubai that passed through Rome." I didn't need to tell him who Shestakov was. Aldo seemed very familiar with him.

"I can't rule it out. In fact, a connection between Shestakov and Sepah Bank in Rome makes sense. The Iranians are trying to get around the difficulties caused by their international isolation and are setting up companies in Dubai that place orders with foreign vendors, including Shestakov, with payments made through Sepah in Rome. I don't think that there are lots of records. The Sepah Bank in Rome has only about twelve employees, and is subject to oversight from a number of overlapping Italian authorities."

I looked at his face, listening attentively. Aldo came from a well-to-do family in Naples, but preferred public service over the family pottery business. I knew little about his private life, other than that he was married and had two young children. At forty-five, he had reached a senior management level position, and seemed very calm and content.

He continued, "The Bank of Italy ensures that Sepah does not create new business, and the Unita di Informazione Finanzaria—Italy's Financial Intelligence Unit—monitors all of Bank Sepah's expenses in Rome. The Guardia di Finanza ensures that Bank Sepah does not sell its fixed physical assets. Sepah's dollar-denominated accounts are blocked, but its euro accounts are still being used for overhead and payment of salaries. The Comitato di Sicurezza Finanzaria can authorize or reject transactions involving Bank Sepah's euro-denominated accounts."

That sounded like a lot of bureaucracy to me. "Is there a way I could accompany the overseer while he's examining the books?" I knew that my request was first-rate chutzpah, but what was wrong in asking?

Aldo shook his head. "No, sorry, but I'll see what I can do regarding your request, which by itself is unusual. Frankly, we should get a formal request through channels." I never got used to that usual objection I get when I try to cut corners.

"Dan," he continued, as he read my mind, "the US and Italy signed an MLAT—Mutual Legal Assistance Treaty—in 1985. If this request is for evidence to be used in a US criminal investigation or prosecution, why don't you use that channel?"

"You are right," I said, accepting my destiny to be entangled in bureaucracy, this time Italian. Last time, an urgent request for evidence took the Italian government three months to acknowledge, and six more months to provide the documents. And the Italians are not an exception. Most countries drag their feet when responding to these requests.

"However," he said with a sparkle in his eyes, "maybe I could help you unofficially. . . ."

He drank another short espresso; I gulped my Campari with orange juice, and we continued chatting for another half an hour.

Five hours later—speed of light in local terms—Aldo called my mobile phone. "Meet me at your hotel in two hours," and hung up.

Thirty minutes past the time of our scheduled meeting, Aldo came with a fashionable leather briefcase. "Please listen to me, don't take notes. After our meeting I'll leave you with documents. But not here."

I just listened.

"Bank Sepah and its military clients have been secretly financing the development of nuclear weapons. We all know that. The Tehran-based headquarters of the bank has handled dozens of transactions totaling millions of dollars for front companies of Iran's missile makers and nuclear parts components traders. Many of the deals have gone through the Rome branch. Iran's use of state-owned banks and front companies is part of its effort to disguise money transfers through the global financial system. It uses front companies to conduct these procurements of needed parts for their missile and nuclear programs. Bank Sepah was the bank of choice for Iran's missile and nuclear firms for many years."

I was losing my patience, although I sat motionless. *Why is he telling me what every reader of a newspaper knows?*

"Can the bank argue they had no knowledge?" I asked.

"Are you kidding?" asked Aldo. "The bank knew full well what sort of activity it was fostering. It's done business over the years; you can presume knowledge solely based on the nature of the companies and the duration of the business and that it's a state bank. Even the UN Security Council determined that Bank Sepah provides support for the Iranian Aerospace Industries Organization and subordinates, including Shahid Hemmat Industrial Group and Shahid Bagheri Industrial Group.

"These companies were not manufacturing or trading in chocolate. The Iranians are smart and use deceptive practices, such as front companies and the stripping of Iranian names off money transfers, which can undermine banks' controls for knowing the identities of customers."

Where is the beef? I wondered again while listening to Aldo. The stuff he was telling was relevant and important, but I already knew it. I needed hard-core documents.

"Can we go to the bank? I don't have a car."

"Why?"

"I simply want to see what it looks like."

"*Bene*," he said.

We went out to the street and entered his Fiat. Well, he entered and I squeezed myself in. He drove to 50 Via Barberini, and found a parking space right in front of the Mussolini-era building. It had a number of businesses. On the top floor was Thai International Airways. The floor below that had a sign for Bank Sepah: SEPAH— IRAN FILIALE DI ROMA in large blue letters. Other businesses included a PCL ticket agency, a local office of France's *Le Monde* newspaper, a branch of the Polish Tourist Office, and, on the ground floor, a men's clothing shop called Extra Large.

We entered the branch. A portrait of Ayatollah Khomeini was hung above the teller window for letters of credit.

Apparently, Aldo was a frequent visitor, because he was greeted by the staff. Not too warmly, I thought, but definitely understood given the circumstances.

We left and drove a few blocks silently. Aldo then pulled over to the curb, and grabbed his briefcase. He pulled out a large brown envelope. "Take it, but open only in your hotel room. I'll deny ever giving you anything."

I took the envelope, and he dropped me at my hotel. I rushed to my room, sat at the stylish desk, and opened the envelope.

There were copies of a dozen or more bank statements, wire transfers, and ancillary banking documents. All were related to Shestakov's company, LSIT, Leonid Shestakov International Trading GmbH. Even with my limited command of Italian, I could see the pattern immediately. Money came into Sepah Rome from Germany—usually a Berlin bank—then was transferred to Sepah Dubai or to the account of Vivian Tenafly Trust at the Bank of Traders and Merchants in the British Virgin Islands.

I felt the thrill of discovery. Which of the treasure troves should I pursue first? They both needed my attention. I thought of a children's espionage book I read in Israel when I was just nine years old. The protagonist suspected a delivery truck that carried hay from the city center to the village, while the normal route should have been the opposite. Why would Shestakov, who sold equipment to Iran—and should therefore be receiving payment into his accounts—*send* money to Dubai? It was not a single transfer that could have a plausible explanation, but it was rather a regular series of such payments, from Germany to Dubai. Who was he paying? The other discovery was of money transfers to an anonymous trust in the British Virgin Islands, an offshore tax haven. I wanted to know who the UTB was, the Ultimate Trust Beneficiary. Definitely a person who wanted to hide those payments, if he created an anonymous trust for them in a tax haven.

The documents were intriguing and had to be investigated, but I needed to decide which way I was going. Continue with my unauthorized investigation, or lay it on the table for Eric, Paul, and Benny to decide?

A phone call to my mobile from Eric made the decision easier. Eric told me to return to Istanbul immediately. He didn't even ask where I was. He either knew, or couldn't care. Something was obviously up. I returned.

XVII

June 2007, Istanbul

In Istanbul, I checked into the Conrad Hotel again and found a message from Benny. I called. Benny asked me to come to the safe apartment that afternoon and promised me a surprise. He also didn't ask me where I'd been or ask me to report my findings.

The safe apartment was in a posh Istanbul neighborhood. When I entered, Benny, Paul, and Eric were seated next to three other men I didn't recognize. Eric was on the phone and turned to Benny, "They're early."

Benny took out a bottle of Yarden, a kosher Israeli wine. He cleared the coffee table and set the glasses out.

"So, what?" I said. "Are we celebrating something?"

"Yes," said Benny, "Madani is coming here."

"Yes, Madani Number Four," said Benny, and I thought he was joking.

"And Madani Number Four likes Yarden wine too?" I asked cynically. I was surprised because Eric had told me earlier that Madani was already in the US.

"Loves it. What he is doing is incredibly dangerous, so we want to make him as comfortable as possible," Benny said cryptically.

There was a knock on the door. Benny opened it. He ushered two men through the door, speaking Hebrew to one of them, to the one who looked Arabic. The other man was Caucasian.

"Meet Madani," said Benny ceremoniously to all of us, but I'd just heard that Madani speaking Hebrew to Benny. I could hardly believe it. A former member of the Republican Guard, a group of sworn enemies of Israel, speaking Hebrew?

Clearly, a sign of the coming apocalypse. Benny turned to me, with our new guest.

"Dan. I'd like you to meet Ittai, aka Madani."

"Ittai," I said in astonishment, hearing that typical Israeli name, "Ittai?"

Ittai smiled. "Yes, Ittai," he said in Hebrew.

Ittai reached his hand out to me warmly. I shook it.

"How was your flight?" Eric asked.

"Good," Ittai said. "I made sure to glance nervously around the plane once or twice. I wore a hat. I definitely looked the part of an absconding Iranian national, if I do say so."

Eric clarified what we already understood. "Ittai was a decoy. He flew here from Damascus as Madani—when Madani was already here—using Madani's passport that we sent back through the US diplomatic pouch to Damascus. It's genuine, the real thing that Madani Number Three gave us when he arrived here and continued to Europe on his way to the US."

"Here's the plan," Eric sat on the couch with Ittai joining him. "Ittai, while in Istanbul, will continue his role, posing as the real Madani and running the usual errands, such as applying for refugee status and getting asylum."

The gravity of Ittai's mission hit me all at once. As the decoy for a defecting Iranian general, it was an extraordinarily dangerous mission. I was overcome with awe.

Ittai looked at the bottle on the coffee table, smiled, and asked, "May I?"

After a brief respite, we got down to business. Benny and Eric were leaving within hours; they had unspecified business in Germany. I didn't ask what. Before they left, though, the two left us parting presents: Benny went to the kitchen pantry and pulled out two handguns. Ittai and I were each given Glock G19s. That compact version of the polymer frame pistol was perfect for self-defense. The heavier artillery would be carried by our security detail and backup. The usual routine. I held the Glock, feeling the heft of it; I hadn't held a Glock in a long time. And, once again, the weight of Ittai's mission hit me. All the dangerous assignments I'd taken over the years, and still nothing compared to this. Ittai looked at me, a serious look, as though reading my mind. He had been in Damascus, and would be now in Istanbul, a walking duck in the shooting range, trying to smoke out any Iranians.

If the decoy operation were successful, it would increase the chances that the Iranians would never realize that the real Madani—Number Three—had already left Damascus because Ittai, the fourth version of Madani, this time courtesy of the CIA and Mossad, was in Istanbul, acting as if he were the real thing. Since Ittai had left Syria and come to Turkey, it was a clear violation of Madani's Iranian exit visa allowing him a Syrian visit only. From the Iranian perspective that meant only one thing: he was defecting and had to be stopped, dead or alive.

"We should go," I said.

"Where is the refugee office?" Ittai asked. "Close?"

Our first stop would be applying for refugee status, and in fact the Istanbul office of the UN High Commissioner for Refugees was on the other side of the city, about as far away as you could get and still be in Istanbul.

"Unfortunately, no."

Why couldn't the office be any closer? *If only.* The longer the route, the greater the danger.

"Ah, well. No matter. Our mission is twofold. You need to apply for refugee status, of course. But, we need the Iranians coming out of hiding," I said, "if they discover that you are here."

"It's not relevant anymore," said Ittai. "I might have seen them in the airport or on the plane. The mind can play tricks. Which means I'm going to be shot at, and that's if I'm lucky. Because if they try to shoot me, it's because they believe I'm Madani. If they shoot, that means that they are sure I'm the real Madani, and that's a good sign. So stay out of my way, or you'll take a bullet, too."

He was serious. We put our bulletproof vests on.

Ittai was right. I cocked my gun, engaged the safety, and stuck it in my waistband. We left the safe apartment, and slipped into the protected, American-style motorcade parked out front. This consisted of three armored black Suburbans, this time chosen specifically to be conspicuous. There were few American-style cars like this in Istanbul. They were ostentatious.

They announced, *someone important is here.*

Armed CIA combatants filled the first and the third in the motorcade, while Ittai and I sat in the second, also with three combatants. And like that, we were off.

Driving through Istanbul was like navigating a minefield. Little old ladies shrunken into their head scarves; women with baby carriages; old, toothless men pushing carts—the weakest, most vulnerable-looking people—were all potential threats. We drove through Nişantaşı, a bucolic neighborhood and a socialite part of İstanbul. It featured expensive shops, cafés with a happy-hour buzz, and sinister windows. Windows, I thought: all the mayhem that can be done out of windows. Guns, grenades, handheld missiles. To name a few.

Ittai sat placidly, it seemed. I couldn't tell if he was nervous or not. Likely he'd steeled himself back at the safe house. His eyes were following the scenery as we drove by. "The scenery." Nothing felt safe, and somehow, ironically, the "nice" parts—the flowerbeds and the minaret-topped museums filled with tourists—seemed especially foreboding. Inside the car, there was silence. I could almost hear the driver breathe.

And then we turned into Surici, the oldest part of town, and the most congested. The streets were narrow and winding. We passed large, crumbling buildings that used to be public baths, groups of begging children, and then an open-air market. Of course we were passing an open-air market. The traffic slowed as we passed, and then slowed again. We inched past two butcher stalls, a stall with dyed fabrics, and then—testimony to our global world—multiple stalls manned by stooped old women selling cheap plastic trinkets no doubt made in China.

The roads, I noticed, were badly in need of repair. I'd grown used to such roads, living in the States. Even with these behemoths we were in—surely these Suburbans had shock absorbers worthy of the price of the vehicle—I could feel every pothole, every bump in the road.

And then traffic ground to a halt. Our windows were smoked; we could look out, but no one could see us. And there we sat, as every other car furiously honked and people began to shout. Off in the distance, in the bustling bazaar crowd, I spotted a young woman who seemed to lock her eyes onto our convoy; she had an intense look of concentration in her face, as least she seemed to from where I sat. She was squinting against the glare of the sun. Was she looking right at us? I couldn't tell. Her hair was long, her clothes simple. I'd place her age at around nineteen. Old enough to kill, surely. I nudged Ittai, *look*. As she stared intently at us, we stared out, unseen, back at her.

Just then, she turned on her heel and walked back inside the little stall she'd come out of; she immediately came back out with another girl, a bit older, also beautiful. The two spoke to each other, then began walking toward us.

How long had we been stopped here? Longer than any traffic light, certainly, so what the hell was it? Maybe this traffic jam had been created for our benefit; maybe an intentional car crash had been staged ahead, designed to keep us trapped here, stopped, vulnerable. And still, the girls moved toward us with singular purpose. For a second I lost sight of them through the crowds of the marketplace. Then I caught sight of the younger girl's scarf, spotting it in the crowd like a shark fin in water.

I grabbed my Glock.

Ittai put his hand on my arm.

"Wait," he said. "We need to know: are they coming for Madani? I need to have proof. I don't see any weapon. They could just be amazed by these massive vehicles."

"And if they have a bomb?"

"One, even if they're not Iranian, it seems that they are after me."

"What difference does that make? Hezbollah does Iran's bidding. So does Hamas. They're not 'Iranian.'" In fact, rarely was there an act of violence committed that was obviously attributable to Iran. The threat of UN sanctions had long ago driven acts of treachery underground. Countries no longer attacked each other openly, or very rarely. Iran had proven itself a master at this kind of battle, inflicting maximum damage, strictly by proxy.

The girls stopped and were chatting with someone, a man.

"Point taken," Ittai went on, "but also, I can see from here they're not Kurds." There was some logic there. Suicide bombers in Turkey were always Kurds. The Turks didn't do that kind of thing.

But of course, there's always a first time.

The girls and the man resumed their beeline, but now a few other men had joined them. One of the girls kept her hand in her purse. So maybe she didn't have a bomb, I thought. Maybe she had a gun. Guns were universal.

"You have to get out," I said to Ittai. "Now. You—"

BAM! Just then someone crashed into Ittai's side of the car. It was filled with thick smoke. "Turn around," I yelled. "Don't open the windows yet, don't let them see us."

It was easier said than done. The smoke was choking us, burning our eyes and throats. It smelled of sulfur. Our driver was not a Sunday driver taking his family to church. He accelerated and used the brakes at the same time, making the Suburban spin 180 degrees. I heard bullets hit the car from two different directions. I knew that the car was armored and light weaponry would not penetrate, but still, every rule has an exception. I knew that every bullet carries an address. However, I was concerned about the bullets that were addressed *To whom it may concern*.

I heard another explosion: an RPG missile just missed us. Our driver pushed the pedal to the metal, knocking over two fruit stands.

I looked back. Two Mercedes sedans followed. One silver, one black, both with tinted windows. There were more shots, but I felt no damage to our car. Pedestrians or no, we had to get out of this mess, and not on a gurney. Our driver raced through an intersection, sideswiping what looked like a small shipping container of clothing, knocking the whole lot over.

The two cars were right on us, crashing into that same container, as well. Our driver swerved. Ittai aimed for the driver behind us, shooting. So did our security detail. The pursuers were shooting back. I handed Ittai my Glock as well.

And then, up ahead, a shock of yellow—*what the?*—yes, it was a massive pile of lemons, spilled all over the road. They'd fallen off a truck, apparently, an entire truckload of them left there, smashed, smearing the street. We *could spin out on those*. We made a fast U-turn over a center divider to avoid them, narrowly missing an old woman. The silver Mercedes drove straight over the lemons and spun out. Bingo! It hit a cement wall. And then it went up in flames.

The black Mercedes was behind us. Obviously, we'd effectively smoked out the Iranians. They believed that Ittai was Madani. Bravo. Mission accomplished. *Now let's get the hell out of here.*

I ducked as a shot rang through the driver's seat window but missed. The driver gunned it; and then Ittai shot at the black Mercedes. I looked back. It was still behind us, but it was listing: Ittai had hit one of its tires.

Quickly, our driver turned toward the bazaar. The Mercedes followed, still listing; it was slower now, but still keeping up. We turned again, onto the road flanking the open-air market; I knew I had seconds, maybe four, five, six, before the black Mercedes would show up. I saw it make the turn behind us, and lurch to a halt. As Ittai had shot out the driver's seat windows, we could see whether it was going to be abandoned. Sure enough, two men came out of the Mercedes, leaving the driver's seat empty, kicking the flat tires and cursing. I heard my little devil say, *The Iranians had to know that Madani Number Three was a fake. Might they have been attacking Ittai to bolster the appearance that Number Three was real?*

A car chase in Istanbul is nothing like you see in the movies. There's nothing easy about an old-world car chase. I always imagined a car chase would be much, much easier in the States, though I've yet to experience one there. The normal, average citizen in the States is a conscientious driver, stopping regularly at stop signs and red lights, nearly always maintaining the speed limit, giving right-of-way to pedestrians. If I were to gun through a red light in the States, I know it's virtually certain that everyone else would be dutifully stopped at that red light, so the coast would be clear to speed off. I would be the one person breaking the laws—along, of course, with the person chasing me—and I suspect every other driver, not to mention every pedestrian, would just instinctively stay out of my way. But if you gun through a red light here in Istanbul, there's no telling what to expect. We're never the only ones breaking traffic laws in a place like this. This is the Middle East. The old world. Chaos comes with the territory, particularly when it comes to driving under a barrage of bullets.

Here we are in the twenty-first century, with new technology sprouting every three seconds. So much of my work is dependent on it. And yet at the end of the day, we lost one pursuing Mercedes, thanks to a bunch of spilled lemons. Never underestimate low tech.

We opened the windows to let the smoke out, coughing. "Is everyone OK?" asked Ittai. A quick head count showed that none of us was hurt. Our driver used the two-way radio to report and, apparently, to get instructions. I just heard the buzzing of the on-and-off exchange. "The first car took an RPG missile at the rear end but managed to drive away. They have three injured."

"What about the car that was behind us?" Ittai asked." He was cool.

"They are fine, with light burn injuries. But we must get the hell out of here. The attack was well planned, and whoever attacked us must have Plan B."

We didn't have to guess who'd attacked us. Forces loyal to Iran made the attempt. They could not allow Madani to get away. He was much too valuable. To national pride and to national security. However, the attack proved that the CIA/Mossad ploy had worked. Our attackers were sure that we had Madani with us, not Ittai, the Israeli decoy.

"We're going to a meeting in Alpha Place," said our driver. "We have a Plan B, too." I knew that Alpha Place was the code word for Istanbul Samandıra Army Air Base, but I had no idea where we were.

"Where is it?" I asked.

"In Kartal district, right here in Istanbul," said the driver, "within the General İsmail Hakkı Tunaboylu Barracks north of the Anatolian Motorway Otoyo Four. We are not far."

Ten minutes later we were at the gate. They were expecting us. We went directly to the heliport. A UH-60A Black Hawk helicopter was waiting for us. We were the last of the three cars from our motorcade to arrive. We rushed into the helicopter, and it took off in a blazing noise.

Ittai was looking out; I was looking out. Men like us are prepared for all kinds of situations. Snipers, grenades, roadside bombs. We understand guns, bombs, and covert war. We know what to do if we're shot at. We know what to do in the case of tear gas. But with all that knowledge and our background in the Israeli Army in combat— still, what the fuck was this? I turned to Ittai.

"Nothing in the Mossad playbook for this?"

"Nope," he said. "Not a thing."

XVIII

June 2007, Ankara, Turkey

We flew to Ankara. After Ittai and I checked into the Hotel Arshan, we were joined by Jay Black, a security officer from the US Embassy in Ankara for security briefing. In the morning we went to the Ankara office of the UN High Commissioner for Refugees to request political asylum for Ittai, aka Madani.

The office was full of people seeking asylum. Most of them were in ethnic clothing typical of their country of origin. I could identify many coming from the combat areas in southern Russia. They were waiting patiently. Following a two-hour wait, a staffer asked us to approach the desk. We quickly filled out the application form and handed it back to the staffer, along with prepared "documents" supplied by the Agency and delivered through Jay Black showing that Cyrus Madani was a subject of persecution in Iran because of his political beliefs, and that his life was in danger. He was requesting asylum in the US.

The staffer quickly reviewed and accepted the paperwork. "Call us in one month for the status of your application," he said, handing

Madani some sheets of boilerplate information with the UNHCR phone number.

"There's one other thing," I said hesitantly. "General Madani doesn't have status in Turkey. There could be questions."

He nodded in understanding. "What would you need?"

"Some paper, a letter or any sort of confirmation that General Madani is being processed by you, if he's stopped by police or any Turkish government agency and asked why he didn't leave Turkey when his visitor's visa expired." I sounded humble and apologetic.

Without a word, the staffer disappeared behind a door, leaving us to wonder if he'd return. Thirty minutes later he emerged and handed us a printed sheet of paper carrying the Commission's emblem. I read it quickly:

United Nations High Commissioner for Refugees

Regarding Cyrus Madani
To Whom it May Concern,
Referrals from the UNHCR for the UN refugee resettlement program for Iranian and Iraqi refugees in Turkey are processed by the office of the International Catholic Migration Commission (ICMC) office located in Istanbul. ICMC is an agency under contract to the American Department of State, and is charged with preparing refugee applications for presentation to US Citizenship and Immigration Services (USCIS) officers. The USCIS officers are responsible for finally determining the applicants' eligibility for resettlement in the United States under the refugee program.

The referred refugee(s) have been scheduled to have their first interview with the agency during the next few weeks. Subject to eligibility determination the case will then be presented to a USCIS officer at the next adjudication in Istanbul. Should the case be approved for resettlement by USCIS then a further 1 to 2 months

are needed for the coordination of the actual departure of the con-
cerned refugee(s).

Any assistance your office may extend to the referred case
during these processing periods shall be appreciated by our agency
and the US Refugee Program.
Sincerely,
Peter K. Schwabb
Director

I thanked the staffer with a nod, not wanting to appear over-joyed, although my heart sang, and walked out of his office. We left the building, relieved that it had gone without a hitch.

The request for the document was a spur of the moment move. I thought that we needed some such document as a sort of alibi. We obviously didn't need a UN agency to arrange asylum for Madani in the US. He was already there with legal status, together with a retirement package that would astonish even the generous souls in the intelligence community. Although issued to a decoy, not to the real Madani, that paper could be a public relations insurance policy against planted rumors that Madani was anything else but a defector. That usually happens in similar instances when rumors, speculation, and anonymously sourced news stories suggest a kidnapping.

There was a risk, though, that the UN—trying to maintain neu-trality—would later on try to distance itself from the document, alleging that it was fake. Obviously, the Iranian government could make that argument as well. But I didn't care anymore. I had the document in my hand, and everything else that could emerge later on would be just propaganda.

In the safe house with Ittai, I reported my achievement to Eric on the secure phone.

"Whose idea was it?" he asked, when I told him about the letter.

Waiting for praise from Eric is like expecting rain in the Sahara: it does come, once in a millennium. Therefore, I wasn't expecting anything. But what followed was bizarre.

"Dan, I think we went through these matters earlier. Although I appreciate your creative mind, in sensitive matters such as this one, you need to clear things with me first."

"Eric," I said trying hard not to lose my temper, "are you suggesting that I had to leave the UNHCR office, call you on an unsecured phone, raise with you the idea of getting something from the UNHCR with Madani's name on it, then return and wait another two hours to ask for the damn letter?"

Eric sensed my anger, but didn't seem to care. Eels don't have feelings, only an insatiable need to hunt their next meal. However, I wasn't about to allow Eric to regard me as his next prey.

"I did what was right under the circumstances," I said drily. "The process as far as Madani was concerned was ended but they gave him no paper or receipt bearing his name. They just gave him a bunch of boilerplate documents with general information, nothing specific to Madani."

Eric didn't respond and moved on to ask other questions. "OK," he finally said. "I'm sending you instructions on what to do next." He hung up.

I no longer take antacids after talking with Eric. I got used to his acerbic conduct. It comes with the territory.

Jay Black called me shortly thereafter. "Due to the sensitivity of Madani's case, and the fact that the US Embassy brought the UN agency in on it, Madani's asylum application will be accepted in a day or two," he said. "After the United Nations accepts his file, it will be referred to Istanbul to a refugee organization called the International Catholic Migration Commission to help him out until the asylum application is finalized." This was basically what was in the letter that I'd got "Madani" from the UNHCR. But Jay Black didn't know that it was in fact Ittai posing as Madani, and I thanked him for the news.

The way back to our hotel from the refugee agency in Ankara was uneventful. As the driver pulled up beside the curb, Ittai sat still for a minute. I knew what he was thinking. We'd crisscrossed the city, he'd been an open target, and we'd escaped unscathed. Did they know? If agents had been watching—and he felt they had—had he done something that had tipped them off? A suspect gesture? Something that had somehow managed to telegraph, "I am not Iranian?" I let him sit. I could see it in his face: he was mentally cataloguing every move he had made since taking on this mission, turning each moment over in his head, looking for the crack, the defect.

XIX

June 2007, Istanbul

We took a commercial flight to Istanbul and waited for three days, under the protection of two US security agents, in a small hotel next to the airport. We were not allowed to leave our rooms, and spent the time reminiscing about Israeli life and food. Then came the word that, with the help of the ICMC, a hotel room had been reserved for Ittai, aka Madani, at the Jiran Hotel—the hotel the ICMC normally uses.

"Are we moving there?" I asked the security detail chief, a bit baffled.

"No. We just made it look like Madani did move over there. Everything has to look like a routine handling of the matter by the UN agency."

We did move, however, together with the protection detail, to a safe house instead. We couldn't stay in one place for too long. The safe house was small but good for the purpose. It was in fact a fleabag hotel where, as European-looking men, we could quite easily blend into the background: this was a red light district. Lots of European tourists prowled the streets at any given time, day or night. Brothels were sandwiched between makeshift tea houses.

There was one upside to this hotel; it did not have computers. They had no way to scan credit cards, though of course we paid cash. They don't input your name into anything; they merely write it down. We made our way to the rooms. They were dark, each with a mattress, threadbare sheet, and worn dresser. My room reeked of urine. A few minutes later, Ittai knocked on my door. He needed to leave Turkey immediately. I reported our location to Eric.

An hour later there was a knock—an expected one. I opened the door. Standing there was a slim man in his forties holding a large satchel.

"I'm Joe and I came at the request of Mrs. Keene."

"Yes, thank you," I said, completing the identification process, "She said you'd bring me a parcel."

He nodded and I motioned to him to come in.

"Joe," I said. "Meet Tango."

Although Joe was an Agency employee and in the loop, for security reasons he was prevented from knowing the real name of Ittai, just as my visitor's name was probably not Joe.

Ittai shook Joe's hand.

"I'm told you're the man," Ittai said.

Indeed, Joe was the one of the best makeup artists in the CIA. Rumor was, before his recruitment into the service, he'd in fact gone to art school—an unusual background for a man in his position, surely. And, as it turned out, one that served the Agency incredibly well: he was amazingly skilled. He was highly sought after, not only because of his skill in completely transforming anyone's appearance, but because he was Arab. He was American born, though his parents were Coptic Christian, from Egypt. He'd grown up speaking both English and Arabic.

"I'm doing both of you, correct?" Joe asked.

"No," I told him. At this Joe looked puzzled.

"I mean you were, yes," I clarified. That's what Eric and Benny wanted, I knew. "But plans have changed, so you'll only need to do Tango."

Joe opened his satchel on the bed. He had a myriad of instruments and tools strapped to the walls of it—brushes, tape, what looked like scalpels, sponges, tubes of pigment, epoxy, containers of putty. He pulled out one small circular jar from a side pocket and held it up for us to see.

"Colored contacts," he said. "You'll be leaving here with green eyes."

He sat Ittai down on the chair. Just as if he were a barber, Joe draped a sheet around Ittai's shoulders, and proceeded, with practiced concentration, to work. Layers of high-tech putty altered the shape of Ittai's face. Joe would mold, shape, then scrape off bits with one of his scalpels. He turned Ittai's crisp jawline into jowls. His nose became bulbous, and arched down. Joe gave Ittai bags under his eyes, and then, as he waited for the epoxy to dry, he mixed skin color until he'd created Ittai's pigment, exactly. And then he mixed a few similar shades, some lighter, some darker. These, he painted over the putty prosthetics he'd so meticulously placed, different pigments for different spots on the face; the results looked naturally irregular. He wove short extensions into Ittai's hair and sprinkled it with gray. As he finished, he stood back, in much the way I imagine a painter would do, surveying his canvas. He held his chin in one hand and squinted. Then he winced.

"No," he said. "Something is missing."

He slipped his hand into a side pocket of his magic bag, took out a small box, and opened it.

"Ah, yes," he said, and, carefully, he gave Ittai tufts of gray ear hair, gluing them into his ear canal with his epoxy, a kind developed just for this, to withstand human sweat.

He stood back again, and indeed the transformation was astonishing. Gone was the trim Mossad agent with the dark-brown eyes and sharp jawline. He had aged considerably, with bags and slight jowls—but the man I was looking at now wasn't simply an aged Ittai. Rather, his face looked entirely different. His profile had been transformed: his forehead was now pronounced, his nose bulbous. His eyes drooped, and deep creases radiated outward, above his now-bushier eyebrows, along his cheeks, surrounding his eyes. He looked hard and weathered, reminding me of the Arab men you see in one of Istanbul's *gecekondus*—those built-on-the-fly housing developments spreading through Istanbul, whole makeshift neighborhoods so dilapidated they seemed to be collapsing in on their occupants. Here, the poor of Istanbul lived, and after a lifetime of back-breaking work, they very often looked broken and ancient by the time they were fifty; Ittai, to me, looked like one of these men.

"How do I look?" Ittai asked, and then he smiled a big, toothy grin. The putty adorning his face—completely invisible now—moved with his smile; it looked entirely natural. But with Ittai smiling, I could see that there was still one thing missing. Joe saw it, too.

"Teeth," he said.

He capped a number of Ittai's teeth with yellow and mottled brown facades. Perfect. And then, like an Italian painter, Joe surveyed his project and kissed his fingertips.

"Beautiful," he said. And before he left, he gave us the pièce de résistance: a passport for Ittai, complete with fake name, and a photo of an old man who bore a striking resemblance to the transformed Ittai.

After Joe left, Ittai and I regrouped. We ate lunch I'd grabbed on our way over. Ittai had to be careful, because of the caps on his teeth—nothing hard or tough to chew, an easy enough prescription in this area of the world. We had hummus and pita.

His mission was completed, but mine was not. He had to get back to the airport in one piece. He was so close, and we needed to make sure he got home safely. There could have been others against us. But those we had tentatively identified had been Turks, which told me a couple of things: One, that Iran had Turks in its service, a trained militia-in-waiting; and two, that there were more out there looking for us, no question; I'd seen the two men from the black Mercedes, and likely there had been two more in the silver Mercedes that had crashed. That made four.

A proxy group trained by Iran, with organized surveillance capabilities—not to mention the funding for Mercedes sedans and Glocks—would have more than four men. No question.

The one place they would know to find us would be our last stop in Turkey. They would be lying in wait outside the airport. This was a certainty. It would make no difference that were we to take a train. They would be there too.

"So, your plan?" asked Ittai.

"Go the airport," I said, and gave him the details.

I thought back to Dubai and Paris. No matter how careful I try to be, someone finds me. Was a disguise—even one by "Joe"—going to change that? And if someone got word that Ittai is in disguise? The way things had been going, that did seem to be a distinct possibility.

Our security detail came with a rented car. Twenty minutes later I was in a big parking lot just outside the airport, driving slowly into the entrance. I passed by the passenger drop-off area and I slowed, surreptitiously checking out all the cars idling there—or rather, I was trying to look like someone who *thought* he was being surreptitious. In fact, I was behaving in a fairly ham-fisted way, craning my neck out the window, nervously looking over my shoulder. Around and around, circling. But, nothing. I pulled off, finally, to a strip in the airport where cars can idle, waiting for late planes. A few cars were there. I made sure there were all within my sightline.

It started to rain. I rolled up my window, watching the rain pour down on this bleak bit of asphalt. Maybe, I thought, I should have gone with the makeup disguise, gone the route Eric and Benny had set up for me. And yet, even still, my gut was telling me no. There were many breaches, so many leaks. It's been rough enough when I've been on assignment alone. Rough, yes, but I handle it. It's a different story now, though. I'm not working alone. I'm on assignment with someone else, a man who has entrusted me with his life. Ittai came here, facing down possible death; his bravery, his willingness, and unwavering dedication reminded me of what drew me to the Mossad in the first place, and now to the Agency.

Again, I felt that something was wrong; I'd been trusted with someone I have tremendous respect for, *and I can't do my fucking job.* There was a risk just openly sending him to the airport. His makeup was impeccable. How could anyone spot him? How would they know? Given the past six months of my life, there's only one conclusion I could draw: they *will* know. I don't know how. But I know they will. They knew in Dubai. In Paris. They knew with the second Tango. They knew with Ittai, the fourth Tango.

Ittai was tense but silent. I started again and kept going. Approaching a red traffic light, I slowed down. Someone started tapping at my window. I jerked my head to the left. It was an old woman. The wrinkles around her eyes were deep grooves. She lifted an umbrella and snapped it open. The look on her face as she backed away, and the umbrella, were signals that she'd identified me.

Ittai and I ducked.

BANGBANGBANG, shots rang through the car, rang through the driver's and the passenger's windows. The shots hit head-high. One just grazed my head. I slammed on the gas. I couldn't see anything behind me. Too gray. Too rainy.

There had been no car behind me, not even the security detail car. Where had the shots come from? Someone standing at the edge of the road, directly behind the car, crouched. Had to be it.

Now there was a car behind me. Clearly, their Plan B. I sped. They sped. We both hit the highway. Traffic was sparse. I jerked from lane to lane and heard shots—but nothing hit the crouching Mossad agent I had in the car posing as an Iranian defector. I found a short-cut.

I took the next exit, made a careening right, then a fast left between two buildings that formed a kind of alleyway, a short one. This was a back way to my interim destination. I shot out between the two buildings, braked, screeched, parked. I was here. My personal FOE were in hot pursuit, racing between the two buildings behind me as one of them got off a few shots. And then, like me, they emerged. We were in the parking lot of a police station. Their car at once made a U-turn and took off. A call to the security detail that lost us in the chase, and within a few minutes a squad car took us to the airport.

I'd had enough being at the top of the Iranians' Hit Parade. Ittai, surrounded by a six-man security detail, entered the airport terminal, turned around, and waved to me.

———

What transpired in the aftermath was expected. Confused and conflicting stories emerged as to whether indeed Madani and his family had left Iran. What followed was an Iranian propaganda effort discounting the idea that Madani had fled Iran of his own volition. Accusations were hurled by Iranian officials in the Iranian press. They claimed that Madani had been the victim of a sophisticated kidnapping plot by Israel, and that the United States had tried to uncover Iran's secrets.

Then Iranian media reported that ten people claiming to be Madani's family—including two women saying they were his wives—protested in front of the Turkish Embassy in Tehran, charging that Turkish security forces had handed Madani over to Israel.

As we idled in the safe apartment, I showed the newspaper to Benny. He chuckled. "In fact," he said, "Madani had three wives—two ex-wives and one current wife. His current wife left Iran with one of their children and is waiting in Europe for the media storm to calm down before they join Madani in the United States. The two ex-wives were forced by the Iranian security services to demonstrate in front of the Turkish Embassy in Tehran, in order to lend credibility to their claim that Madani was kidnapped."

Tango Number Four is OK, but what about the third Tango? Was that mission entirely successful? The escape from house arrest, to Damascus, to Germany. No breach. No ambush. And just how is it that *that* mission—the most important of them all—went off without a hitch? I was out of the loop. Only Paul, Benny, and Eric were all over that mission.

I, however, was not.

It was time to do some soul searching. How did the Iranians know that Ittai—who they thought was Madani—was coming to Turkey? Was that a security breach, or a leak? And—if there *were* a leak up on high, wouldn't it have been leaked that Ittai was in fact a fake Madani? Wouldn't the leak instead have pointed to the real Tango?

So, I reasoned, this can't be a leak from on high. It has to be something else.

A nagging feeling began welling within me—a feeling that I was the link. Good god.

It was me. It had to be. I was out of the loop with the Third Tango. I was in the loop with every other mission—and every other mission has been ambushed. I was the through-line: the one common element connecting the compromised missions. *But still, where did these breaches come from? How did they happen? How—*

Although Benny and Eric were certain that "their Madani," whom they told me was already en route to the US, was the genuine Madani, I was doubtful. I was even willing to take the heat from Benny and Eric, who'd most probably accuse me of being stubborn and blind to the facts, or even crazy.

XX

June 2009, Paris

I left Istanbul without telling anyone, and flew to Paris. There, I could start down the path to solving the mystery.

Women in tight skirts and heels, espresso, escargots in butter. It was good to be back in France, even better to be back with my old friend, Pierre Perot. An afternoon meal with Pierre, running down my past mission—it was like my own kind of debriefing. I always appreciated his opinion. He was one the sharpest people I knew. And today, I was hoping to get some information from him.

But first came a long lunch, and conversation about everything but what I wanted to ask. That seemed, as far as I could tell, to be the French way—everything in leisure. And indeed, after what I'd been through, taking my time felt damn good.

"Tell me," Pierre asked, glass of wine in hand. I'd just finished my story of Istanbul; Pierre had listened with rapt attention. I knew that Pierre had already read the official confidential circular the CIA had sent its intelligence allies, but Pierre wanted to hear the details. I had no problem with telling him, particularly when what Pierre wanted to hear was whether there were any good restaurants to recommend, or . . . well, I know he wanted to hear about women.

"It all went without a hitch." *Like fun it did*, said my inner devil.

"Wonderful to hear, Dan. Let's drink to that. And of course, to your survival."

I raised my water glass. He raised his wine glass. I noticed the wine he was drinking was—Chianti?

"You're drinking—Italian?"

"Yes, well, a man can grow, no? Experience all life has to offer."

Indeed. I knew Pierre well; I knew immediately his latest mistress had to be Italian.

"Her name?"

"Giuletta." He smiled that impish smile of his. "But enough about my life, as wonderful as it might be. You, Dan, seem not yourself. Shouldn't you be feeling triumphant? You're here; you're safe. The man you were charged to protect is safe. And of course, let's not forget, the world was made just a bit safer, all because of you, my friend. Are these not reasons to celebrate?"

Yes, we had made it. Because of me. But if he hadn't made it, that would also have been because of me. Running down hypotheticals like this—what might have happened if X or Y or Z had happened—was a trap. I knew that. Mossad training intelligently warns against hypotheticals. Young recruits can get too easily mired in them: *If that bullet had been flying a sixteenth of an inch to the left*, or *If I had taken a different train*, and on, and on. A trap.

I was in that trap. I was stuck.

"A woman, Dan," Pierre said. "That's all you need. To cheer you."

I shook my head, smiling in spite of myself.

Pierre looked serious now.

"What, then? How can I help?"

"You know, I came this short of thinking either Benny or Eric had been contaminated."

"So? It happens. Even to our friends, it happens."

"True. But the thing is, I used to be able to rely on gut instinct, and for a while, it was making me very leery of them. Very. But I was off—way off."

"We all have off days, Dan. No one is perfect. Not even you." He smiled. "Listen. I know what you're thinking. We've all heard the stories about agents who've lost it. Their edge, their mind. Every agency has stories like that. In the RG, there was a man who thought that every person he met in the street was attempting to recruit him. We had to let him go. You're not that kind of man."

"How do you know?" I was teasing, but being half serious.

"Because what you just described, Dan, is a perfectly normal reaction to being in the Agency. Or the Mossad. Paranoia, Dan. A normal reaction for those of us who do what we do."

I nodded. Of course, he was right.

"There's more though, isn't there?"

Again, I nodded.

"I was so worried about where the contamination was, I missed the most obvious answer: it could be me. I've been under surveillance for a good six months now, which has jeopardized every one of my missions. Every one. I should have seen it. How could I *not* have seen it."

"You're seeing it now."

"I was compromised in Dubai. And right here in Paris—remember?"

"Ah," Pierre said. "Well, I could certainly make an educated guess who this person is. Leonid Shestakov, yes? From Russia, illegally brokering German-made nuclear parts in Dubai, for Iran, and the German girl working for him, yes."

"And twice," he continued, "during jobs that involved Iran."

"Exactly. I lay it out in the simplest terms possible, instantly you know. But me, it's taken me. . . ."

"Dan. Don't get stuck like that. You must look forward. To the future."

I took a deep breath.

"I wanted to ask you something, Pierre. About looking to the future—about Leonid. Maybe you can help."

He nodded.

"As I said, we've known for more than a week now that the man I escorted out of Tehran was fake. How did the Iranians know what we were about to do?"

"Start the search back process again," suggested Pierre. "I'll also look up some records at the office. Maybe there was something that you overlooked."

Only later I realized how right he was.

XXI

June 2007, Dubai

I flew from Paris to Dubai. Immediately after checking in into a hotel, I walked into the Sepah Bank to confront Ali Akbar Kamrani, the assistant manager in charge of export document financing. He was the person with the clues, and I was about to extract them from him.

"Sorry about your brother, or was he your brother?" I asked sarcastically and loudly, when I walked unannounced into his office.

Ali Akbar Kamrani seemed shaken to see me. "Please," he said. "People are watching."

"I don't care," I said. "If you want this conversation to be quiet, you'd better talk to me."

"What do you want to know?"

I took the big flower vase off his credenza. "I'm going to smash it right now and raise such a scandal that you'd find it difficult to explain to management."

"What do you want to know?"

"All."

"Like what?"

"I think that you are a VEVAK agent under deep cover, and that's OK with your bank management because the bank is owned by the Iranian Revolutionary Guard, and VEVAK is a close affiliate. I want to know how and why you contacted me."

His eyes were puzzled, trying to see what leverage I could have on him, and consequently should he concede to my statement.

"Get out!" he said. "Get the hell out!"

"If I walk through that door, you'll be sorry for the rest of your miserable life that will probably not last too long after I tell the world, VEVAK included, what I know."

"You know zilch," he said defiantly.

"Really?" I said mockingly. "You're doubled. You have double loyalty. The VEVAK is not going to like it." I put the vase back on his credenza. I noticed a slight tremor in his right hand. He was sweating.

"Doubled? What do you mean? I don't work for VEVAK, and I'm not sure I understand what you mean by doubled? I'm just an assistant manager in charge of export document financing in the bank." There was also a slight tremor in his voice. He licked his lips.

"Are you sure?" I asked in clear contempt. "Don't give me that bullshit. I know that Firouz Kamrani was not your brother—you just have the same last name, and even that could be intentional, I don't care. I also know that your story that you found me through your brother-in-law or some other funny connection, is also crap.

"You received my name from VEVAK and they came up with this cover story that has more holes than in my grandfather's net when he went fishing. My friend, you work for VEVAK and, without telling them, also for a Russian agent working for the Russian foreign intelligence service."

"Who?" he asked, breathing hard.

"SVR, the Russian Foreign Intelligence Service, Служба Внешней Разведки *Sluzhba Vneshney Razvedki.*" I repeated it in Russian.

"Never heard of them," he became defiant again.

A thought crossed my mind: perhaps Ali Akbar never realized that Shestakov was building his own nest, but was also working for SVR to smooth his activities.

"What do you want from me? I lost my brother and now this?" Ali Akbar tried again.

"I shed tears for you," I said mockingly. "You were recruited to work for the SVR. Was it Leonid Shestakov, the owner of LSIT—Leonid Shestakov International Trading GmbH—who recruited you?"

"Never heard his name."

That Kamrani continued with this conversation rather than calling security to throw me out, just as any legitimate bank executive who had gotten no closer to espionage than a James Bond movie would do if I came bolting into his office with accusations taken directly from a spy manual, spoke volumes. Clearly, Kamrani was negotiating with me in his own subtle way to find out what I knew about him, and to discover what I wanted, and if that was below his cost of being exposed as a double agent cheating VEVAK.

"Never heard of him? So maybe it was Monica Mann who got you into this?" I decided to first use that name, which appeared on the passport of the German girlfriend of my "son" in Paris. "Or maybe it was Gerda Ehlen?" I deliberately did not show that I knew that it was the same person.

"Mr. Van der Hoff," he said slowly, "I really don't understand what you want from me."

There we go again. He's playing dumb. "Fine," I said, "Unless you start leveling with me, VEVAK's security officers will receive copies of payments you regularly received from Shestakov and SVR, his masters, directly or through Monica into a bank account in the British Virgin Islands. They will also highly appreciate the information that you were successful in saving $13.5 million in just two years from your salary at a midlevel management position at the bank. They will also get word that these savings represent 'commissions' from Shestakov on each sale of equipment to the Iranian Bushehr reactor."

I partly was bluffing, of course, or at least shooting in the dark. But only partly. I had bank statements from the Italian branch of Sepah, transferring 15 percent of the amount of each of many transactions to the bank in the BVI. Though they did not prove a tie to Ali Akbar personally, that each transfer was exactly 15 percent of the money transferred each time to Dubai served to suggest that it was the customary 30 percent commission, split fifty-fifty.

And who'd be a more suitable partner with whom to share a commission than Ali Akbar, who was in a perfect position to enjoy both worlds? All that mattered was that Ali Akbar Kamrani believed that I had proof. And if he hadn't thrown me out of his office by this point, it served as proof that he had something, or maybe a lot, to lose by letting me make good on my threat.

"Get out! Just get out," he said quietly, as if he'd read my mind and wanted to prove me wrong.

"Thank you," I said and left his office. I had a better plan. A floor show without the audience around us.

———

That evening, I waited for him next to the employees' exit from the bank building. As he walked out the door, I came from behind him, stuck my finger at his back, and said, "You're coming with me now. If you make a wrong move, you'll get a bullet so fast that you won't even have time to think about how you ended up in hell. Trust me, I won't hesitate or miss."

I pushed him lightly toward a car I had rented earlier and made him sit next to me. I repeated my threats to hurt him if he acted foolishly. I drove to the Jumeirah Beach, next door to the Burj al Arab and the Jumeirah Beach hotel. I stopped the car, turned off the engine and the lights. "Get out," I barked at Ali Akbar, flashing my gun.

Shaken, he exited the car. "Walk," I ordered him, signaling to get closer to the sandy beach with the palm trees. I looked around. The area was devoid of people. There were just a hot breeze and cicadas.

"This is your opportunity to stay alive," I said. "Either you talk to me, or you're a corpse." I cocked my gun. He shivered when he heard the metal clicking.

"Please, Mr. Van der Hoff, please," he begged.

"Sit," I ordered. I pressed the video recorder in my pocket. The tiny wireless camera attached to my lapel should capture our conversation even when the only light came from the full moon. Ali Akbar sat on the sand. I remained standing.

"I'm going to ask each question only once. If I don't get a satisfactory answer, you'll meet my ugly side."

Ali Akbar didn't answer. But his black eyes reflected his fear.

"What do you want?" he asked, and I knew that I'd scored.

"Where is General Cyrus Madani?" I dropped the bombshell.

Ali Akbar was stunned.

"Who?" His question seemed like a futile attempt to gain time.

"You heard me, General Cyrus Madani. Where is he?"

Kamrani let out a big sigh. "He's here."

"What do you mean?" I was too overwhelmed by my success to take that information in. I was clearly shooting in the dark and hit a jackpot.

"Here in Dubai."

"Doing what?" I asked hastily.

"Waiting."

"For what?"

"For travel arrangements."

"To where?"

Kamrani became silent. "Please, Mr. Van der Hoff, I can't tell you more or I die."

"Where is Madani?" I insisted, lowering my gun to his neck, letting him feel the cold metal.

"In a safe house in Dubai, that's all I know."

"Who's holding him?"

"Shestakov's men. Please," he begged, "they will kill me, please let me go, I told you all I know."

"You are not going anywhere until I get the whole story. How did Madani end up here, and where is Shestakov holding him and why?"

He didn't answer. I switched to another topic that was burning in me, making him believe—falsely—that he was off the hook.

"How did you know who I was when you first approached me with your story about your supposed scientist brother who allegedly wanted to defect?"

"Mr. Van Der Hoff, I'm sorry, I can't answer you."

I knew I had only a one-bullet gun. If I informed VEVAK about their bad apple, he would die—and so would my only source of information. So I made a tactical withdrawal. That seemed to astonish him more than anything.

"How did you know to approach me when we first met?" I repeated the question.

He hesitated.

I lifted my gun toward his face.

"Wait," he cried. "I'll tell you."

"I'm listening," I said.

"When you first came to We Forward Unlimited company in Dubai to rent their services, you gave them your passport, which they copied and scanned. As routine, they sent your image to VEVAK in Tehran."

"Why would they do that?" I asked, although I knew the answer.

"Because VEVAK owns them."

"Why did the request come?"

"It's a routine procedure applied whenever a new client hires the company's services. That helps VEVAK to identify foreign agents snooping around the Gulf States, since they are more likely to use services such as We Forward Unlimited to mask their identity. They are particularly interested in American agents collecting proof of embargo violations."

Smart idea! I thought. That service gave VEVAK information about potential foreign intelligence agents, but also an open door to read all their mail. Obviously, intelligence agents don't discuss their subterfuge matters on third-party vendors' service platforms. But sometimes, some of their counterparts' names and addresses are revealed, and at times secret information falls between the cracks without being ciphered.

Ali Akbar paused.

"Go on!" I urged him.

"VEVAK used sophisticated facial recognition software to match your photo with all photos they have on file."

"How did they have my photo to compare to?"

"You gave the Iranian Consulate in Vienna your passport photo when you applied for a visa a few years back."

Ha! I remembered that. It was during my preparation to infiltrate Iran chasing the Chameleon.

"When VEVAK had a positive ID on you, they told We Forward Unlimited to send them your mailbox services application and saw your listed Paris address."

"And then?"

"They told Shestakov that you were likely to expose his secret dealings. So he sent Monica, the German woman, to befriend your son and move in with him to get access to you."

"Does she work for VEVAK?"

"I don't know. I know she works for Shestakov."

I was amazed. That means that I was under the prying eyes of VEVAK as soon as I set foot in Dubai. I also didn't have an answer yet as to how VEVAK identified me as an American agent. Just by comparing photos? Well, they were right to suspect, because they saw the same person using two completely different names, and even with different nationalities.

I also delved into my memory to ascertain what had happened to André's rent payments. I knew they ended up in at the Agency's coffers, but could André know about it and tell Monica that the CIA cashed his rent checks? I made a mental note to ask Eric about it.

"You still didn't answer my question. How did you know to approach me?"

"After VEVAK identified you as a suspected foreign operative, their agent instructed me. He showed me your photo, told me where you were staying, and directed me to talk to you about my letters. When the letters were sent to the US Consulate in Dubai, saying that my scientist brother wanted to defect, VEVAK didn't know who the CIA would send. When you came, they had no proof that you were the one the CIA sent for that mission. There are so many foreign agents here. But for them it was enough if you exposed yourself as an American agent so that they could kidnap you."

My stomach lurched, but I kept on going.

"Was Firouz really your brother?"

"No. We just happen to have the same last name. It is very common in Iran."

"But the brother story came up first through your letters to the consulate!"

"That's true. It was the beginning of the VEVAK operation to apprehend an American agent in Dubai."

"Were you the one to post a warning on my account with We Forward Unlimited to make me leave Dubai?"

"No. VEVAK did that independently to make you panic, do unexpected things, then try to kidnap you. But if you managed to leave, they would follow you to your next destination."

"Did they follow me?"

"I don't know."

"I need the address of the place where Madani is held."

Ali Akbar didn't answer. Without a warning, I hit his face with the gun. His nose started bleeding. "Answer me!"

"Shestakov has him."

Although he'd told me that earlier, still, this was breaking news. But I didn't blink, as if I'd expected Ali Akbar to tell me that.

"Where?"

"In a villa right here in Dubai."

So, there's a new Madani revealed every way I turn. Who's the right Madani and who's fake? I was getting confused.

"Why would Shestakov hold him?"

"Shestakov orchestrated, along with Madani, Madani's escape from Iran. Madani in return was expected to advise Shestakov about the Iranian government's military and nuclear purchasing plans, to enable Shestakov to continue sales of the parts for the reactor and initiate additional sales of military goods."

"Madani wanted to leave Iran?" I asked a dumb question. Ali Akbar didn't need to know what I already knew about Madani.

"Yes, and it was impossible for Madani to leave." If what Ali Akbar was telling me was accurate, it seemed that Madani's contact with the Mossad agents who attempted to recruit him earlier in Italy was loaded. Madani knew that the price of betrayal could be very heavy and that he could face summary justice Iranian style—at the end of a rope. And he had already been in contact with Shestakov, who wanted his services. So great discretion was needed. Madani must then have played off Shestakov and the Mossad. Perhaps the textile business that Madani thereafter started was only a cover? If Shestakov was indeed holding Madani, then it seemed that he'd got tired of the games Madani was playing and had had his men abduct Madani.

"Did Shestakov abduct Madani?"

"You can say that," answered Ali Akbar. "Shestakov smuggled Madani here through the Iranian port of Kharg Island, across the bay from Dubai. They hid Madani in an empty container that had earlier brought Iranian reactor equipment shipped by Shestakov, and therefore anchored in a separate place for security reasons. Shestakov's men had free access to the ship, and it sailed the four-hundred-and-thirty-mile distance to Dubai."

"Why is Shestakov holding Madani? For ransom?"

"I don't know. All I know is that Madani cannot leave the villa and that there were some angry exchanges of words between him and Shestakov. I was there just once."

It was clear to me that Shestakov knew he was holding a treasure, and if he was holding him in a secluded villa, it could mean that Shestakov was negotiating to sell Madani to the highest bidder.

I wouldn't be surprised if Shestakov had given SVR a right of first refusal. After all, Shestakov was Russian, and he brokered between Russia and Iran re the reactor in Bushehr. Therefore offering Madani to the SVR would make a lot of sense. From the SVR's perspective, "buying" Madani had its advantages. First, to prevent a knowledge-able Iranian general from defecting to the West. Second, to strike a blow at the CIA, which had failed in the race to get Madani, when he was discovered to be in the SVR's hands. Third, Madani could give firsthand information that he possessed regarding the Iranian government's nuclear bomb plans though obviously, by now, Shestakov must have sucked from Madani everything he wanted to know.

"Does Madani understand what will happen?

"I don't know. Shestakov's men bring him food and entertainment."

"Women?"

"Yes."

"Are you married?" I asked.

"No."

"Any children?"

"No."

"Do you live alone?

"Yes."

"Get up!" I snapped, "We're going."

"Where?" he was frightened. "I already told you everything."

"Home, to your home."

If Ali Akbar thought I was done with him and was about to give him a free ride home, he would soon find out he was wrong.

He directed me to his home. An apartment in a high-rise. When he exited the car I followed him.

"Where are you going?" he asked when he saw me next to him.

"To your place. I just accepted your kind offer to serve me with tea."

He had no words. We entered the elevator and went to the ninth floor. He opened his apartment door. I grabbed his keys from him and locked the door from the inside. So much for any attempt to escape and call the police to arrest an intruder.

"I need documents," I said. "Show me your files, and I promise I'll be out of here in no time."

He pointed at a two-drawer gray metal file cabinet. It was not locked. I flipped through the files. Most of them were personal. "Show me your bank account records in BVI."

He was dumbfounded. "I don't have any," he finally managed to say.

"But you own that account in Traders and Merchants Bank!"

"No, I only have an account with Sepah Bank here."

"Who's your insider officer?"

"I don't understand."

"Insider officer, your VEVAK case officer who handles you."

"Mustafa Hadid."

"Do you have a file on him here?"

He shook his head. I quickly ran through the files, but there was nothing of interest, except, except . . . a fat file with the initials "LSIT." Ha! These were the initials of Shestakov's company. I pulled it out and flipped it open. The first thing I saw was a lease agreement for a single-family house in Arabian Ranches for AED 275,000 per year (approximately $58,000.) The renter: Ali Akbar Kamrani.

"Is that where Madani is being held?"

Pale and shaking, Ali Akbar nodded.

"Who instructed you to rent this place?"

"Shestakov."

I looked at the date of rental. September 1, 2006. That meant that an operation to kidnap Madani had been contemplated before Madani was about to defect. Unless, of course, the house had other uses. I continued sifting through the file. In fact I didn't exactly know what I was looking for. I knew that Ali Akbar was a self-confessed VEVAK agent, a clandestine recipient of money from Shestakov—and maybe also from SVR—for "fixing" things.

Did he have a third loyalty?

Where were the documents regarding the BVI account?

There was nothing in the file cabinet. It was only my speculation that he was the owner of that BVI account, just a hunch with nothing to back it up with. I turned around. Ali Akbar would be my compass. His face would tell me if I was approaching the hot stuff. When I closed and shut the file cabinet I saw an expression of relief on his face. I looked behind the cabinet, but saw nothing other than spider webs.

I opened it again. There must be something here. I pulled the upper drawer out completely and ran my hand under the top. Bingo. Taped to the flat metal was a file, half an inch thick. I looked at Ali Akbar. He was shaking. I pulled out the file. It was full of documents, most of them in Arabic or Persian, but the few that were in English looked promising. Wire transfers between Sepah Rome and Tehran of significant amounts, and I mean millions. There were also official-looking letters with the Revolutionary Guard emblem, but although I could read them, I understood little.

"Mr. Van der Hoff, please, I ask you to leave. You are going through my personal records. These files have nothing to do with the materials that you are interested in."

"Really?" I asked and continued with my search. A white office envelope felt as if it contained more than just paper. I looked inside. It contained a green American Express credit card that looked as if it had never been used.

There was a tense look on the face of Ali Akbar. Although he tried hard to keep me from noticing, my Mossad body language course told me that I was holding something that caused him great concern. The card looked just like all American Express cards. The little devil inside me was also curious. *Why would he keep the card secreted?*

Before I could answer, I felt a blow to my head that shook me. I fell to the floor. Before losing consciousness briefly, I saw Ali Akbar holding a table lamp with a heavy base. I opened my eyes and closed them again. The headache was splitting. The apartment was quiet.

I opened my eyes again. Ali Akbar was crouching close to me, searching my pockets. The keys to the apartment! I'd locked it when we'd entered. I half closed my eyes so as not to alert him. But Ali Akbar was too busy looking for the keys. Luckily I'd put them in my pants' back pocket and was lying on my back. Therefore he couldn't get at them.

I thought of Amos, my martial arts instructor during Special Forces training at the Mossad. Amos was a short guy with red hair, cross-eyed, so you never knew where he was looking. That helped him to kick us hard when we least expected it. He would say:

When your enemy is very close to your body, that limits your options. Look for the available vital points or vulnerable points. They can kill, or cripple your enemy. Therefore use them only when it's either your or his life, and you cannot escape. Don't be a hero. You have an assignment to carry out. If you deliver your enemy a crippling blow, you will be the survivor, not the winner. Choose the target carefully.

I did.

As Ali Akbar leaned toward me closer, until I could smell his body odor, I hit his ears suddenly with both my slightly cupped palms. That created a painful and serious vacuum effect that could burst both his eardrums. Injury to the inner ear and the cochlea also means loss of balance. He gasped in pain and fell backwards. I turned on him and pushed upwards with my fingertips into the hollow areas just under his ears, and finished him with an elbow strike to his nose. He was out instantly.

I got up, breathing heavily. Ali Akbar was showing signs of returning to reality from the temporary serenity I had imposed on him. I looked for the file I'd retrieved earlier, and, most importantly, the envelope with the credit card that seemed to be the immediate trigger for his attack. The contents were scattered on the floor. I picked them up and left the apartment, locking it from the outside.

I didn't know if Ali Akbar had called for help while I was knocked out. I left the apartment building, entered my car, and waited. My camera was ready. If Ali Akbar had summoned help, it would not be the police. They could ask too many questions. I wanted to take a good look at any people he'd called, for future reference. After ten minutes of sitting in my car, lights off, I saw a black Buick stop next to Ali Akbar's apartment building. The man who exited the car looked familiar, but I couldn't place him immediately or get a good shot of him. He rushed into the building.

I started my car and returned to my hotel, headache and all, but with significant prizes. I sent a short message to Eric, reporting where I was and that I'd made serious progress, and went to bed. I had to think about how to break the news to Eric that if Kamrani was right, Madani was in Dubai, and, therefore, the person Eric had in the US—Madani Number Three—as well as his wife and son still waiting in Europe, were also fakes.

I woke up a few hours later. It was still dark outside. My head was hurting but my mind was clear. I sat at the small desk, turned on the banker's lamp, and looked at the scanned photo Pierre had given me in Paris of Christian Chennault. *Gotcha!* I said to myself, that's the man I saw a few hours ago rushing into Ali Akbar's apartment building, Christian Chennault, Leonid Shestakov's henchman. If I needed further proof of the Shestakov-Ali Akbar connection, I didn't have to look any further. I'd just seen it.

Then I looked at the credit card I took from Ali Akbar. I was troubled, but didn't know why. "Let's play a game," I said to myself, "let's look at the account number." I turned on my laptop, keyed in the twelve-digit password and logged in through a secure server to the office. I ran the account number on the database. The response came in immediately: *No data is available. Check the account number as it appears to be invalid.*

I compared the numbers on the card with the numbers I keyed in. They matched. I'd made no mistake. I tried again. The same auto-response came. The only conclusion I could make with my head hurting was that there must be a mistake. Either American Express issued a card with an erroneous account number, or the Agency's database was screwed up, or the card was forged.

I went back to bed. I was still bewildered and uncomfortable about how to break the news to Eric. But, what the hell, I thought and fell asleep.

———

When I woke up, I sat on my bed trying to collect my thoughts. What if Kamrani was lying about Madani's being held in Dubai? What if the credit card was a simple amateur forgery? Anyway, nobody can use it because every card-reading machine would reject it immediately.

Then what's the use? And what is the real reason for printing this card and then secreting it so carefully?

A blow to my head again, this time metaphorically. *You're an idiot,* my little inner devil told me. *After all those years with cipher training you couldn't see it? The credit card is a code card, a key, not a credit card!*

I looked at the card again. This time I counted the card number's digits. Sixteen! American Express cards have fifteen. This one was never meant to be used for charging champagne. To make sure, I followed the routine of manually checking the validity of the card. I wrote down the sixteen-digit number and doubled every other digit from right to left. I added the new numbers to the undoubled digits. Now all double-digit results should be added as a sum of their component digits; sixteen is actually one plus six. The result I had was seventy-two. Since the final sum on a valid card must be divisible by ten, and the result was seventy-two, then the only conclusion was that card was a fake. The Agency's database was correct.

Ali Akbar had made no hostile moves when I interrogated him over very important matters. But when I found the credit card, that blew his top, and he'd hit my head. I copied the numbers and sent them to Eric and Paul, suggesting that they also copy NSA—the National Security Agency, the US agency that encrypts and deciphers all communications that further the interests of the United States.

XXII

July 2007, Washington, DC

It was time to leave and go home. I decided to break the news to Eric, Benny, and Paul personally about Madani's allegedly being held by Shestakov in Dubai.

I flew to London and I called Eric, asking to have a meeting as soon as I arrived, then caught a connecting flight to Washington, DC. An Agency car met me and took me to Langley. In Eric's office, I put an envelope on the coffee table between us. "It's all in there," I said, "all my findings."

"Tell us now," said Benny. "We'll read it later."

"OK, Benny, do you remember telling us that your men approached Tango while he was in Italy on a business trip?"

Benny nodded. "Yes, he was identified by our talent spotter. We did a target study that marked him as a suitable and worthy target for recruitment."

"Well, it was business, all right. There were some requests for bidding made by Tango, or maybe a better term would be double-dipping. During the same time he talked with your men, Tango was already working for Shestakov. The immediate reason for his visit to Italy was to set up a bank account to receive Shestakov's payments. Obviously he couldn't open an account at Sepah Bank, knowing that the payments he'd receive would be reported to VEVAK. Therefore he opened an account at Banco di Luigi, a small and discreet bank in Rome."

"Do you have these statements?"

"No. But I have intelligence telling me the account has several million euros. The US can ask the Italian government for authenticated copies of these statements if we establish that the request falls under the US-Italy Mutual Legal Assistance Treaty."

"Where did you get the intel?" asked Eric.

I wasn't about to tell him that Aldo had told me. Eric would crucify me for cutting corners. "Ali Akbar Kamrani told me."

"Voluntarily?" asked Benny with a surprised smile.

"Yep. Another squeeze of Kamrani's balls can get you surprising results. I went to Dubai for that. Tango received a one-time amount of one million dollars, and additional frequent payments. Ali Akbar hinted that Madani had partners."

"But Kamrani is an Iranian agent. Didn't he report this to VEVAK?"

"Apparently not. He was more afraid of Shestakov's thugs, who are next door to him, than of VEVAK, which is across the bay. Anyway, I suspect that Ali Akbar Kamrani himself was double-dipping, working for VEVAK and getting 'bonuses' from Shestakov."

"Meaning?"

"A few days after Shestakov made payments from his account at Sepah Bank in Rome to Tango's bank account in Luigi Bank, there was another transfer, of exactly fifteen percent of each transfer, to a bank account in the British Virgin Islands."

"Got details?" asked Benny, with increased interest.

"No, just the name of the account and an account number. I know that the bank account is held by a trust, and British Virgin

Islands law is very strict in defending the anonymity of the ultimate beneficiary of the trust, unless . . ." I paused.

"Unless what?" asked Benny.

"Unless you can show that you have been wronged by ways and means that you can only partially understand or by persons unknown. If so, you can apply to the BVI High Court for a document disclosure order against any third party in the BVI who is not a mere witness but who has gotten caught up in, facilitated, or become involved in a wrong. In the BVI, there are more than 470,000 active offshore companies. Such a third party is almost inevitably a locally licensed and regulated trust company, or a company formation and administration agent.

"BVI trust companies are expected to hold ultimate beneficial ownership and 'Know Your Customer' documentation. Such documentation should reveal who actually stands behind any BVI company that is administered by a regulated BVI trust company. Such a court order should lead us to the disclosure of this type of documentation."

"How do you know all that?" asked Benny, a bit suspiciously.

"Well," I said with a smile, "don't forget that I'm a lawyer," and when Benny's facial expression signaled *Oh, come on!*, I continued: "I consulted Martin Kenney, a leading fraud attorney in BVI and the local member of FRAUDNET, a worldwide network of attorneys created by the International Chamber of Commerce. I told him that I'm a Tel Aviv lawyer acting as an estate's executor trying to invade a BVI Trust that the estate was suing.

"Kenney told me that if my client was the apparent victim of a breach of a fiduciary duty or an apparent victim of a fraud, we can seek disclosure orders against any third party in the BVI who has apparently gotten mixed up in or become involved in the handling, transfer, or concealment of the fruits of the fraud or iniquity complained of. He warned me, though, that sometimes hard-core fraudsters will anticipate the possibility of the use of such orders, and may therefore interpose a further layer of fraudulent data by the use of a nominee ultimate beneficiary owner—a totally illegal method of concealment. Kenny said that he is able to get around this problem and place us on a path of inquiry to show who stands behind a nominee ultimate beneficiary owner."

"We can't go to court just now," said Benny. "The whole case is super confidential at this time."

"I thought of that as well," I said. "According to Kenney, he can ask for a seal and a gag order, to protect the integrity of a fraud recovery or similar investigation. We can move quietly in the BVI court, by filing ex parte—without the other party present, just us and the judge. However, all ex parte orders in the BVI require the applicant to make full disclosure of all material facts. This requires a very full, detailed, and objectively supported application. And therefore we may have a serious problem."

"Still, nice job, Dan, but I don't think the Israeli government would allow that, and, frankly, I don't think that the US government would go for it, either."

"Then there's the ultimate solution," I said smiling, anticipating the obvious. I enjoyed toying with Benny, for once, after being subjected to his little games throughout our decades of friendship. "There are no alternative ways to obtain the disclosure of documents that show who actually stands behind a BVI company available to a private person, except for foreign government financial intelligence units. They can issue requests to the BVI Financial Services Commission for the same data. Any such request is heavily guarded and protected."

Benny looked at Paul and Eric. "Can FinCen do it?" He was referring to the Financial Crimes Enforcement Network established by the US Department of the Treasury to provide a government-wide multisource financial intelligence and analysis network.

"Sure," said Paul, "will do."

"And now, to the main news," I said. "According to Ali Akbar Kamrani, General Cyrus Madani, the real one, is being held captive in Dubai by Shestakov." I expected the sky to fall, but it did not. "If he's right, then the person you are holding, Madani Number Three, is a fake."

Eric took the initiative. "We already know that Number Three is fake. It took us one day to discover that. He's in a federal prison now."

"On what charges?"

"Multiple. For example, making false statement to a federal agency about a matter within the agency's jurisdiction. Let me have all the information you have regarding Madani in Dubai."

XXIII

September 2007, Washington, DC

Two months went by. I was busy reducing my caseload, looking forward to spending a vacation with my children, when I was called to a meeting in Washington, DC, with Benny, Paul, and Eric. I wondered if there was something to run my blood hot and to cool off my vacation plans.

"Dan, this meeting is intended to wrap things up. The Tango case is closed," said Eric. "Madani was pulled out of Dubai. He is here, he is the real thing, and he is talking. And," he added, probably anticipating my usual skepticism, "he is not a dispatched agent."

"How did he get to the US?" I asked. I'd heard nothing since I'd given Eric the address in Dubai that might have been where Shestakov was holding Madani.

Paul answered, "A team of Navy SEALs raided the villa. He was flown to the USS *John C. Stennis* of the Fifth Fleet. In South Africa he boarded a US military plane to Washington, DC. The Iranians have no clue where he is, but they are, uncharacteristically, keeping quiet about it."

Benny said in a philosophical tone, "You probably remember the biblical story of Saul, who went looking for lost donkeys and found himself becoming a king?"

"Yes?" I said, waiting for the punch line. "Explain the connection."

"Well," said Benny, "you went searching for the security breach and found the real Madani."

"Does that make me king?" I asked ironically.

"No, just our hero for the day."

That was good enough for me.

"Dan," said Paul, as if he'd just remembered, after listening to Benny, "I also want to thank you."

"Oh, it was my duty," I said in an atypical modesty.

Paul smiled, "Let me finish. There were plenty of things you did right—and a few that you did wrong, but the second most important achievement was retrieving the fake credit card, while the first was of course discovering where Madani was held."

I'd almost forgotten about the credit card.

"Was it valuable?"

"Definitely. You assumed, correctly, that the card's supposed account number was a key—a parameter that determines the functional output of a cryptographic cipher. Without it, the cipher cannot be broken.

"Here it seems that the Iranian mathematicians used the numbers they imprinted on the fake card. They built in a formula as an encryption key. However, they made two mistakes. One, by hiding it in a credit card with a combination of numbers that do not exist in a genuine card. They should have known better. Second, by not generating a truly random sequence of numbers, but by following the credit company's formula. And then they misdid it.

"It took NSA's cryptology experts just a few hours to run the number crunchers, break the code, and use the key to decrypt crucial communications between Tehran and its agents throughout the

Middle East and Europe. It took Ali Akbar Kamrani a full day to report to Tehran that the card had been taken, and they immediately changed the key.

"But since NASA already had on its computers thousands of encrypted messages that could not be broken without the key. Now they were able to crack these messages and the intelligence fruits derived were abundant, and . . . juicy." He smiled.

I knew I couldn't ask what they were. But the pat on the back was pleasant. Eric, on the hand, just smiled—a rare occasion—and said, "So much for the Stimson dictum."

We all laughed. In 1929, during the administration of President Herbert Hoover, Secretary of State Henry Stimson had closed down the State Department's cryptanalytic office. "Gentlemen do not read each other's mail," he reasoned.

"What about the BVI account?" I asked. It all sounded like ancient history now.

"There was no need to go to a BVI court," said Benny. "Once we broke the cipher with the key you brought, we had all the information. The account's ultimate beneficiary was a high-ranking Iranian politician who benefited from each sale of equipment to Iran. Ali Akbar wanted Madani to give him a portion of the commissions Madani was earning from Shestakov. Madani refused. Therefore, Ali Akbar tried to blackmail Madani by threatening to tell the Iranians about the commissions Madani was receiving from Shestakov.

"So, as a precautionary countermeasure, Madani decided to defect. He had to choose between us and Shestakov before he was arrested by VEVAK. He chose Shestakov, and with the help of Shestakov's men, he was smuggled out of his house arrest."

"How could they do it?" I asked.

"Remember that Shestakov was highly esteemed by the Iranian regime because he was such an important figure supplying them with nuclear reactor components. Therefore, his men could roam in Tehran without any problem. I'm sure they found a hole in the security detail that was watching Madani and hoisted him out to Dubai." He paused.

"I'm listening," I said. "Please continue." In fact, I was extremely eager.

"We think that Madani escaped from his house arrest very close to the time of your arrival, which he wanted to avoid, due to his earlier agreement to side with Shestakov. However, VEVAK knew you were coming. Madani told us that he confided to Shestakov that we were about to extricate him from Iran, but that he—Madani—preferred to go with Shestakov, who promised him a European passport and asylum.

"By that time, Madani had amassed a fortune from commissions paid to him by Shestakov, and therefore giving up the three million dollars we promised was not that difficult."

"How did VEVAK know I was coming?" I asked.

"First, they control all airline traffic in and out of Iran. Second, Shestakov tipped them off, hoping that they would take care of you."

"The son of a bitch," I said, thinking of Madani. Well, at the last moment I also added Shestakov.

"Anyway, where are Shestakov and Chennault?"

"We know that Shestakov managed to flee Dubai. He was not in the villa during the raid. We think he might be hiding in Russia. We've asked for the Russians' help. However, the list of countries that want to 'talk' to him is rather long, and I'm not sure we are anywhere near the top. We do have Christian Chennault, though. He's a small fish and we'll soon release him to whoever wants him enough to extradite him. We are consulting with INTERPOL."

I poured myself some water from a bottle that was on the table. But the taste was stale. There was also a bowl of apples. Benny took one, and bit into it.

Eric continued, "VEVAK therefore had a problem. The real Madani had disappeared and you were coming to meet him. The plan was to arrest you both and try you as spies. Without the real

Madani, however, they turned the problem into an opportunity to fool us again. They located a former major in the Revolutionary Guard who has some physical resemblance to Madani and placed him in the high-rise apartment in Tehran to pose as Madani, to make you escort him out of Iran."

"Aha," I said, "Now things fall into place. Do you know if Hammed, the Kurdish Mossad contact that I met in Damascus, was bona fide?"

"We don't know, but assume he was," answered Eric.

"He connected me with his cousin Khader in Tehran, and Khader was holding the fake Madani who I escorted out of Iran." I was still unsure of who was good and who was bad in the scenario I'd just heard. "Where is Khader?"

"The Khader you met in Tehran was fake," said Benny.

"And where is the real Khader?"

"Sad," said Benny. "VEVAK apprehended him and we don't know what happened to him, or whether he's even still alive. He was an important link threatening the success of the VEVAK ploy operation. He knew you were coming, and he knew Madani; therefore, he had to be removed from the scene one way or another. Instead, VEVAK placed one of their men, called him Khader, and instructed him on how to treat you."

"That's why they moved me to the apartment," I said.

"Right, because VEVAK didn't know what arrangements we had made for you at the hotel."

"And they were angry when I returned to the hotel once without their permission," I said.

"Exactly. You'd never met Madani before; you only had his photos. The Mossad combatants who were in contact with Madani had left Iran immediately after he disappeared, fearing that a megasearch by VEVAK for Madani could uncover them. Therefore, it was easy to introduce the new face of the fake Madani."

"That explains also the bizarre incident on the train when he disappeared."

"Right," said Paul. "While you were asleep, he went to report to a VEVAK agent on the train."

There was a tad of criticism in his tone. I chose to ignore it. The final successful result is what should count. *You're wrong*, said my inner little devil, but I ignored him too.

"And even stranger was what happened after he was taken off the train, and then released on one hundred dollars bail. Was that part of the charade?" I asked.

"Of course," said Benny. "Madani had to be inspected by the police to increase his bona fide appearance, and taken off the train for some reason. But the stupid cop at the police station didn't realize that the one million rials that he asked as bail—to him a huge amount—would translate to a mere one hundred dollars, and so that backfired, because it made you suspicious. He should have asked for an amount a thousand times bigger to force you to seek help and enable them to follow your steps to more of our operatives."

"What about the Iranian politician who was bribed as well?" I asked, sensing it'd soon be a new case for us.

"We are working on it," said Benny with his signature sly-fox smile.

"Anyway," said Paul, "Good job, Dan. The Iranians are still in the dark regarding the whereabouts of Madani."

"You said that before, but how come? Didn't the Dubai intelligence services help them discover what happened?" I asked.

"They tried, but got nowhere, because even they are in the dark," Benny chuckled. "The Dubai border control records cannot show whether Madani is still in Dubai. When Dubai offered that explanation to the Iranians, it created friction with Iran, which questioned whether Dubai was hiding Madani, or, worse, selling Iran out to the US for some unknown benefit."

I smiled. "Iran and Dubai are neighbors, and you sowed suspicion between them."

"It's never a bad move. They shouldn't get too chummy," concluded Benny. He took another bite of the apple, and winked.

Acknowledgments

The publication of *Defection Games* coincides with news of clandestine operations—attributed to the CIA and the Mossad—to identify and block Iranian efforts to develop a nuclear bomb. In *Defection Games*, Iran is a key player in the roster of bad guys and rogue states operating in the murky world of international espionage and terrorism.

Dan Gordon, an Israeli lawyer and a former Mossad agent, is now working for the US government in foreign intelligence gathering. Gordon faces sinister plots, corruption, intrigue from a power-hungry, manipulative rogue government that constantly threatens his life—and the national security of the US.

Gordon faces multiple layers of secrecy, subterfuge, and treachery, which are not the exception. They are the rule.

But Gordon is no team player. He's an indefatigable lone wolf, alert to hostile moves even by those he should be able to trust. Therefore, he must sleep with one eye open. Always.

Like all of the other thrillers in the series—*Triple Identity, The Red Syndrome, The Chameleon Conspiracy*, and *Triangle of Deception*—*Defection Games* was inspired by my twenty years of intelligence-gathering for the US government, performed undercover in more than thirty foreign countries. Obviously, in my years working for the US government, I could not share the spine-tingling aspects of my work with anyone but my supervisors, and in some adventures, not even with them. Sadly, these events, which are sometimes more intriguing and thrilling than the best fiction I have ever read, are buried in reports submitted throughout the years. The story of Dan Gordon and his battle against the invisibles is my idea of the next best thing. However, *Defection Games* is not an autobiography, but a novel. Apart from historic events, all names, characters, personal histories, and events described in this book have never existed and are purely works of fiction.

During the past three years, I found it increasingly difficult to find time to complete *Defection Games*, the fifth installment in the Dan Gordon Thriller® series. With a demanding international legal practice that included a complex litigation schedule, and a big family, the mission looked almost impossible. During those years I also researched, wrote and completed a legal textbook in international law, *Foreign Judgments in Israel: Recognition and Enforcement*, published by the Israel Bar Association. I also wrote dozens of op-ed articles for the *Huffington Post* and the International Herald Tribune. However, with the tenacity usually attributed to Dan Gordon, the fictional protagonist of the series, I completed *Defection Games*.

Many thanks to hundreds of readers who repeatedly asked me when the new Dan Gordon thriller would be released. These consistent inquiries were the fuel that moved me to continue writing, my busy schedule notwithstanding. Special thanks to Sarah McKee, the former general counsel of INTERPOL's United States National Central Bureau, who, as always, was gracious enough to read the manuscript and make important comments. She is not only an astute lawyer but an excellent reviewer. I am grateful for the special efforts she made, and for her unfailing grace, professionalism, and friendship.

I am eternally grateful to David Epstein, who for almost two decades was my supervisor while he headed the Office of Foreign Litigation at the US Department of Justice. His trust and support were an important motivating factor in my work. With utmost professionalism and the long leash he allowed me, he became a major partner in the successful results of my work for the US government. During the earlier stages of writing *Defection Games*, Sharon Lintz and Tova Piha made important suggestions and amendments. I am indebted for their efforts.

The time I spent writing this book was taken from my wife and law partner, Rakeffet, and our five children; and my everlasting gratitude is the least I can offer for their sacrifice.

Haggai Carmon

About the Author

Haggai Carmon is an international attorney sharing his time and practice between the United States, Israel, and the rest of the world. Since 1985, several US federal agencies have given him worldwide responsibility for legal intelligence-gathering outside the United States in complex, multimillion-dollar cases, mostly involving money laundering and megafraud. He has performed this sensitive investigative work undercover in more than thirty foreign countries. He has also represented the US Department of Justice in its Israeli litigation, and acts as legal counsel to the US Embassy in Israel.

Carmon was born in Israel, where he graduated cum laude from the Tel Aviv University Faculty of Law. He earned a certificate in international law and diplomacy as well as a master's degree in government and politics from St. John's University in New York. He is married to Rakeffet, who is also his law partner, and they have five children.

Made in the
USA
Lexington, KY